Captain Marvelous

"Marvelic is down here on special assignment, looking into the trouble," Valetta told her. "I'd like you to help him."

"Trouble?" she mused. "An odd way of describing women being murdered and dumped along I-88 like last week's trash."

"Now, Annie." Valetta's patent sigh made Ronen cringe.

Offering the man a glacial stare, she said, "I'll ignore that patronizing response, Major, because I know you would never deliberately piss me off."

"You're right on that account," Valetta muttered.

"And I'm sure, had you seen the condition of the bodies as I did, you would agree with my professional opinion that it was a blessing none of the women survived."

"I would," he said.

Ronen felt Annie's cold gaze scan his body from forehead to shoes. "Special assignment, Marvelic? Guess you picked the right butts after all."

From her, the comment stung. "The less people who know why I was assigned to this area the better."

"That your way of telling me to keep my lip zipped?"

What They Are Saying About
Captain Marvelous

In *Captain Marvelous* Kate Henry Doran has created a wonderfully—or should I say marvelously?—entertaining story. As a hero, Ronen Marvelic makes your mouth water, and Annie Wolf is a complex, driven heroine. The villains are about as nasty as anyone could wish for. The story is touching, scary, and funny. When I wasn't biting my nails or wiping away a tear, Ms. Doran had me laughing out loud.

—Patricia Frances Rowell
A Scandalous Situation, August 2004, Harlequin Historicals
A Dangerous Seduction, Available, Daphne Finalist 2004
A Perilous Attraction, 2001 Daphne Award, 2003 Rita Finalist,
2nd Place Barclay Gold
www.patriciafrancesrowell.com

Wings

Captain Marvelous

by

Kate Henry Doran

A Wings ePress, Inc.

Romantic Mystery Novel

Wings ePress, Inc.

Edited by: Lorraine Stephens
Copy Edited by: Leslie Hodges
Senior Editor: Lorraine Stephens
Executive Editor: Lorraine Stephens
Cover Artist: Pam Ripling

All rights reserved

Names, characters and incidents depicted in this book are products of the author's imagination or are used fictitiously. Any resemblance to actual events, locales, organizations, or persons, living or dead, is entirely coincidental and beyond the intent of the author or the publisher.

No part of this book may be reproduced or transmitted in any form or by any means, electronic or mechanical, including photocopying, recording, or by any information storage and retrieval system, without permission in writing from the publisher.

Wings ePress Books
http://www.wings-press.com

Copyright © 2004 by Kathryn Doran Cottrell
ISBN 1-59088-717-4

Published In the United States Of America

August 2004

Wings ePress Inc.
403 Wallace Court
Richmond, KY 40475

Dedication

To Bunny and Mary Kate,

mother and sister of my heart,

who give new meaning to strength,

wisdom and perseverance

against incredible obstacles.

You are my heroes.

12/04
To Dale & Carol,
Hope you enjoy the ride down I-88 with the Wolfgirl and her Captain!
Enjoy your trip!
Kate Henry Doran

Kathy Cottrell

Prologue

Fifteen year-old Luba Sanko did not die easily.

Battered beyond endurance, her body gave up the battle just as the ambulance stretcher hit the Emergency Room doors. The trauma team worked like demons to save her. Only after no signs of life remained, except for a few agonal respirations and the occasional non-functional blip on the EKG monitor, did they finally accept the obvious. Nothing would save Luba, on this night or any other.

Dr. John Latimer checked the clock on the Trauma Room wall. "Let's call it. Time of death, twenty-two-fifteen hours."

Physician's Assistant Annie Wolfe covered the girl's body with a clean sheet, hiding the ligature marks around her elbows and livid bruising across her shoulders and torso. The Sankos would want to see their child.

They don't need to see everything.

Gently wiping a trickle of blood from the corner of Luba's mouth, she murmured, "I'll talk to the family, John."

"Sorry, Wolfgirl," the aging doctor announced. "It's your turn to take the coppers."

"You really know how to spoil a girl's night."

The comfort of John's hand was exactly what she needed. For brief seconds, Annie resisted the urge to turn into his arms and weep for another dead woman. "When you have MD after your name, and one of these days you will," he rumbled, "you can call the shots. Until then, little girl, view it as building character."

Annie could list a hundred ways to build her character—like surviving medical school. Talking to uncaring police officers ranked lower than root canals. Nevertheless, she squared her shoulders and straightened her spine, and felt only semi-prepared for the offensive task ahead.

For late March, the ER was reasonably quiet. No DWI's for a change, and only two domestic assaults. Annie took her time walking the length of the work lane. As she passed each treatment room, she mentally listed the patients inside for presenting symptoms, differential diagnoses and treatment plans.

The uniformed *patients*, who routinely gathered in the last room on the left to share war stories while scarfing down raunchy hospital coffee and stale doughnuts, were undiagnosable. It had long been her opinion, personal and professional, that any male, police officer or private citizen, who needed to prove his masculinity by carrying a weapon, was beyond redemption. From before she could walk, Annie knew all about misogynist bullies who considered it their inherent right, as well as sacred duty, to abuse those in a powerless position.

As she reached for the doorknob to the staff lounge, unease niggled its way up her spine. Unable to ignore the sensation, she cracked the door open but proceeded no farther. Eavesdropping. A skill she'd honed to a science during her childhood, perfected to an art form during adolescence, had saved her life on more than one occasion. Something was telling her to wait. Annie always paid attention to those little... somethings.

"My clients are dying, gentlemen," a familiar voice said, "and you're telling me you have nothing to go on. Why is that?"

Barb Thompson, social worker extraordinaire and advocate for the disadvantaged, sounded angry, as well as frustrated, Annie thought. Maybe even a little frightened.

"Because we are clueless, Barbie-doll," Randy Terrance, ranking officer on the Nohmensville Police Department, replied. "But don't you worry. We know how to take care of business."

"Oh, really?" Barb said with a frost in her voice that could shatter glass.

Terrance's sigh was loud. "Not many folks know this. We wanted to protect the parents and all. But we picked up the Sanko kid more than once for strutting her stuff. Didn't we, Bobby?"

"If you say so, Randy."

Annie rolled her eyes. Bobby Claun, called Bozo by those who knew and loathed him, would stand shoulder-to-shoulder with his idol, Raging Randy Terrance, no matter the circumstances, no matter the opponent. God Herself wouldn't stand a chance against these two.

"Strutting her stuff," Barb repeated slowly. "If that child was a pross, I'm Queen of the May."

Using the same measured tones usually reserved for the acutely psychotic, and Family Court Judges, Barb spoke through, what Annie was sure were gritted teeth. "Luba Sanko was an honor student who worked several part-time jobs so her family could eat well-balanced meals and sleep in a house that hadn't been bombed out by rebel forces. Is that how it goes in this town, Officer Terrance? A woman walking alone is begging to be pinched for soliciting?"

"So she was a hard worker," Randy said. "Didn't keep her from getting the snot kicked out of her, did it?"

Anticipating the squawk of an outraged feminist, Annie threw open the door and barged in. "Barb! John Latimer sent me to find you. He'd like you there when he talks to Luba's family."

"One second," her friend snapped.

"He wants you now," she lied.

Over Barb's shoulder, Annie focused her gaze on Bobby Claun whose receding Crayola-red hairline and perfectly round face gave him an uncanny resemblance to the cartoon character, hence the nickname Bozo. Having no respect for the odious Randy, she ignored him. It was the presence of a third officer, a state trooper, that came as a surprise. The ER staff called him Howdy Doody because of his square jaw, freckles, and perpetual goofy grin.

"You're over-stressed, Barb." Terrance's schmoozing tone was so blatantly false, Annie wanted to throw up. "Help Doc Latimer with the family, go home, and have a stiff drink."

"I meant what I said, Randy." Barb jerked her purse over her shoulder. "Five dead women in the space of eighteen months and your department hasn't done squat. If you can't do it, I'll find someone who will."

Randy's face turned to stone. Annie put a Vulcan death grip on her friend's arm. "Let's go. Now." She followed Barb out the door. Just before the latch clicked, she heard Bobby Claun grumble, "Since when do we break a sweat over an NHI?"

"Since never," Terrance replied.

"Bastards," Barb growled. "I'll have their badges."

Annie hissed, "What's an NHI?"

"No Human Involved. When the cops don't consider the victim to be human it gives them a reason to not *break a sweat*."

Annie tasted bile as they moved down the work lane. "No human involved. Because the victims are women? Or because they're immigrants?"

"Probably both."

A belligerent voice from behind stopped the two of them in their tracks. "Do yourselves a favor, girls," Randy Terrance said. "Don't tell us how to do our jobs."

Without bothering to mask her contempt, Annie turned on him. "Looks like someone should."

One

"Your job sucks."

With his own thoughts running along similar lines, New York State Police Captain Ronen Marvelic kept his response clear and concise. "It's one year, Chris, not twenty-to-life."

His son pulled another box from the cargo hold of Ronen's Bronco. "Nohmensville. *No Man's Land* is more like it."

Ronen tried to remember what it was like to be eighteen years old, his entire life ahead of him, and knowing it all. "Remind me to call your grandmother as soon as the phone is connected."

"To let her know we arrived safely?"

"To apologize."

He dropped a crate filled with cleaning supplies on the top step of the porch of the Victorian mansion that was to be his new home, waiting patiently for Christopher's comeback.

As usual, his son didn't disappoint him. "Did you check out all the trucks with rifle racks as we drove through town? The beer joints lining both sides of Main Street?"

Five taverns and double that number of four-by-fours were only a few of the things he had noticed. "So?"

"Dad. The town's okay, I guess. I even saw a couple satellite dishes. But the outskirts look like something out of *Deliverance*. Wait'll one of these hicks comes barreling down the street at three in the morning, blasting *Dueling Banjoes*."

"It won't be that bad." *Please, God. It can't be that bad.*

"Why did you accept the transfer, Dad?"

"We've been over this fifty times. It's my job."

A rote answer, granted, but lately, Ronen had been trying to figure that one out himself. Why would anyone take an assignment to the rural area bordering New York State's Catskill Mountains?

Because something needs to be done and, despite past screw-ups, the brass picked you to do it.

"Help me get the rest of this stuff upstairs," he said. "The landlady indicated she'd be here at noon to drop off the keys for the apartment and show us the alarm system."

"Hooterville has alarm systems? I'm impressed."

"Watch it, pal."

The two worked in silence, carrying boxes and crates up the polished oak staircase inside Grover Mansion. After neatly stacking their things outside Apartment 2-A, Chris followed his father down the stairs into a July sun hot enough to fry eggs on the pavement. "How are you planning to handle this tour, Dad? I didn't see a whole lot of museums or gourmet restaurants as we cruised through town."

"I'll live," Ronen growled, yanking open the Bronco's rear passenger door, cursing silently when he saw the amount of stuff still to be unloaded. *I will survive this. Even if it kills me.* "You mind telling me where all this crap came from?"

With a laugh, Chris hauled another crate from the cargo hold and surveyed the remaining contents. "Classical CD's. Stereo equipment. Your computer. I believe you consider them essential tools of survival."

Ronen made a mental note to trim the number of tools in his life.

"Knowing how much you love the twang of steel guitars," the boy went on, "hokey songs about hard-hearted women and soft-brained men, you'll do well here. Yessiree-bob, real well."

"Whatever their choices in music, most of these folks are honest and hard-working. Don't let that big-city ego overcome your good sense and discretion."

"We're talking hayseeds here, Dad. Hicks who wouldn't know discretion if it came up and bit them in the—"

"Christopher! Enough!"

"No, Dad. It's not enough."

Ronen executed an exact military about-face. With a broad gesture for the empty parking area, he offered, "The asphalt is yours. Speak your piece."

Chris hedged for a second, then let it out in one sustained breath. "When Mom died you almost killed yourself to make sure things stayed the same for me all the while keeping the Troop brass happy."

"Your point?"

Chris stood his ground. "Nohmensville smells like a demotion. After all you've done, why are they punishing you?"

His son's belief in the demotion fantasy was all right with Ronen. Rarely during his fifteen years with the Troops, first as an undercover grunt, tracking drug smugglers and crooked cops for the Bureau of Criminal Investigation, later as a crime profiler, did he share the gory details of his work with Chris. It was safer that way. For both of them.

The voice of the Deputy Superintendent rang in his ears. *Take the Cats, Marv. We need your skills and experience to clean up the mess down there.*

Ronen recalled his hesitation in accepting the assignment.

You won't let anything like the Collins case happen again; we're sure of it. When you're done, you can write your own ticket. Anywhere you want in the state.

The brass' confidence was compelling. Determined not to repeat the past, Ronen couldn't say no. *Anywhere in the state.*

With Chris going off to college in a few months, it was the right time for a change. But when he thought about what he was walking into, a community's apathy over murder and mutilation of women, followed by incredibly sloppy police work, he shuddered.

It was too late to turn back now. "I'm choosing to view this as a challenge."

Taking a box of computer components in his hands, Chris headed back inside. "Dad. You'll be bored out of your gourd."

Between the poverty and deprivation he'd witnessed just a few miles outside the Nohmensville town limits, honky-tonk bars, rifle-toting good-old-boys, and brutalized corpses, Ronen doubted boredom would become an issue.

Chris whined his way to the top of the stairs. "Did you know No Man's Land has more cattle than people? The way my luck's been running lately, the cows'll look better than the girls."

"Golly gee," a female voice drawled. "I can't recall the last time I mooed."

~ * ~

If hell had a special place for eavesdroppers, Annie Wolfe claimed a ringside seat. After all, listening in on others' conversations was one of the few things she did well.

So after she flew up the back stairs of Grover Mansion and overheard the new tenants dissing her town, the chance to decimate a couple of big-city boys with big-shot attitudes was a challenge too juicy to ignore.

"Mrs. Grover?" the older of the two croaked while the younger one turned the color of ripe strawberries.

"Sorry, no." She gestured at the door across the hall. "I'm Annie Wolfe from 2-B. Miz Grover's tied up with final plans for next week's Kumquat Festival. The Kween was late for parade practice; Miz G. had a regular hissy-fit."

Without missing a beat, she directed her attention to the younger of the two city boys. "See, the Kween was late 'cause one of her daddy's heifers slipped a fence and trampled a patch of prize-winning kumquats. Took Miz Grover near to an hour to calm the poor child down. Around here, gentlemen, we take our kumquats serious."

Annie took note of the solemn look on the older city-boy's face as he stood back, arms folded across an impressively broad chest. The hooded gaze was almost as impressive as the body. She yanked her Nuggets jersey farther past her hips.

"Miz Grover asked me to run over and show you boys the alarm system, help you get settled." She went to hand the keys to the younger one. "Here you go."

Mr. Serious stepped forward to take the keys from her hand. As he did, his fingers brushed her palm. "I'm Ronen Marvelic. The tactless young man is my son Christopher."

Son? Except for different eye color, their builds were identical—huge. Sandy-blond hair and engaging smiles made them look more like brothers. Annie's gaze drifted to the small tower of crates stacked outside the door leading into 2-A. "Packed kinda light."

Christopher grinned. "That's my dad. Mr. Spartan."

"My furniture arrives tomorrow." In addition to moss green eyes, Mr. Marvelic came equipped with a voice warm enough to take an iceberg to an ice cube in ten seconds flat. With a glance over his shoulder, he unlocked the door to 2-A. "Being on the other side of the mansion means you've got the turret. Is it as great on the inside as it appears from the parking lot?"

"Architecture?" the boy groaned. "Get a grip, Dad."

Annie swallowed a laugh before lifting a suitcase in each hand while nudging a crate of towels and sheets through the open door. "Better. At night I can lie in bed and survey the galaxy. And the sunsets are spectacular, unless—" She glanced at Chris, then gave the father a wink. "—the local manure patch overheats and steams up my view."

"*Manure patch?*" The boy swallowed visibly, several times.

"Doesn't happen very often," she qualified. "Worst comes, I'll lend you a spare gas mask."

The father chuckled. "Think we could let Mr. Short-On-Tact off with community service?"

"Maybe." She headed to the door for another crate. "Most likely, they'll assign him to the festival's bull-chip throwing contest. Last year's winner went more than two hundred feet."

"You don't say."

"Is she serious?" the boy squealed, his face going from its former crimson hue to the green of newly-picked asparagus.

"Ask her," the father suggested.

"Are you serious, Ms. Wolfe?"

Annie checked her watch. "I'd love to stay and debate proper manure temperatures, but I've got a hot date with a softball."

Pulling a ratty Mets cap from her pocket, she slipped it on with the brim facing backward. "You're both welcome to stop by the game. We're at the VFW field across from Dell's Emporium and What-Knot Shoppe and the Curl Up and Dye beauty parlor." She grinned at the boy. "I promise, Chris, not one of the players has ever chewed cud. Hers or anyone's."

"Yes, ma'am," he gulped. "Thank you, ma'am."

At the bottom of the staircase, Annie sensed someone was watching her, and turned. Heat from Ronen Marvelic's green eyes radiated all the way down the steps. "Good luck, 2-B."

Ka-chink.

Recognizing the sound of armor cracking, Annie resolved to shore up the cast-iron enclosure around her heart. His face wasn't beautiful, not in the male-model sense. It carried a lived-in look, all ridges and planes, with deep creases at the corners of his mouth. That aura of understanding and patience surrounding him was going to be tough to ignore.

"Is there something you wanted, Mr. Marvelic?"

"Many things." The hint of humor that creased the corners of his mouth sent the hem of her jersey that much closer toward her knees. "If we're going to be sharing living quarters—so to speak—you could start by calling me Ronen."

It was the heat, Annie concluded, causing the sudden onset of tightness in her chest. Just heat. Nothing more. She was sure of that.

"All right, Ronen," she agreed, finding that his name rested easy on her tongue. "We'll probably run into each other again, us being neighbors and all."

His nod was brief, that of a man used to having others follow his orders without question. "Count on it."

~ * ~

"Welcome to *No Man's Land*." Ronen surveyed the large, raucous crowd gathered at the VFW field. "Just what I wanted to do on my first day in town—watch a softball game."

"Get used to it," his new boss, Major Jim Valetta, advised. "It'll grow on you."

Like mold, Ronen imagined.

Without warning, Valetta let out a lung-bursting shout. "Way to go, baby!"

Even to Ronen's untrained, and definitely uninterested eye, he could see the second base-person had made a spectacular play.

"That's my little girl," Valetta crowed. "Fields a ball better than any of her brothers."

"I'm sure." Ronen could see she was good, not that he knew the first thing about women's softball—or any other sport for that matter. He'd always considered working up a sweat over a ball, no matter the size or shape, to be an exercise in futility.

The crowd, and his boss, obviously disagreed. On the next play, spectators erupted in screams after a Nohmensville player collided with the runner coming from second base and went to the ground in a magnificent three-point landing. Nugget players crowded around her. The coach rushed across the field carrying a medical bag.

Murmured speculation that this was it for the Nuggets moved through the stands in waves. After several moments, the player came to her feet. Chorused sighs of relief were followed by roars of, "Go, Wolfgirl!"

"That Annie," Valetta said. "She's a pistol."

Ronen took a closer look at the slim, long-legged woman who sported a fanny-length ebony braid, grime-covered uniform, and spit-in-your-eye grin.

"Where you staying, Marv?"

"It appears across the hall from... Wolfgirl."

"Convenient."

"How so?"

Valetta guided him away from the crowd. "Walk with me. I'll fill you in on an idea I've been kicking around."

After five minutes, Ronen decided one year couldn't end soon enough.

~ * ~

Annie looked into the anxious faces peering down at her. "I'm fine, you guys."

The coach grumbled, "Get her up."

Two players pulled her to her feet. One said, "Man alive, check out the hunk."

Brushing away the coach's probing fingers, Annie tested her weight on her sore knee. "We're here to play ball, not—"

"I saw him," second base gushed. "Pleated trousers, oxford shirt. Standing next to my dad by the bleachers."

Annie didn't need to look. Pressed slacks and button-down collars were dead giveaways in a community largely populated by poor, hard-working farm families.

"How's the knee?" Coach asked.

She gave it a couple practice lunges. "Not bad."

"Take your time," he cautioned. "Let the ump know when you're ready to resume play."

First base trotted over to commiserate. "You okay, Wolfgirl?"

"We were discussing the hunk," second base advised before Annie could respond. "The one with the glow-in-the-dark smile."

"Did you catch the hands on him?" first base moaned, giving Annie's sore hip a nudge. "Know what they say about a man with big hands, doncha?"

Aw, jeez.

"Big hands, big—"

"Ladies," Annie interrupted. "Let's play ball and leave the wives' tales to the old wives."

Careful not to be obvious, her gaze sought out the man who was now deep in conversation with Major Valetta, commander of the state trooper barracks in the nearby town of Sidney. Big as a mountain, 2-A carried the healthy look of a jock, moving with the presence and purpose of a commanding general. His shoulders were as wide as a silo. His hands—

"Play ball!"

The game continued with the lead trading back and forth in the remaining innings. Whenever the Nuggets were on the bench, the primary focus of discussion, to Annie's disgust, continued to be the *hunk* with Major Valetta. The top of the seventh ended with the score tied. She was gingerly lowering her aching butt to the bench, her only thoughts on ice packs and a cold drink when third base pondered, "Wonder who is he is?"

"New neighbor," she grumbled, more from pain than thirst. "Probably stopped by to check out the action."

Never one to miss a little action, particularly where it concerned someone with measurable testosterone levels, the hot corner said, "He can check me out any time he wants. Miz Grover got any vacancies?"

Just what the mansion needed, Annie decided as she fashioned ice packs for her knee and hip. A bottle-blonde barracuda whose male-seeking radar was legendary throughout the Catskills. "Sorry, all filled up."

"Probably married," the catcher offered around a mouthful of ice chips. "All the good ones are."

Don't think so. The absence of a wedding ring was the first thing she'd checked.

"Gay, then," third base decided.

Doubt it! Annie accepted a cup of Gatorade from the bat girl before forcing her thoughts back to the game. She was here to play ball, not get all hot to trot over a man.

The opposing pitcher had an arm like a laser, putting down the first two Nohmensville batters with ease. The third Nugget took her base after deliberately stepping into a pitch and got dinged. What the team needed was a hard line-drive into the outfield to score the runner from first. A win today would put them into the regional play-offs. If they nailed the regionals, it was a trip to Syracuse for the state championship.

After the umpire called a time out, Annie left the bench to walk off the ache in her knee. Her hip was killing her; her shoulder smarted like no tomorrow. Nothing that rest, aspirin, and a few strategically placed ice packs wouldn't cure. As a medical professional who'd treated more than her share of sports-related injuries, most of them her own, she ought to know.

"You okay, 2-B?"

The sun's relentless glare forced her to squint into Ronen Marvelic's killer green eyes. She recalled the gentleness in his touch when he slipped the keys from her hand. The way he looked at his son that made her heart ache for things she'd never have.

"Oh... hi. I didn't realize you were here."

Jamming his hands into the pockets of his slacks, he rocked back on his heels. "How's the leg?"

Concern from a man. A new experience for someone whose batting average with the opposite sex ranked well below dismal.

"Chris decided to pass?"

"Mrs. Grover arrived home shortly after you left. She put him to work weeding flower beds."

"Stella's real picky when it comes to her plants. She'll probably keep him busy until dark."

"After the cow remark, he deserves a taste of hard, manual labor."

Annie made a close inspection of the cleats on her left shoe. "Did I go too far with the kumquat business?"

Besides a smile as genuine as a May shower, he had a wicked, sexy laugh. "Naw. He deserved that one, too." He paused, then gave her a rueful grin. "Kumquats are tropical fruits. I wasn't aware they could grow in a cooler climate."

"They don't. I'm—"

"Wolfgirl!" the coach bellowed. "Yer up."

She reached for a batting helmet, chewing back a curse when the metal hat slipped from her hand then bounced several steps beyond 2-A's massive legs. Agony erupted from body parts she'd forgotten existed. Annie swore silently. With no time or energy for a man, she had even less for injuries.

"Thanks for stopping by, 2-A. We appreciate the—"

"In this century, Wolfgirl," the coach yelled.

"Can I walk you home?"

"I've got my car," she said, too quickly. "Thanks any—"

"Then, could I catch a ride with you? I'd hate to get lost my first day in town and fall into the manure patch."

"Manure what?" Then she remembered what was probably one of her better scams. "I guess. If you want, I mean."

The grin on his face was like the sun. Bright, shiny, and dangerous to any woman who basked in it too long. "I want."

Whoa. Put that smile on the list of controlled substances. "Okay, I guess. Uh... stay right here. I guess."

Dammit, how could one man jam her up so bad?

"Knock it out of the park, 2-B."

She did. Only because the opportunity came. Not, she reminded herself as she rounded the base path at a slower pace than usual, because the best looking thing to hit the Catskills in this century was cheering her on.

~ * ~

Stella Grover and Christopher Marvelic bolted off the mansion's wrap-around porch as soon as Annie pulled her car into the driveway.

"Lordy, Lordy," the landlady crowed, her Georgia roots showing in her voice. "When Sophie Jackson phoned me with the news, I about pitched a fit. Are you all right, child? Should we get you to the hospital?"

Annie was tempted to bang her head on the steering wheel. The delights of living in a small town were many. The drawbacks included a grapevine that moved at warp speed. Mr. Big City was sure to get off on this.

Glancing at her passenger, she found him looking more amused than cynical. "In this town," she explained, "a person can spit on the sidewalk at the south end of Elm Street; by the time they reach the north end—"

"Don't tell me," he said. "They've launched a terrorist assault on City Hall."

"Exactly."

Stella Grover attacked every assignment with the speed and efficiency of a four-star general. "Mr. Mar-vel-itch," she ordered in a crushed-gravel bark. "Bring that girl upstairs. Chris, get the door for your daddy. I'll load up on the ice packs."

Annie squawked, "What about me?"

"Sugar," Stella cackled, "you just sit back and relax."

Not so easy to do, Annie decided, after the man plucked her from the bucket seat and lifted her in his arms. "I can walk."

"If you say so."

"A simple bruise," she maintained. "No big whoop."

He continued striding toward the porch. "You're an expert on simple bruises and no big whoops?"

"Sort of."

"Chris," he directed, "wipe the spit from your chin and get the door for the next Surgeon General of the United States."

"Sure thing." The drooling young man pulled his gaze from Annie's '68 Mustang before taking the porch steps two at a time.

"I don't really."

Glancing down at her, 2-A paused on the first step. "You don't really what?"

Wow, he had great eyes. Deep and dark and sad. Made a woman want to take him in her arms and—

"I... don't consider myself a physician." His hold tightened as they entered the mansion. "Please, Mr. Mar—"

"It's Ronen. Be quiet and enjoy the ride."

Fun was fun, but this guy wasn't listening. If there was anything worse than a man who didn't listen, it was one who figured he knew what was best for a woman. "Put me down. Now."

He did nothing of the kind. "You wound me, Ms. Wolfe."

She pulled back to stare at him. "I wound you. How?"

"By inhibiting my unfulfilled Rhett Butler fantasy."

"Mis-tur Mar-vel-itch," Stella bellowed from the top of the staircase, fists planted on her ample hips, a George Patton glower on her face. "Is there a problem here?"

2-A used a grin on the glaring General Grover that would melt the tarnish off a brass doorknob. "We seem to be having difficulty with the concept of pampering."

"For land's sake," the woman squawked. "Great big man such as yourself should know how to handle a stubborn woman."

"Yes, ma'am, I do." He crossed the foyer, then placed Annie on her feet at the foot of the stairs. "Show me."

With one eye on the incredibly long flight of steps that led to her apartment, she swallowed hard. "Show you what?"

"Make it to the top under your own steam, we'll leave you alone. That's the deal. Take it or leave it."

Nothing like a dare to help a woman make up her mind. "I'll take it."

Grasping the hand rail and girding her loins, Annie placed a foot on the first stair, then stepped up. Pain instantly shrieked up her leg, taking uninvited occupancy in her knee. Dammit, she'd done it this time.

2-A was there, taking her under the knees and around the waist. Again. "Put your arms around my neck."

"I told you," Stella crowed. "Didn't I tell you?"

"Mrs. Grover," Ronen asked, "would you run a bath for Annie? I'm sure she'll rest more comfortably after she loses some of the sweat and grime from the game."

Damn. Here she was, reeking like a gym locker while Mr. Picture Perfect smelled good enough to nibble on, one small bite at a time. "I could do this on my own if you'd just let me lean on you. A little," she added with regret.

One elegant eyebrow rose in question as he proceeded up the staircase. "Are you trying to permanently damage your knee?"

"Of course not."

"I believe I heard someone say the Nuggets will play in a regionals game next week. Is that correct?"

"Yeah, but—"

"No yeah-buts," he warned after they reached the landing. "I've carried you up the stairs. My son is playing doorman. Mrs. Grover is preparing ice packs and a warm bath. If you behave, I'll cook you dinner."

"Geez, Dad," Chris said. "You've never—"

Marvelic pinned him with a look. "The door, Christopher?"

Annie handed the boy her athletic bag. "Keys are in the inside zipper pocket. Thanks." She then focused her attention on the man who'd carried her up a full flight of stairs as if she'd weighed no more than a bouquet of flowers. "Did you say *behave*?"

"Yes, ma'am. I did."

"Christopher?" she said, politely as possible, given her rapidly rising blood pressure.

The boy covered his mouth, coughed delicately. "Yes, ma'am?"

"For future reference, some women don't care for men with patronizing, sexist attitudes."

Sighing deeply, Chris held open the door to her apartment. "He's a never-ending embarrassment to me."

Ronen began to hum the opening bars to "I Am Woman, Hear Me Roar". Annie's withering glare only served to egg him on.

"A second point of reference, Chris," she offered with a sniff. "A real woman takes care of herself. She gets herself out of her own jams—" God help her, her voice had risen to a harpy's shriek. "—and isn't influenced by an XY chromosome pattern. Have I made myself clear?"

Ronen breezed into her apartment like he owned the joint. "Crystal. Ma'am."

~ * ~

"Let me fix your hair," Stella offered after helping her out of the tub.

Annie unknotted the waist-length braid, shaking it out until it covered her shoulders and arms in a heavy black cape. "My hair's fine. No one's going to see it except me."

"I wouldn't be too sure of that."

Annie sat on the lid of the commode to dry off. "What's that supposed to mean?"

"Oh... nothing," Stella twittered. "If I didn't have the pot-luck supper tonight, I'd stay home and take care of you."

"You don't need to do that. Thanks any—"

"Not that I mind missing the dinner," came the hasty reply. "Lord knows the food will be paltry at best, but my blackberry crumble is entered in the dessert contest, and you know how I hate to miss the annual VFW bake-off."

"Absolutely." Her landlady's blackberry dessert was known throughout the surrounding three counties. Its chances for taking the blue ribbon landed somewhere between zip and none.

"I'll be sure to tell everyone you'll be in top form for next week's game." Stella peered at her over the rims of her rhinestone-studded glasses. "You *will* be ready by next week, won't you?"

She certainly hoped so. "You bet."

"Good. This town hasn't had anything to put it in the headlines in a sow's age."

Annie was well aware that most of Nohmensville didn't consider the deaths of five women—two of whom were runaways, the other three prostitutes—if one were to believe the bullshit dished out by the local cops, important. Call it what you want, denial ain't only a river in Egypt. The prudent person picked the battles which stood a chance of being won. She wasn't stupid enough to debate basic tenets of civil rights with the widow of the town's former mayor. "We'll do our best, Stella."

The landlady stood back, giving the clothes Annie put on after her bath a jaundiced look. "Sure you don't want to wear something a little more... stylish?"

This from a woman who regularly dressed in skin-tight Capri pants, iridescent tank tops, spike-heeled sandals and sported a beehive hairdo the color of an over-ripe pumpkin.

Glancing down at her favorite LA Laker's jersey and matching shorts, Annie grumbled, "What's wrong with it? It's functional and cool as well as comfortable."

"It's butt ugly."

Needing only the comfort of her davenport, a bunch of ice packs and the remote control for the TV, Annie said, "Go on now, Stella. Have a good time at the VFW."

The landlady worried a rope of multi-colored beads hanging from her scrawny neck. "I'll check on you once I'm back home."

Attempting to manipulate a pair of crutches and carry several ace bandages at the same time, Annie lumbered out of the bathroom—only to discover the reason behind Stella's suggestion that she change into something more *stylish*.

Ronen Marvelic was standing in her living room, surveying the decor that many claimed resembled a locker room. "Quite a place you have here, 2-B."

One of the aces spun out of her hand, tangling with a crutch tip as it unrolled. Annie stumbled, then found herself caught up against Marvelic's tempered steel chest.

"Steady there, slugger. You okay?"

She was. Until she felt the muscles of his chest rippling beneath her fingers, the solid bands of his thighs cradling hers. "Despite what you've seen today, Mr. Marvelic, I'm not usually so clumsy."

"I'm sure." Steel vibrated against her palm. "Ready for bed?"

The other crutch clattered to the floor. Unable to formulate a logical, coherent response, she stammered, "I... uh, yeah, I guess I want—"

"What?" he murmured in that iceberg-melting voice. "Tell me what you want, Annie Wolfe."

"Oh my," Stella squealed behind them. "*Oh... my!*"

Annie felt his hand cup the back of her head, urging it to the hard plane of his chest. "She's fine, Mrs. Grover. Just about to lay down."

"I'll just... uhm... pop these pice acks—I mean, ice packs—into the freezer. You be sure to—" Stella cleared her throat, pulled at the beads circling her throat. "—get off your feet and—do whatever it is you two want to, uh, do."

Ronen lifted Annie in his arms and carried her to the battered couch. Stella handed him bags of ice after he elevated Annie's leg on throw pillows. "Thanks, Mrs. Grover." He looked up into Annie's eyes and smiled.

For a second, the world tilted on its axis. She found herself struck dumb. The phone's ring cut through the heavy silence.

"I'll get it," Stella offered quickly, giving them both a queer look. "Want I should take a message, sugar?"

Annie leaned her head against the back of the couch. Until this moment, she hadn't realized how bone-weary she was. No doubt from too many back-to-back twelve hour shifts, capped off by a grueling softball game. "Please."

Hands resting at his hips, Ronen towered over her. "Is there anything you need before I leave?"

Stella handed Annie the portable phone. "Dr. Latimer would like a word with you. I'll check on you after I get home."

"I'll leave my door open," Ronen said as he followed Stella out the door. "Holler if you need me."

Annie watched his broad-shouldered frame move out of sight. With a sigh that was part-wish, part-regret, she raised the phone to her mouth. "Yes, John?"

"How's the knee?"

After a quick visual exam of the flagrantly swollen part, she chirped, "Just peachy."

"Tell me another fairy story, Wolfgirl," the elderly, take-no-crap-from-anyone physician muttered. "You know what to do. RICE it and relax."

Rest, Ice, Compression, Elevation. Annie knew the drill. Better than most. "I've already started."

"MRI in the morning," he rattled off. "Need to check out the collateral ligaments. Just in case. Agreed?"

She would have gone the same route, were she the physician of record. "I'll get somebody to drive me to the hospital."

"Now. As to the second reason I called."

Since she was on call for the Urgent Care Center, Annie prayed it wasn't a patient emergency. "Who is it?"

"Got home from the game, found a message from the med school at Syracuse on my answering machine."

Her heart stopped for several seconds. *Please, please, don't let this be another rejection.* Her pulse resumed a hard, thumping beat. "And?"

"Dave Murray wants to interview you."

Annie nearly came off the couch. "Yess!"

So many schools had looked only at her academic records and test scores before summarily dismissing her applications. SU was her last chance at making her dream of becoming a doctor come true. Tears of relief scalded her eyelids. "Thank you, John, for whatever strings you pulled, for whatever it took to convince Dr. Murray to interview me."

"Didn't do anything, Wolfgirl. Dave only sees the best. You're it."

"I hope so."

"Yeah, yeah. After I told him about your work with the immigrant community, the mobile medical unit you organized, the last three rape trials that ended in convictions only because of your forensic exams, the man couldn't move fast enough to rearrange his calendar."

"I don't know what to say."

"This is your chance, Wolfgirl. Don't let me down."

Now she was really going to bawl. "I'll do my best."

"Stay sharp, stay focused," Latimer advised in his customary growl. "Don't let anything or anyone stand in your way."

With a short glance for the empty doorway of her apartment, Annie drew a shuddering breath. "I won't. I promise."

She hung up the phone, wishing she could share the good news with someone other than John.

Her thoughts went immediately to Barb Thompson, whom she knew would dance circles if she knew this latest event.

Christ, where was she?

Barb had moved back to Albany shortly after Luba Sanko's death, promising to stay in touch with Annie, let her know how she was doing. But Annie hadn't heard from her friend in months. The New York State Department of Social Services in Albany refused to give out any information on Barb's current whereabouts. With no family, that Annie was aware of, to contact she was at a loss as to what to do next. And how she loathed waiting.

"Dammit, Barb! Where are you? Why haven't you called?"

Two

Throwing open the door to his son's bedroom, Ronen delivered the threat with appropriate decisiveness. "Turn it down or that CD becomes the latest thing in Frisbees."

Chris glanced up. With a flick of his thumb, the decibel level on the boom box dropped from brain-melting to merely eardrum-rupturing. "Sorry, Dad."

"Save the sorries." His gaze hardened on the piles of clothes, throw pillows and books strewn across the room. "Clean this mess up before the Health Department shuts us down."

"Yes, sir. Watcha doin' out there?"

"Thinking."

"Feeling reckless, are we?"

"Very funny." On his way out, Ronen snatched a pair of earphones off the doorknob. "Here." He tossed them in the direction of a tattered sleeping bag. "Use them or lose them."

He slammed the door, then headed into the kitchen to finish putting away crockery and glassware. There was little else to occupy his mind while performing the necessary, no-brainer chores that accompanied moving into a new place—other than thinking about the case, this town and its people...

And a woman whose knee currently resembled an eggplant for size, shape, and color.

Annie Wolfe was bright, funny and intriguing. It had been a long time since he'd felt such an immediate, intense attraction to any woman. As his entire family, including Chris, were reminding him with increasing frequency, it was time for him to get a life beyond witness statements, crime scene photos and autopsy reports. Lisa had been dead for ten years. Ten long, lonely years.

Shelf paper in one hand, scissors in the other, Ronen found himself staring through the screen of his new kitchen window overlooking the landscaped area across the street from the mansion. Earlier in the day, Stella Grover proudly informed him the park was named after her late husband, Henry.

A miniscule breeze barely ruffled the starched curtains hanging from the rod above the window. He'd known before heading down here that the northern Cats was in the middle of a brutal heat wave. This was no aberrant temperature rise.

This was hell.

Two elderly gentlemen, sharing one of the park's wrought-iron benches, argued over a checker game. Two kids, shouting dares and taunts at one another, raced their bikes over the winding asphalt paths. Just watching them made him sweat.

After the last verbal challenge, a woman vaulted off a tree-shaded bench. "Caleb Parker!" she yelled. "Use the F-word again, there'll be no chicken barbecue for you tonight."

"Aw, Ma!"

"I mean it, young man. I won't have your mouth makin' folks think we're poor white trash."

Ronen could only wonder about a mother who voiced more concern over her son's language—admittedly raw—than his riding without a safety helmet. In the distance, a fire siren competed with the roars from souped up four-by-fours tearing down Main Street. Ronen glanced at his watch. "Five o'clock. Time to get happy."

He pondered the vagaries of small town life. How did people survive the slow pace without going stark raving mad? Where did a man, if he was so inclined, take a date in this town?

One of the ever-charming Main Street taverns for a couple of boilermakers? Perhaps the local drive-in theater for a Rambo marathon? He shuddered. "I don't think so."

Socializing, he decided, would have to take a back seat in order for him to do his job and get back to civilization. What's another year when you've already been alone this long? Even if there was something remotely interesting to do in Hicksville, USA, he was so out of practice, he wouldn't know how to approach a woman for a date.

A knock on the apartment door interrupted his train of thought. He entered the living room to find Annie standing in his open doorway, looking embarrassed. "I'm sorry to bother you," she mumbled.

Discomfort lined her face, and set off an immediate protective-male response. He walked to her, hand out. "What's wrong?"

"After all you did for me today, I hate to bother—"

"That's what neighbors are for, Annie."

She fidgeted on the crutches, as if she were trying to find a more comfortable position. Or maybe turn and run. "My doctor booked me for an MRI in the morning. I was wondering if you could—"

She shifted the crutches again. He couldn't help but look at her knee. Even wrapped, it was swollen to twice the size of the other. "What can I do?"

"It's short notice. I'd understand if you couldn't drive me. See, my car is—"

"Standard shift, I noticed." Unlike most men, he hated sports. But, like most men, he appreciated classic cars. Her cherry-red Mustang was a honey.

Annie shrugged, then turned away. "No big whoop. I'll ask Stella."

Given the way she responded to his carrying her up the stairs, what she said to Chris about a woman getting herself out of her own jams, he imagined it took a lot for her to ask for help. Her manner was one of resignation, like she expected him to turn her down before the request was out of her mouth.

"Tomorrow is my first day of work, Annie, I'm sorry." He raised a palm. "But... there is an alternative. Chris?"

The boy appeared at his bedroom door. "You bellowed?" The smart-aleck grin faded when he saw Annie. "Geez, Ms. Wolfe, you look like shi—"

"Christopher!"

Annie chuckled. "No need to spare my sensibilities. I've used the word a time or two. God knows I feel like it."

"Chris," Ronen explained. "Ms. Wolfe needs our help."

"Sure thing. What's up?"

"Do you drive?" she asked.

"Me? I can handle anything on wheels."

"Ever driven a stick shift?"

The boy gaped at her. "Are you serious? You want me to drive *your car*?"

A slim smile creased her mouth. "That's the idea."

"When, where, how far and how long?"

"This is a trip to the hospital in Oneonta," she advised. "Not a moon launch."

"Serious?" he wheezed. "This isn't a joke?"

"No joke, Christopher. My car."

"Man, oh man," he crowed. "I'm gonna get to drive a V-8, tweaked suspension, Shelby mag wheels and dual hood scoops?" He stopped to examine the toes of his sneakers. "I kinda checked it out."

"Smart man always checks out his wheels," Annie murmured.

Chris tucked his chin; Ronen didn't miss the grin on his son's face at the word *man*. "Could we put the top down?"

She nodded. "Only way to go, kid."

"Man, oh man. This is so phat."

"Excuse me?" Ronen asked. "How does being overweight enter into driving a classy car?"

A bubble of laughter erupted from Annie's throat. "*Phat* means cool, 2-A. As in super, out of sight, fabulous. You know."

Sure. He knew that. From the look on his son's face, Annie Wolfe had just made Chris' day—if not his entire summer.

Perhaps job responsibilities could afford a short detour. But, first things first. Annie's knee was looking more swollen by the minute and, from the deepening lines at the corners of her mouth, she looked to be in some serious pain.

Ignoring her squeak of protest, he scooped her into his arms and let the crutches fall where they may. "I'll take Ms. Wolfe back to her place, Chris. Find my wallet and car keys. Make a food run to the supermarket we passed on our way into town. Get enough for three."

"No problem. While I'm out, I'll look for the dry cleaners Major Valetta told you about. If it's still open, I'll drop your uniforms off."

"No ramming around," Ronen warned. "Come straight back."

"Dad. Please."

As Ronen carried Annie back to her place, he noticed many things. A whiff of lilacs from her hair, the narrow waist, the suppleness of her skin. And the long, lean legs that would wrap a man's waist in—

He cleared his throat before settling Annie on her davenport, then packed her leg in fresh ice. The look she gave him was sheepish. "I feel like an idiot."

"Is it so hard to lean on others?"

"Hard?" She laughed mirthlessly. "Try penance."

Chris appeared in the doorway, arms filled with Ronen's uniform shirts and trousers. "Anything in particular you'd like for dinner, Ms. Wolfe?"

The gentle smile she gave Chris twisted Ronen's gut into a pretzel. "You choose."

"How about you, Dad?"

Needing space and distance, Ronen stepped back from the couch. "Watch the spices and the fat. If you find the cleaners, ask for extra starch in the shirts."

Seconds after Chris left, Annie murmured, "You're a cop, Mr. Marvelic."

Caution settled over his shoulders like a mantle. "Is that a problem?"

"Of course not. I work with cops all the time." Her wry smile gave the knot in his gut another twist. "A state trooper. Whose butt did you forget to kiss?"

"I'm sorry?"

"Not many would consider No Man's Land to be the grand prize in assignments."

Having already felt her barbs where it concerned small town life, the last thing he wanted was a debate over career choices. He took a seat in a nearby Papasan chair. "Let's say there were probably several pair of buttocks I neglected to address in the appropriate fashion."

Her sigh was deep, as well as provocative. "A lone ranger. My kind of man."

"Beg pardon?"

"Forget it," she mumbled, playing with the hem of her shirt. "Doesn't matter."

~ * ~

Over spinach salads, flame-broiled vegetables, and fresh fruit, Christopher did a superb job of interrogating Annie about her duties and responsibilities as a physician's assistant. His father, she noted, just sat back and listened.

"So, you get to boss nurses around?"

"We prefer to call it writing orders."

"I always wanted to know how you figure out what's wrong with people just by poking and prodding, taking blood and stuff."

She wanted to laugh, but feared it might stifle his natural curiosity. "I find it helpful to listen to my patients. Get an idea of how long they've felt ill, what made them better and, more important, what made them worse."

"Sounds good." Chris pushed the bowl of melon, purple grapes and fresh strawberries out of his way. "Why do you need an MRI? I mean, can't they tell what's wrong with your knee with a regular x-ray?"

The kid was bright, inquisitive, and asked all the right questions. "How old did you say you were?"

"Eighteen."

"Going on thirty," Ronen offered.

"Dad."

"Sounds like you're interested in medicine," Annie said, watching his father's face go from placid to queasy.

Chris nodded. "I think I am, yeah."

"I have a couple old textbooks in the living room if you'd like to look at them."

"No lie? Could I really?"

"Christopher," Ronen cautioned. "Don't—"

The boy was out of his chair like a shot. Annie raised a hand. "It's okay. There's nothing more fascinating to a budding medical professional than really gross pictures. If they don't turn him off, nothing will."

After a few moments, Christopher flew into the kitchen, clutching an ancient dermatology book to his chest as if it was spun gold. "Check this out, Dad. It's great!"

The big, tall trooper turned as green as the salad in front of him. "Thanks, son. Maybe another time."

"But, Dad, this guy's got something called Hee-dra-adeen-eye-tis Super something. The picture's too gross for words. They have to cut out all the infected scar tissue, then—" His eyes went to the size of saucers. "Too gross!"

Annie explained treatment options for Hydradenitis Suprativa, long-term antibiotic therapy versus wide-angle tissue resection as she diagrammed the surgical procedure on a paper napkin.

"Yeah, but—" Chris breathed. "If they have to take out all that infected tissue, how do they close it back up?"

She was about to explain the principle of undermining the top layers of tissue to approximate the skin edges when she saw that Trooper Marvelic was beyond green. Cold and clammy had entered his clinical picture. "Maybe you should look at the book on your own, Chris."

He glanced at his father. "Sorry, Dad." Then he looked to her. "Sure it's okay if I take it with me?"

"Keep if for as long as you like." An idea came to mind. "Would you like to observe the MRI tomorrow?"

If it was possible, his eyes got even bigger. "About as much as I want to breathe."

"I'll fix it," she promised. "We need to leave here by ten at the latest."

"I'll be ready." Chris rose from the table with his hand out. "Thanks, Ms. Wolfe."

She returned the handshake. "The name is Annie, and you're very welcome."

By the time Chris was out the door, Annie saw that Ronen's color had improved. The area beneath his jaw was no longer chartreuse. "Sorry for getting carried away with the clinical stuff."

He carefully aligned her mismatched salt and pepper shakers with a napkin holder that held only bills and junk mail. In a murmur she'd likened to the devil's, he said, "For the past four weeks, I've watched my son take pouting, whining, and sarcasm to new heights. It's a new experience, seeing him enthused about something other than acid rock and the latest horror movie. Thank you."

After taking several deep breaths to settle her pulse, she asked, "For what?"

"Paying attention to him, answering all his questions." He paused. "For not treating him like a kid."

Man, this guy pushed all of her buttons without even trying. And if he continued looking at her that way, she might ignore John Latimer's words of caution.

Don't let anyone get in your way.

~ * ~

"Man alive, Annie!" Chris Marvelic shouted as he took the Mustang flying down Interstate 88. "Driving this car is better than looking at pictures of nasty skin diseases or watching an MRI any day."

Compelled to put a death grip on the door handle for a third time since they'd left the hospital, she clenched her teeth and gritted, "Who taught you how to drive a stick?"

"My aunt Rachel. She's a marshal."

Annie gulped. "As in Tommy Lee Jones and Wesley Snipes *US Marshals*?"

"You got it," he crowed against the wind buffeting his face. "Cops run like water in my family. My Dad, Aunt Rachel, and her husband. I'm the renegade."

"I don't understand." When he slowed to take the exit for Nohmensville, Annie relaxed her hand.

"I know cops help people," he said, "but I want to help them in a different way."

Cops help people? Not in this town.

"I think I want to be a physician's assistant like you, maybe even a doctor."

"What does your father think about your plans?"

"He says if I try hard, I can be anything I want."

"Good for him. Where are you going to college?"

"Cornell."

Whoa. Good grades and big bucks were the only things that got somebody into that school. She was lucky to have slugged out barely passing marks at City College of New York. "You must be smart."

"I did okay," he mumbled over a rising blush. "Dad had to put in a lot of overtime to make the fall tuition payment. I'd like to find a job this summer so he won't have to work so hard."

An eighteen-year-old who put others ahead of himself. She didn't need to look further than a pair of solemn green eyes and a smile that shook her resolve to avoid relationships to know the source of that particular value.

"Let's stop at the Urgent Care Center, kid. There's someone I'd like you to meet."

~ * ~

Annie wasn't surprised to find Trooper Marvelic pacing the mansion's parking lot when she and Chris arrived home from Urgent Care. Having a son driving all over hell's half acre with a near stranger would turn the most understanding of fathers into raving lunatics.

"How'd it go?" he asked.

Chris bolted from the driver's seat. "Dad. Living down here might not be so bad. Did you know there's two colleges in Oneonta and the Baseball Hall of Fame's only a few minutes away? Why didn't you tell me No Man's Land had babes *and* baseball?"

"I was saving it for a special occasion," Ronen murmured, jutting his chin toward the Mustang. "Did you forget something?"

"Not that I—oh." Chris raced back to the car to open the door for her. "Sorry. Guess I got carried away for a second."

"Babes?" Annie chuckled. "We'll discuss the politically correct terminology for women later, Christopher."

The kid gaped at her. "Politically correct? Didn't I—?"

Annie could only laugh as she maneuvered her way out of the Mustang. "Go. Tell your father what else you learned on your travels. I can manage here."

Then, Ronen was there, at her side, holding her crutches in one hand while helping her to her feet with the other. And oh, that hand was warm. And strong. "Feeling steady?"

Jesus, Mary, and Joseph, the man had eyes that could drive a nun to the nearest condom rack. "I'm fine."

He glanced over his shoulder at Chris. "Fill me in."

"Annie got me a job at the Urgent Care Center!"

The kid was so excited, she thought he might start dancing his way across the parking lot. "You did it all by yourself."

"And what, pray tell," Ronen asked quietly, "is an Urgent Care Center?"

Chris looked to Annie, then ducked his head. "Go ahead," she urged. "Tell him."

Scuffing the pavement with the toe of his sneaker, Chris mumbled, "It's where people who aren't sick enough to need an ER, but still need to be seen, can receive care. Annie works there sometimes."

"What else is it for?" she prompted.

"Oh, yeah," he said, seeming to regain some of his former confidence. "If folks don't have a regular doctor, they can go to Urgent Care. It's open evenings and weekends. It's great, Dad."

During Christopher's explanation, Ronen's face had taken on the inflexibility of granite. Something told her it might be wise to avoid that particular look in the future.

"You took him there?" he asked her in clipped, precise tones. "Without consulting me?" The quietness of his voice was deceptive, and infinitely more menacing than a shout. Had she been able, she would have run for the next bus out of town.

"Chris looked around and spoke with Dr. Latimer," she explained, growing increasingly more uneasy with Ronen's body language. "He filled out an application. John hired him on the spot. No big whoop."

"I believe I should be the one to decide on *no big whoops*, don't you, Ms. Wolfe?" He turned a cold gaze on his son. "What will you be expected to do there, Christopher?"

She wondered what effect that tone of voice had on suspects. Probably scared them into confessing. She started to answer, then changed her mind.

"Cool stuff, Dad. Mop up blood and guts. Hold broken bones while Annie or Dr. Latimer slap on a cast. Take blood pressures and pulses—after awhile—if I'm good enough." The next came on its own. "Best of all, Dad, Dr. Latimer will pay me eight dollars an hour. Eight bucks! Can you believe it?"

Annie wasn't about to let the glower on Marvelic's face scare her off. Chris needed all the support he could get. If he didn't get it from his father, he'd sure as hell get it from her. "You'll be good enough for blood pressures and pulses. Give yourself time."

"We've discussed this before," Ronen said. "You need to devote your time to studying and enjoying college life. It's my job to worry about finances."

Annie watched the light fade from the boy's eyes. "But, Dad, I really want to—"

"We'll discuss this later."

"But, Dad—"

"Later."

With that one single word, she moved quickly to avoid what appeared to be an imminent explosion. This was not her place. It was none of her business. If Marvelic wanted to act like an insensitive jerk, he could do it on his own time.

"Mutant pinhead," she muttered, angling the crutches in the direction of the porch. "All the flair of amoebic dysentery."

"Annie, wait!" Chris called. He caught up with her at the front sidewalk. "Thanks for today. You're the best."

She wanted to take him in her arms, give him the hug he deserved. "You're pretty phat yourself, kid." Surveying the perimeter, radar on full alert for arrogant fathers, she leaned toward Chris. "Sorry if I caused you trouble with your dad."

"Nah," he said, but studiously avoided her gaze. "He's a little old fashioned sometimes. Need help getting upstairs?"

This morning, she managed to get herself down the stairs by sitting with her bad leg extended out in front of her and sliding her fanny down one step at a time. If it worked going down, it ought to work going back up.

"I'll be fine. Go back to your fathead—I mean, father."

Chris whooped. "I like you, Annie Wolfe."

Instead of hugging him like she wanted to do, she reached out a hand and stroked the side of his face. Chris grinned. Regret reared its ugly head. Just as quickly, she tamped it down. "I like you, too, pal."

"I'm going to take a walk," he said. "Try to figure out a way to make Dad listen to me."

That should only take the rest of his life. "Good luck."

She was halfway up the inside flight of stairs when Ronen appeared one step below her. "Need help?"

Not from a Neanderthal, thank you very much. "I'm fine."

"I appreciate what you did for my boy."

Buttocks held in midair by locked and braced arms, Annie stared at him. "Appreciate? I must have missed that part of the conversation, Mr. Marvelic."

"I shouldn't have allowed private matters to go public."

Remembering the way the light faded from that beautiful child's eyes, she spat, "God forbid we should let family secrets be known to anyone outside the family."

"What's that supposed to mean?"

"Do you have the faintest idea of what a terrific, sensitive kid you've raised? Are you aware he's worried you'll work too hard after he leaves for college?" He raised one brow; Annie plowed ahead. "Your son loves you, Marvelic. Do you understand just how lucky you are?"

Back went the shoulders, out went the chest. The man might look smashing in the spic and span, hyper-starched uniform. He fell a tad short when it came to taking criticism.

"I know exactly how great Christopher is." She could see the muscles of his jaw working overtime. He'd have a headache tonight, she decided and grinned inside. Good. "No one need tell me how lucky I am."

She edged up another step. "You'll forgive me if I have doubts about that particular proclamation, Mr. Marvelic."

"You don't understand the way it is between him and me."

"Bullshit, I don't understand! He's a bright, caring boy who wants to take the load off his overworked parent."

"I'm not overworked."

So much for communication between parents and children. "Chris needs to hear that, not me."

"You don't understand what it's like to raise a child all..." His voice faltered. "Alone."

He was right on that point. She would never experience the joys and heartaches of raising a child. "Is it such a sin to back off a little and let him do something to help himself? If it turns out to be a mistake, he'll learn from it."

"Let him learn from something other than flunking out because he had to work his tail off for tuition money."

Ah, ha, she thought. Now comes the truth.

"He is eighteen years old," she said. "Isn't it time he learns to consider options, weigh them, then make a choice?"

Marvelic's sad, sweet smile battered the armor enclosing her heart. With blinding clarity, she realized it wasn't arrogance she was seeing on his face. It was worry and anxiety. Uncertainty.

It was love for his son.

With recognition came a softened manner. "You're correct, Ronen. I've never had a child, probably never will. Please don't expect an apology for my helping Chris do what he felt was right, what he felt was his fair share."

"I never expected—"

"Yes, you did," she said sadly. "If you'll excuse me, I need to get upstairs, rest my leg."

"Let me carry you the rest of the way."

Never in a million years would she let this man take her in his arms again. "I'm perfectly capable. Thanks anyway."

Ronen plunked himself down beside her. Running his fingertips over the brim of his Stetson, he offered, "Appreciate the time you took with my boy."

"However," she muttered, "you'd just as soon me stay out of your business."

"Not exactly. It's just—"

Pushing up on her hands, she hauled her fanny to the next step. "This is getting old, Ronen. Kindly go away."

"At the rate you're moving, slugger, it'll take you the better part of a week to get upstairs."

"Aw, hell. Haven't got anything better to do."

She needed to be by herself right now, not arguing with a man who didn't know the first thing about her understanding of family dynamics or filial affection and respect. At the moment, feeling quite sorry for herself, she needed comfort from junk food and a double header on ESPN. After reviewing the MRI, John Latimer insisted she take a week off. No matter how loudly she protested, he refused to budge.

Exactly what was she supposed to do for an entire week? There was only so much preparing she could do for Dr. Murray's interview. Over-rehearsal might diminish the spontaneity of her responses, and that would put her dead in the water as far as med school was concerned.

Twiddling her thumbs was not her style. With her bum knee, cleaning the apartment was out. Not that housekeeping, tasks she loathed more than root canals, would have entered her mind.

Marvelic persisted. "Sure you don't want a lift?"

He didn't have to grin, as if that killer smile would make things all better between them.

"Don't you have something more important to do? There must be an illegal search and seizure out there with your name on it, someone whose civil rights are begging to be violated."

"You have a warped view of law enforcement, Ms. Wolfe."

"Comes from long, painful experience."

A voice barked from the foyer below. "Am I interrupting something?"

In the dim light Annie spied another tan Stetson, another arrow-straight body clothed in gray trousers and shirt bearing a load of fruit salad medals above the breast pocket. The voice, of course, identified him immediately. Only one man had a voice that sounded like his vocal cords had been buffed with sandpaper. "Major Valetta?"

"It ain't the Easter Bunny, Wolfgirl. What are you doing with my officer?"

"Having an argu—"

"Putting me in my place," Ronen cut in.

"Was not."

"Were too," he replied, then grinned.

"Creep."

"Harpy."

"All right," Valetta barked. "Neutral corners, both of you. Annie, we need to talk. In private."

"Do I need an attorney for this private conversation?"

"Cute," Valetta retorted. "Marvelic, you know the drill."

"Wait a minute," she yelped after Ronen scooped her up in his arms. Again. "Is there some part of 'No' that's escaped your comprehension?"

Dammit, did he have to smell like he'd just stepped out of the shower?

"Burn your brassiere on somebody else's time, missy," Valetta directed. "We need your help."

~ * ~

"You want me to what?"

Ronen heard the shock in Annie's voice from where he stood at her living room window. "Are you out of your mind, Major?"

"Marvelic is down here on special assignment, looking into the trouble," Valetta told her. "I'd like you to help him."

"Trouble?" she mused. "An odd way of describing women being murdered and dumped along I-88 like last week's trash."

"Now, Annie." Valetta's patent sigh made Ronen cringe.

Offering the man a glacial stare, she said, "I'll ignore that patronizing response, Major, because I know you would never deliberately piss me off."

"You're right on that account," Valetta muttered.

"And I'm sure, had you seen the condition of the bodies as I did, you would agree with my professional opinion that it was a blessing none of the women survived."

"I would," he said.

Ronen felt Annie's cold gaze scan his body from forehead to shoes. "Special assignment, Marvelic? Guess you picked the right butts after all."

From her, the comment stung. "The less people who know why I was assigned to this area the better."

"That your way of telling me to keep my lip zipped?"

Valetta broke in. "Annie, are you aware the Nohmensville Police Department is being dissolved come the fifteenth of the month and that the Troops will take over ensuring public safety?"

"Can't come soon enough for me," she said. "Five dead women and nobody's done squat. Five dead men would be different. Hell, five dead cows would create outright panic in this town."

"Why is that, do you think?" Ronen asked.

She challenged him with a look. "You tell me, city boy. The first two were crossed off as runaways because no one could ID them. As long as it wasn't a girl from the area no one had cause to be concerned, because—"

If they hadn't run, they wouldn't be dead, Ronen finished silently. He'd heard the excuse. Too many times.

Annie worked her hands around the crutch handles until her knuckles blanched white in the midday sun. "The third was a migrant worker from Harbaugh Farms who liked to party, occasionally with some not so nice guys, so nobody got too excited. The fourth lived in town, only she was from El Salvador; she obviously didn't count. By the time the fifth murder occurred—well, you tell me."

The fire of indignation was alive and well in her eyes. "I'd prefer to hear it from you," Ronen murmured.

She glanced up at him, chin set at an obstinate angle. "All right. I want to know who else has to die before this town opens its eyes and demands appropriate police response."

Valetta growled, "You've run your mouth, Wolfgirl. Gotten it all out of your system. Will you help us?"

"I don't think it's such a good idea."

Ronen's head snapped up in both surprise, and relief, at Annie's response. Personally, he thought it was a lousy idea—but Valetta wanted her involved. And what the brass wanted, the brass usually got.

"I don't have the qualifications," she protested. "I'm not a medical examiner; I'm not a physician."

"Didn't you work with torture victims when you lived in New York City?" Valetta countered.

Her reaction was instant, and defensive. "How did you find out about that?" she demanded, eyes narrowed, shoulders grazing her earlobes.

"Doc Latimer."

"That man needs to have his mouth sutured shut," she snapped. "If it were to come to trial, any defense attorney worth his salt would laugh my testimony out of court."

Victims of torture, Ronen groaned silently. So that's why Valetta picked her. "You wouldn't have to testify, Annie."

The fire in her eyes had not dimmed one iota. "Exactly what would I be expected to do?"

"I need you to look at the coroner's photographs to correlate wound patterns, help me gather background information on the last victims. We call it profiling."

"I don't know how much help I'd be."

Valetta worked the brim of his Stetson. "Annie, we know you were acquainted with some of the women. You just said you saw the bodies."

"Oh, yeah." Ronen heard the despair in her voice. "I saw them all right."

Jim Valetta played his trump card. "John Latimer said to tell you David Murray would shinny up a flag pole if he knew you were helping us on this."

At the mention of this Murray guy's name, Annie went from guarded to all-out aggression. "Son of a bitch!" Fists clenched on the crutch handles, she demanded, "Where's Tom Moran in this picture?"

"Local Medical Examiner," Valetta advised Ronen. "Took off after the last vic was recovered."

Annie's grunt showed her disgust. "The local cops did zip on that case so Tommy told the county legislature to take his job and stuff it."

She stepped back and glared at Valetta. "Tom was the best. Can't you call him? Ask him to help?"

"Far as we know, Doc Moran's somewhere in Alaska," he responded. "No forwarding address."

Mounting frustration showed in her voice. "So get Big Mouth Latimer to help. He's acting coroner these days."

"Acting," Valetta emphasized. "John is the first to admit he can tell if somebody's croaked or not—but it ends there. Besides, he was only involved on the fifth case. The teenage prostitute, I forget her name."

Despite the crutches, she was across the room in seconds, and in Jim's face like a terrier after a rat. "Luba Sanko," she hissed, "was little more than a child who *did... not... hook*!"

Palms up in a sign of surrender, Valetta moved back a step. "Settle down, Annie. If you say she didn't work the circuit, we believe you. Don't we, Marv?"

Surmising the Major was in imminent danger of having his throat ripped out, Ronen moved to his commander's side. "It doesn't matter what any of the victims did or didn't do. None of them deserved to die. Certainly not like that."

Moisture glistened at the corners of Annie's chocolate-brown eyes. She blinked, once. "I have to think about it."

"Take all the time you need," Ronen said.

She began to pace the room on the crutches, mumbling to herself. After shaking her head a few times, she spun around on her good foot. "I'll only look at pictures?"

"Correct," Ronen said.

"No one outside the three of us will know I'm helping?"

"Absolutely," Ronen promised, wondering why secrecy would be a concern to her.

She looked directly at him. "You won't ask me to come up with theories on the perps or any of that other profiling stuff."

"That's my job."

"Can we do it soon? Latimer's making me take a week off to rest my leg. It'll keep my mind occupied."

"How's the knee?" Valetta asked.

"MRI was negative. Just a strain. No big whoop."

"You're good, Annie," Valetta pronounced. "Make my little girl look like a champ."

"She does the work, Major. I'm only there for moral support."

Valetta grinned as he stuck out his hand. "Deal?"

Ronen saw her slide a glance in his direction. "I may regret it," she said, "but we've got a deal."

Three

"You don't like men very much."

Leaning her weight on the kitchen table, Annie shuffled through morgue shots and grimaced. "Where did you get that idea?"

After three incredibly long nights working with her, he was used to her sarcasm, suspecting she used it to keep people—meaning men—at a distance. He'd seen it before, particularly among victim advocates.

When she spoke of the dead women, even the ones she didn't know, sarcasm rapidly switched to soft and serene. Ronen had to wonder if she was aware that the change in her tone was sending him on a slow trip around the bend. He doubted it. Highly.

When it came to the killers, her voice and body language took a one-hundred-eighty degree turn. "I look at these photos," she said, "and ask myself where were the cops? What steps did they take after the first death to prevent the rest?"

"It's my understanding the locals had little to go on," Ronen cut in, uncomfortable with what felt like a lame excuse. "The first two bodies were seriously decomposed by the time the hunters found them. There were no missing persons reports to correspond with Dr. Moran's descriptions of general body build, ages and coloring."

"Why weren't they sent to Albany?" she countered. "Let the forensics people work on fingerprints and reconstructing the faces? Don't you think there are families out there who deserve to know what happened to their children?"

"When they couldn't ID the girls as being from this area, it was logical to assume they were runners. Sorry—" he said quickly. "—I meant to say—"

"I know what 'runner' means, Marvelic," she snapped. "They were runaways."

"If you know what runner means," he offered, "then you know most kids don't take off because mom refused them a second helping of dessert. Some families simply don't care, Annie."

"Tell me about it." She flipped through the next series of photographs. "Some people should be sterilized at the onset of puberty. Wouldn't know how to care for an animal—much less a child."

Where did that come from?

Annie continued. As she got going, Ronen didn't attempt, didn't want, to stop her. "Okay, so nobody got all nervous and jerky about two runaways. I can live with that. Don't like it, but I can live with it."

The muscles in her face tightened. "Then, local women started turning up dead, and still nothing happened. I can't help but believe if English had been their first language, the cases would have been handled differently. Maybe the town would have been more vocal."

Sadly, Ronen couldn't disagree. It was human nature for people to turn their heads when crime victims practiced different lifestyles, or came from the less affluent part of town.

But when one of their own was victimized, no one pushed for police action louder, or harder, than 'concerned' citizens. He'd seen it happen, too often, in Rochester, as well as other cities across the state.

Human nature. Sometimes Ronen hated it.

Annie took a deep breath, letting it out it a slow whoosh. "Have you read the investigator's reports?"

Another piece of the puzzle to grind his teeth over. The police reports on the deaths were MIA—or so Jim Valetta had been informed after he requested copies of all major case files in preparation for the change-over in departments. Valetta told Ronen to be patient, to wait for the Troops to take over the Nohmensville PD before taking action. As much as he hated delays, one minute after the change-over, he planned to tear the damn place apart.

"I haven't had the opportunity as yet."

"I'm sure they'll be quite helpful."

Sarcasm was the last thing he needed. It wasn't the first time she'd hinted the police had more than a passive involvement in the murders. That was all. Just hinted.

Though it had been five years, flashes of the Collins case still singed his conscience. The prolonged investigation into police corruption, loaded with blind alleys and one-way turns, went sour after the civilian consultant on the case shot off his mouth in the middle of a cop bar. While bragging about his part in the case, he disclosed confidential information to the wrong people. Word spread through the department like a case of VD. After hearing that his name had been mentioned by the civilian, police officer Ted Collins—later proved innocent—panicked, then committed suicide.

Seeing Collins' body, half his face missing, was bad. The widow's screamed accusations that Ronen was responsible for her husband's death was ten times worse.

Never again would he trust a civilian, no matter how crucial their information was to the case. And *never* would he trust any civilian to keep their mouth shut.

"Do you have names, dates, times, Annie? If you do, I'll act on it. If not—"

Raising a palm, she said, "That was unfair of me. No more nasty comments about the Nohmensville cops." She gave him a grimace of a smile. "To answer your original comment, I like men just fine—as a group."

"Individually?"

"Bullies who don't care enough to keep their families—or the citizens they're hired to protect—safe and free from abuse go right to the top of my hit list." She loosened her shoulders with a quick shrug. "Can we get back to the file? I've got places to go, things to do."

With a leg she could barely stand on for more than fifteen minutes at a time, she had things to do? "Really? Like what?"

"Elimination rounds for the World Cup start tonight."

Was there nothing, he wondered, more inane, more trivial, than group sports? *Pass the beer and pretzels, honey. And don't forget the remote.*

Outside what she'd done during the enforced time off, he had to wonder, between her shifts at the local Emergency Room and Urgent Care Center, in addition to her obsession with sports, if Annie considered anything other than contagious diseases, sudden death shoot-outs or compound fractures worthy of her attention.

"Anyone ever suggest you get a life, Ms. Wolfe? Outside medicine and sports, I mean."

"Big talker, Mr. Law and Order," she jeered. "Working ten hour days, then coming home to—" She cleared her throat before giving the hem of her T-shirt, whose message suggested the observer Eat Dirt And Die, a hard jerk. "Can we please get back to victim number four?"

Had she been about to say *coming home to me* before she caught herself?

Even after putting in long days at the barracks, he'd found himself looking forward to her greeting him at her door. Each night, he discovered another facet of her personality. Each time he became more intrigued by Annie's drive to fulfill the request from Jim Valetta, as well as her limitless passion to help the abused and disadvantaged.

Cop's instinct told him her background featured neglect, if not actual abuse. It wasn't uncommon for a kid to rise above rotten beginnings, turning into an obsessive overachiever along the way. Annie Wolfe was obsessive with a capital O.

He needed to understand what made this fascinating woman tick. Examining graphic details of hideous abuses was not the way to pursue a relationship. For three nights running, he'd tried his best to persuade her to see him as more than a cop. He needed Annie to see him as a man.

What did he have to show for it? Squat.

He dropped the pictures of victim number four on her kitchen table. Adjusting the crutches beneath her arms, Annie fanned them out like a deck of playing cards. One look had the color draining from her face. A soft whimper left her throat.

"Ann." He touched her shoulder. "We've been going at this non-stop. Let's take a breather."

She tilted her head in his direction, narrowed her eyes. "Do you need a break?"

"I'm fine." This was his job after all. He'd been doing it for years. Someday, he might even get used to it.

"Same goes, Ronen. I need to get this over with."

Tough-women personas didn't deter him. Ronen covered her trembling hand with his. "We both need a break. Now."

"And do what?" she demanded, pulling away. "Discuss the weather? Talk about this heat that will drive me up a wall if we don't get some rain soon? Maybe the Nuggets' chances at the regionals? How about hog futures?"

"What in hell are hog futures?"

"Sorry. A little Nohmensville humor. Did you have any special thoughts about this set of photos?"

Did every assignment consume her like this? Did she attack every patient problem with the same single-minded intensity?

He was the supposed expert on crime scenes, but Annie was showing him a thing or two about restraint devices and pre-morbid bleeding patterns. Her ability to understand and accept what the immigrant women had endured in their countries of origin, and how those experiences influenced their new lives in Nohmensville, was staggering. She set an exhausting pace for herself, one that would bring most men to their knees.

"How about we go for a ride, come back to this later?"

She looked at him like he'd sprouted a second head. "I'd like to finish up, Ronen, if you don't mind."

Of course he minded. The only thing he didn't mind was that she was calling him by his first name, not the ambiguous "2-A", or worse, "Mr. Marvelic".

Resigned to being shot down, again, he asked, "How did you come to know Maria Salvado?"

One slender finger slowly traced the photograph of the bruises on Maria's shoulders and elbows. Her voice, filled with regret—and something else he couldn't identify—seared his heart.

"She was a teacher in El Salvador, held a master's degree in early childhood development. Her husband was a journalist; they had one child, a son. One night, government troops forced their way into the Salvado's home and took Maria's husband and son away. She never saw them again. And two more names were added to the list of *los desaparecidos*, the disappeared ones."

"It must have been very difficult," he murmured.

"Yes." She fingered the remaining photos; her shoulders sagged. "Missionaries smuggled Maria out of the country; the underground movement here in the States helped her get settled. When she felt stronger and was ready to make a fresh start, she came to Nohmensville to open a nursery school for the workers on Abner Harbaugh's farm. The children and their parents, everyone, adored Maria. After a few months, word spread about her innovative teaching methods. Some of the younger, more astute townspeople began to enroll their children in *La Escuela de la Luz,* School of Light."

At a loss for words to comfort Annie's obvious pain, he touched her shoulder again. When she looked at him this time, he saw the frustration in her face, heard the rancor in her voice. "Maria Salvado survived a vicious gang rape during her journey to the States. In my heart, I know she would never have willingly gone off with any man."

"I don't understand."

"After the last death, word spread that both Maria and Luba Sanko worked as prostitutes. The rumors," she added with cold derision, "were based on facts that could have only come from the Nohmensville cops."

"Did you hear these facts personally?"

Her chin came up in a defiant posture he was coming to know well. Ronen couldn't avoid her stare. "The night Luba died, Randy Terrance told me he'd picked her up a couple of times. 'Strutting her stuff' was the enchanting term he used."

Ronen swallowed his revulsion for the officer who would be out of a job within a few days. Inaction. Lack of respect. Obvious stupidity. Did those things point to a killer? He didn't know. Yet.

"Is there anyone else who knew Maria as well as you?"

"One of the girls from the compound helped out in the nursery school. I'm not certain how much Danuta would know about Maria's activities—or with whom she spoke."

Annie was sharp. She'd picked up very quickly that he would want to track Maria's movements in the days prior to her death. "Would you introduce me to this person named Danuta?"

"If she's willing." She stopped for a moment, then said out of the blue, "Thanks for letting Chris keep the job at Urgent Care."

"I should have explained myself better that day," he said. "I figured you weren't in a mood to listen."

She turned to face him. "I'm listening now." Her voice softened to a caress. An invitation.

It had never been easy to open up and reveal himself to anyone. Annie's invitation prompted him to give it his best shot. "I didn't go to college right after high school. Late bloomer, you might say."

"Bet you were more motivated when you finally went."

He grimaced at the memories of balancing a colicky baby in one hand and a textbook in the other. "I had a wife and baby to support. I worked nights and took courses during the day. Motivation came in there somewhere."

"Your wife didn't work outside the home?"

"Absolutely not!" He quickly erased the vehemence from his tone. "After Chris was born, Lisa and I agreed she would stay home until all the kids we planned to have were in grade school. Children need their mothers," he said. "Particularly in those formative years."

"I agree completely. Kids need a full-time mother."

He took a seat at the table. "The day I graduated from college, Lisa and I promised each other that our children would never have to kill themselves in order to get an education. I suppose I am overprotective when it comes to Christopher's working while going to school."

"Sounds like you don't want him missing out on the fun and freedom of college."

"Exactly. I want him to stay a kid. Have fun, do all the things—well, maybe not all of them—that college kids do."

After Annie blew up at him in the stairwell of the mansion, he and Chris worked out a compromise about school, work, and misplaced responsibility. His son was now strutting around like the king of the hill, whistling. Whistling!

Chris couldn't wait to get to the Urgent Care Center each morning, no doubt to perform duties too disgusting to share with polite company. When he arrived home each afternoon, he couldn't wait to share all that he'd learned. With Annie.

Her responses to Chris' million questions were unfailing in their patience and encouragement. Thinking about it now, she seemed as eager as Chris to talk. Ronen figured it was like the trooper who's temporarily out of commission, dependent on his buddies to keep him up to date on happenings, arrests, *the action*.

He'd never seen his son this excited about anything. If working at UCC promoted Chris' new found enthusiasm, Ronen was all for it. Annie was right. No matter how much he wanted to protect his only child, the boy needed to field some of the responsibility for his future, take pride in a job well done.

"He seems to be handling the work," she murmured, aligning the photographs in precise order. "John is very pleased."

Her sweet, understanding smile renewed his courage. "I'd like to spend more time with you, Annie. Outside the case files, I mean."

There. He'd said it. If she didn't want to have anything to do with him on a personal level, he'd make her spell it out in clear, one syllable words.

Something that resembled sadness, perhaps resignation, entered her big, dark eyes. "Have you ever wanted something so much you could taste it?"

Anywhere you want in the state. "Yes."

Taking a step back from the table, she said, "That's how I feel about medicine, Ronen. I want to be a doctor. I want it so bad, I can't think about anything else. I don't have time to date. Even if I did, I wouldn't do it."

"Have you applied to medical school?"

She chortled. "About a hundred."

"Been accepted?"

"Not yet."

"Let me get this straight," he said. "There's a chance you might be accepted into medical school. Until you are—which could be any time in the distant future—you'll deny yourself a social life. That about right?"

Annie lifted her shoulders once, then let them fall. "On the money."

"As my son would say, that sucks."

"It's my life, Ronen. I live it on my terms, not the way others think I should."

"But—" Why would anyone give up the chance for a home? A loving family? Babies?

Ronen offered no more on the obviously touchy subject, but his son was right in his description. Annie's choices sucked, big time.

"I need to move around," she said. "Moving helps me think." Her crutches squeaked as she took several turns around the narrow kitchen. After a moment, she came back to the table. "Let me see Maria's pictures again."

She turned the top photograph from one side to the other, then upside down. "Son of a bitch!"

He nearly came out of the chair. "What? What?"

"Her hands! Ronen, look at her hands."

"What about them?" He looked closer at the area beneath the tip of her finger. And knew instantly what she meant. "The thumbs."

"Exactly." As she leaned over his shoulder, her braid brushed his cheek. "Check out the lines of demarcation at the base of her thumbs."

He cocked his head and found himself staring into her incredible eyes. For the first time he noticed tiny points of gold circling the pupils.

Annie cleared her throat. When she spoke, it was in a soft croak. "Someone tied a thin wire around—"

"Restraining captives by their thumbs," he murmured, unable to look away from those enchanting eyes, "was a torture method favored by the Contra rebels in El Salvador."

She straightened, patted his shoulder. "There's more."

Before he could take another breath, his arms were pinned behind his back. *Handcuffed.* "What are you doing?"

Those gold points of light danced at him. "I wrote the training manual for pick pockets, pal. You don't want your stuff pinched, don't come into my house in full uniform."

She'd lifted the cuffs from the back of his belt with such ease he'd not felt a thing.

"I didn't have time for a shower and change of clothes," he grumbled, unwilling to admit he'd been in such a rush to be with her again, he didn't think about how he was dressed. Pulling at the restraints, he demanded again, "The cuffs?"

"Not till I've made my point."

"Make it and let me go."

"Keep your shorts on."

Her hair swept the side of his face again. He breathed deeply and inhaled the same fragrance he always smelled whenever he was close to her. Lilacs. Sunshine.

He squirmed to ease his forearms away from the hardware clipped to the back of his belt: 9mm. Glock, extra ammo clips, the pager and... cuffs. "Get on with it, Wolfgirl."

Something smooth slid between the bend in his elbows and the small of his back. He quickly looked to each side and found the ends of a broomstick sticking out. "Your point?"

The stick jerked up, hard and fast. He came off the chair if only to prevent both shoulders from dislocating. "Dammit, Annie!"

"Sorry." She pressed a hand on his shoulder, easing him back into the chair. "I didn't intend to hurt you, but I need to demonstrate something."

"You did that, real well. Unlock the damn cuffs."

"Not into S and M," she mused, giving the stick another jerk. "Tying the thumbs together behind their backs left them helpless. Then—" she went on, "—the broomstick, or a similar device, was slid between their arms and the small of the back and suspended from the ceiling, leaving the women hanging like a—"

Her point was more than clear. "*Piñata*. It accounts for the bleeding patterns at the shoulders."

"Exactly." She removed the stick. "At least one of the killers has military experience—government or private hire. And he's no kid, Ronen, because the broomstick thing is straight out of the Viet Cong's book on interrogation techniques." After he came to his feet, she asked, "Where are the keys?"

Turnabout is fair play, he decided. "Right front pocket."

She didn't speak for several seconds. "I don't suppose you mean the pocket of your shirt?"

He smirked, enjoying her narrow-eyed suspicion. "Cuffing me was your idea, madam. Go fish."

Her hand slid into his pocket, then paused. "Deeper," he advised.

A grunt rumbled in her throat before her fingers moved south and encountered his arousal. "I don't find this one bit funny."

"You're the one who had to show and tell."

"Some men are able to control themselves."

Once his hands were free, he rolled and flexed his shoulders with a reminder to spend more time with the weights. "Do you see me acting on a basic physiologic response to a specific set of stimuli?"

She cleared her throat. "That's beside the point."

"All your own doing," he reminded her. "It is the wise woman who doesn't fish in unknown waters."

"Yeah, yeah. No big whoop. Let's just forget this ever happened, okay?"

No big whoop? Pigs would fly before he forgot. Pigs would fly real high.

"Whatever you say," he murmured, then focused on the issue at hand. "The Vietnam era ran from the early sixties to the middle seventies. El Salvador erupted in the mid-seventies, lasted into the eighties. The mess in Nicaragua was approximately the same time. We could be talking about regular enlisted, something we jokingly called 'military advisors', or—"

Annie cut in. "We could be talking mercenaries, Ronen."

"Mercs in No Man's Land," he grumbled, flexing and rotating his shoulders again. "The hits just keep on coming."

"This profiling stuff is kinda cool," she chirped. "Want I should check around town? See who served time in 'Nam or Central America? Jeez, I could even—"

Ted Collins' death mask flashed before his eyes. "No!" he bellowed. "For a very bright woman, that's a pretty stupid, idea, Annie. Use your head, for Christ's sake!"

It was the wrong thing to say. Instantly all prim, proper, and rigid, she sniffed, "Excuse me for taking an interest in stopping murder."

Civilians. Shit.

~ * ~

"He's baaack."

Annie grunted, "Who's back?"

"The hunk from last week," Sue Valetta said from second base. "Only—"

"Only what?" Annie barked.

She wasn't in the mood for this. She'd spent an entire week with Marvelic, trying her damnedest to keep her hands off him. Did he help? Hell, no! Hinting around that they should relax, go for a ride, take a breather. Each time he asked, it became that much harder to say no.

The man made her itch in places she hadn't used in years.

To make things worse, he had to show up at today's game in uniform. No pressed chinos or oxford cloth shirt for him. No sir. Standing straight and razor sharp, looking impeccable from the peak of his Stetson to his short-sleeved, extra starched shirt with its cluster of medals, to the trousers with a crease sharp enough to cut glass, the man oozed power and control.

Third base joined the conference between second and short. "Great ass."

Annie fixed her with a steely glare. "Who asked you?"

"*Play ball!*"

The Nuggets hunkered down and set out with the style of Althea Gibson, the grace of Peggy Fleming and flair of Rosie O'Donnell to cream the onions out of the Walton Rockets. Annie took a couple lunges to test the elasticity in her knee and was delighted to feel not so much as a twinge. *Yessir, all is right in Wolfe's world.*

Except for the uniformed idiot in the crowd who displayed an annoying, not to mention unhygienic, act of sticking two fingers in his mouth and giving off ear-shattering whistles every time she made a play. Even if a couple of them were spectacular, he didn't need to make a total ass of himself.

The man was as focused on his job as others claimed she was on hers. Spending the last five evenings with him, examining illegible coroner's reports and graphic autopsy photographs, wasn't easy. Ronen never pushed her. In fact, he often encouraged her to stop and take a break. With him, of course.

Thankfully, they completed file number five last night. Now maybe she'd sleep without the nightmares that had plagued her since she agreed to help him. Good thing. It was time to focus on the game, then the med school interview.

At the bottom of the seventh, the coach made a change in the batting order. With two outs, the score tied and two Nuggets on base, it was crunch time. Do or die for the greater glory of Nohmensville.

"Gonna put you in for Dwyer, Annie."

"Whatever you say, Coach."

"How's the knee holding up?"

"Great. Couldn't be better."

"Sure?"

"I'm sure," she promised. She hoped.

"You wouldn't jive me, would you, Wolfgirl?"

"Dr. Latimer," she asked the physician-cum-coach in an aggrieved tone. "Would I do that?"

"In a New York minute."

She took a couple bounces to prove the strength in her knee. "See?"

"Then what are you waiting for?" Latimer blustered. "Get out there and knock their socks off."

Ronen sensed the power in Annie's long, deceptively lean body as she stepped to the plate. With a swish of her waist-length braid, she dug in a toe and took her stance. After a wiggle of those fine hips, she waited—then poured all her weight into her swing—and sent the ball soaring into the next zip code.

The crowd exploded in a rhythmic chant. "Go, Wolfgirl. Go, Wolfgirl. Go, Wolfgirl, go."

He found himself shouting and whistling as loud as anyone, uncaring to find that he'd developed a sudden keen interest in women's sports.

Throughout the game two men stood beside him, discussing crop rotation and milk prices, when they weren't knocking back beers like Prohibition was about to be reinstated.

As Annie took the bases, one of the men slapped the other on the back. "Told you, Clyde."

"Told me what, Three-J?"

Jimmy-Joe Jackson, Ronen grumbled beneath his breath. After clocking the jerk doing a hundred down an isolated stretch of I-88, with a herd of little kids in the back seat, not a seat belt on any of them, he wasn't likely to forget this bird.

Three-J hiked up his pants, spat a stream of tobacco juice, then drained the can of Coors in his hand. "Wolfgirl is gonna take this town to the states. If I'm lyin', I'm dyin'."

Clyde responded to that profundity with a belch that had to come from his toes. "Jackson, you lie like a dead skunk in the middle of the road. That girl ain't takin' this team down I-88 much less to Syracuse. She's hurtin' like my prize steer after he's split a hoof."

Ronen never took his gaze off Annie. As she rounded third base, he had to agree with belching Clyde. She was running with a catch in her gait, but a determined grimace on her face. The Nuggets crowded around home plate, catching her in a group hug before hoisting her to their shoulders for a victory lap around the infield. Dodging the onslaught of frantic fans who rushed the team, Ronen stayed where he was. And waited.

Christ, it was a mistake coming to the game. Mooning after a disinterested, career-focused woman had to be one of the dumber moves he'd ever made. But trying to push Annie Wolfe out of his head was like trying to tell his heart not to beat.

He was lonely. When Chris left for college in the fall, it would be twenty times worse. All he wanted was to spend time with someone his own age, someone who made him laugh out loud, someone who could take his mind off the job. Not just any someone—Annie.

The rush was still there every time he put on the uniform, each time he walked into the barracks. Rush or not, a smart man knew when to take time away from criminal profiles, death and destruction. What better way was there to unwind than spending time with a long-legged woman with midnight-dark hair and eyes the color of fresh-brewed coffee?

"Good game, Wolfgirl!"

The shout refocused Ronen onto the woman slowly walking toward him. The hitch in her gait, in addition to the tight frown on her face, told him several things. Stepping directly into her path, he said, "Nice hit, slugger."

She looked everywhere but straight at him. "Thanks."

Townspeople passed by, touching her shoulder, offering congratulations. One patted her truly remarkable butt. She accepted it all with a brisk nod of her head, even the fanny touch. If he tried that, she'd probably deck him.

"I was in the neighborhood," he bluffed. "Wanted to help cheer the Nuggets to victory."

She continued looking everywhere else. "We appreciate the support."

They'd not spoken, because there had been no reason, in almost twenty-four hours. He'd become so used to spending every evening with her that being without her was like withdrawal. Right now, he would do anything, *anything*, to keep her in one spot. "If you don't mind riding in the unit, can I give you a lift home?"

"Thanks, I've got my car," she mumbled, jerking on the hem of her team shirt. "I'm giving some people a ride home."

"Could I see you later tonight? After I'm off duty, I mean."

"I don't think so. See, I—"

"Nothing heavy," he interrupted. "Maybe have a cup of coffee, watch a video—or something?"

Man, asking a girl—woman—out was a whole lot simpler at sixteen.

"That's not a good idea," she murmured. "I... gotta go."

"Hot date?"

That put the spark back into her body language. "As a matter of fact, I do. His name is Ronaldo and I'm supposed to meet him at four-thirty." She tossed her braid over one shoulder, then checked her watch. "If I'm late, he'll start without me. Believe me, Trooper Marvelic, I never let Ronaldo start without me."

Ronen reassured himself he wasn't the jealous type. "I make it a practice never to stand in the way of lust."

An odd look entered her eyes. "Yeah, me, too."

He watched her walk away, wondering what he could do, what he could say, to make her rush anywhere for him.

Four

"Could you could go any faster?" John Latimer bellowed against the wind blasting his face.

Annie ignored the man's one-handed death grip on the door handle. "World Cup final starts at four-thirty."

"A soccer game is worth risking your life?" he shrieked. "Not to mention those of your team-mates and coach?"

To celebrate their victory, Annie caved in to passenger demands that she put the top down on the Mustang for the ride home. Kathy Baker, the Nuggets catcher, leaned over the back of Annie's seat to yell, "Who you taking, Wolfgirl?"

"Brazil, who else? Ronaldo is my hero."

"Cute little bugger. If he was old enough to vote," the all-league catcher added, "I'd take him on in a second."

John Latimer braced his free hand on the dashboard. "If you don't slow down, Annie, I swear I'll make you see Old Man Harbaugh the next time he comes in with his piles in a pinch."

Feeling the way she did right now, it'd take more than the threat of Abner Harbaugh's thrombosed hemorrhoids to scare the Wolfgirl off. "Been there, done that."

"What about Sophie Jackson's pessary check?"

Mrs. Jackson's sagging uterus was another story.

"Oh, all right." Disgusted with John's histrionics over a little speed, she eased up on the accelerator.

"Thank you."

"Man, this is the nuts," Kathy crowed. "First we beat the Rockets, then I get to ride in the Wolfmobile with the top down, doing eighty in a sixty-five. Am I in heaven, or what?"

"Hey, Wolfgirl," another teammate yelled. "Can I use your cell phone? Gotta call home."

"Sure. John, get the phone from the glove compartment."

"We're doing eighty?" Latimer screamed as he handed the phone into the back. "Are you crazy?"

"No. I'm in a hurry."

Latimer checked his side-view mirror. "Guess what, little girl? There's a cop on your tail and he's signaling you to pull over."

Annie checked the side and rear-view mirrors before pulling to the shoulder of the road. "A trooper. Just my luck."

"Keep your mouth shut," John cautioned. "Take the ticket and go."

The trooper took his time getting out of the unit. Annie decided long ago it was a deliberate attempt to heighten the driver's anxiety level, get him so nervous he'd confess to anything, including the bombing of Pearl Harbor.

Whomever this guy was, he went by the book. Being thoroughly familiar with traffic stops, Annie knew what came next. He radioed in his location and her license number, then parked the blue and gold unit with the front tires pointing out into traffic, leaving the motor running. *For a fast getaway?*

Fear teased every instinct for self-preservation. Fight or flight. From the looks on the faces of the other Nuggets, the fear was contagious. "Take it easy," she cautioned. "Don't do anything stupid—like crying."

There was something familiar about the trooper's stride as he approached the Mustang. His carriage was too perfect. She muttered something pithy after he pushed his knuckles on the trunk of the car, then slapped the silver posse box against his thigh.

"Do you know why I stopped you, ma'am?"

Because he was standing behind her and at an angle, Annie was forced to crane her neck to look up at him. "Trooper Marvelic, what a surprise."

"License, registration, and proof of insurance, ma'am."

She passed over the forms without comment.

"I repeat, ma'am. Do you know how fast you were going?"

"Not... exactly."

He gave the passengers a solemn nod. "I'll ask all of you for your names and dates of birth, please."

After writing the information down, he strutted back to the unit to radio in the information. Annie knew he was checking for wants and warrants on all of them.

In the same straight-legged, tight-assed gait, he returned to the Mustang. "Step out of the car, ma'am. Please."

She complied, but not before making a big deal out of handing the keys to John, ensuring the cell phone was still turned on, and checking the back seat passengers for bats and helmets. If she was going for the gold, she'd go all the way.

"One hint of trouble, you guys book out of here," she said, strictly for Marvelic's interest. "Keep the phone in your hand," she told the outfielder. "Call 911. They won't send anyone, but they have to record every call. The rest of you make sure you've got your bats ready."

Latimer unbuckled his seatbelt. "I'm coming with you."

She felt compelled to squash the martyr-for-the-faith look on the old man's face. "Stay there. Anything, I mean *any thing* starts smelling funky, take off."

The good doctor agreed, grudgingly. "Whatever you say."

Marvelic escorted her down the shoulder of the road, past the trooper unit, positioning himself with the sun at his back. Annie figured it was to maintain a clear view of her, her car, and its passengers. "That was somewhat excessive, don't you think?"

She glanced into the mirrored shades covering his eyes and wished she'd kept hers on. "The speed or the precautions?"

"Both." He removed the sunglasses, hanging them from the breast pocket of his shirt. "I'll have to ticket you."

Avoiding the effect of his eyes was next to impossible. Any number of things showed in those big green pools. Purpose.

Frustration. Humor. "Look, Marvelic, I admit I was speeding. Give me the ticket; I'll be on my way."

He checked his watch. "Looks like Ronaldo will have to start without you."

"He'll survive. So will I."

Marvelic blinked once before continuing to check off the tiny boxes on the ticket pad. "What's that supposed to mean?"

It meant, for reasons she didn't care to examine, that she trusted him. Maybe not the rest of the cops in town, but Ronen was different. Perhaps it was the sensitivity he'd displayed for the dead women, or the understanding in his face when he looked at his son, or the respect he always paid Stella Grover.

"Look, Trooper Marvelic, I—"

"It's Captain."

Several seconds passed before his response sank in.

Yessir, she always went for the gold. "You're a *captain*?"

The impressive chest pumped out a few inches, his posture went a tad straighter. "Going on two years now."

"Captain Marvelic," she said slowly, stretching out the syllables. The expected tie-in followed. "*Captain Marvel*," she croaked, then doubled over in helpless, gut-busting laughter.

"Exceeding the speed limit by fifteen miles an hour," he said through clenched jaws, "is hardly a laughing matter."

"Fifteen. Is that all?" she squeaked. "I'll be damned."

"Better than dead." Marvelic handed her the ticket, tipped his hat, offering her a professional, by-the-book nod before striding toward the unit. "See you in court, Ms. Wolfe."

"In your dreams, Captain."

He glanced over his shoulder one more time before tipping the brim of his hat. "Every night for the past week. Ma'am."

~ * ~

Yes! Oh, yesss! More, Ronaldo. I... want... more!

If those weren't the sounds of a woman in the throes of sexual agony, Ronen Marvelic wasn't exquisitely familiar with the confines of self-imposed celibacy. Girding his loins for another rejection, he knocked on her door. "Open up, slugger. It's me."

After a second knock, one that came with more than a moment's hesitation, the door flew open. Hunched over a pair of crutches, wearing a hockey jersey and little else, it appeared, Annie glared at him. "What now?"

"After hearing your screams of—whatever it was I heard, I felt it my duty to check on your welfare before the grapevine went into warp drive and had you murdered—" His gaze swept her tanned legs from the hem of the black and red jersey to the tips of her bare toes. "—in that incredibly unattractive outfit."

"My welfare is fine," she grumbled. "And the grapevine's only concern is my ability at shortstop. Thanks for stopping by."

Anticipating her next move, Ronen braced a palm on the door. "So where's the guy you tried to break the land speed record for?"

"Excuse me?"

"Ronaldo? Four-thirty? Start without you?"

"Oh, yeah, right." She took a quick look at someone or something behind her back, then sighed. "Come in. If you must."

Yes, he really must.

She limped into her living room which, in his opinion, held enough junk to stock a good sized sporting goods store. "Ronaldo, honey," she yelled. "Put your pants on; we got company." She glanced at the TV screen before turning to him. "Sorry, Cap. Looks like he started without me."

"You snooze; you lose."

Annie sank to the davenport where she raised her leg on several pillows before repositioning a giant ice pack on her knee. "Have a seat, Captain Marvel. The man'll be back in a second."

"I can wait." Feeling stubborn enough to outwait Lucifer himself, Ronen weaved a path between assorted pieces of sports gear scattered across the floor before reaching a worn recliner chair. Thankfully, Wolfgirl was into comfort as well as the sports pages.

"There he is!" she crowed, pointing the remote at the TV.

Ronen glanced at the screen. She'd scammed him again.

"Oh yes, baby," she crooned in a voice designed for dark nights and wrinkled sheets. "Now, sweetheart. You want it. Come for me. Bring it home. Come, Ronaldo... Yesss!"

Arousal came instantly. Savagely.

"You mean to tell me," he croaked, "that you risked your life on an interstate to watch a bald-headed runt play soccer?"

The look she gave him might have crushed small bones. Thankfully, he took a daily dose of calcium along with other vitamin and mineral supplements. "Do you know who you just called a *bald-headed runt?*"

"I'm sure you're about to tell me."

"Second only to Pele, Ronaldo is the greatest player in the history of soccer. You suggested I should get a life," she scoffed. "Look at your own, Captain."

A commercial came on the screen that featured the *runt* kicking a soccer ball through an airport to the tune of one of Ronen's favorite sambas. He had to admit after a few seconds, the guy was good.

Edging to the side of the davenport, as if she was about to get up again, Annie groaned. Some puffiness had returned to her knee, though the vibrant purple from the previous week had quickly faded to a putrid green.

"Sit down," he sighed. "I'll get whatever you need."

"Beer. Can't watch World Cup play without cold beer."

If she was trying to turn him off, it wasn't working. Between the living room and the kitchen his erection eased, though it wouldn't take much for a recall to active duty.

The refrigerator's contents were some of the most pathetic he'd ever seen. A dried-out wedge of cheese and a head of wilted lettuce, plus a tube of tomatoes that had seen better days. And —two cases of beer.

"High-test or non-alcoholic?" he yelled after checking out the labels.

"I'm not going anywhere. Gimme the real thing."

A cupboard over the sink held a collection of Loony Toons glasses. His hand paused over Wile E. Coyote. "Would you like a glass?"

"Please. Only sissies use glasses."

Is that so?

An alternative choice in glassware caught his eye. The evil in the Tasmanian Devil's smile matched Ronen's mood as he headed back into the living room. Ignoring the heat that raced up his arm when their fingers touched, he leaned close enough to smell Annie's shampoo. "What else do sissies use, Ms. Wolfe?"

"Nothing that interests me."

Something crossed her face—only for a moment before being lost behind those Hershey-brown eyes. It was there long enough to confirm his suspicions. "Liar."

Satisfied he'd made his point, he moved swiftly to the cushy recliner. "It's only fair to warn you, slugger, I play to win."

"Is that so?"

Raising the Taz glass in toast, he smiled. "And I rarely play fair."

"Thanks for the warning. Why are you here?"

"Told you," he said after draining the glass. "I came to check out Ronaldo. Now that I know the competition's a twerpy kid, how about a date?"

~ * ~

Needing time to ease the nerves created by the resolve in his cool green eyes, Annie repositioned her aching leg on the pillows before taking a long pull on her beer. "It seems to me we've had this discussion once already, Captain. In case I forgot to ask before, why on earth would you want to go out on a date with me?"

"It certainly isn't because of your retiring demeanor, chic fashion sense, or impeccable style of decorating."

The beer eased the dryness in her throat, relaxed more than a few tight muscles. "Dating is passé."

"It's only dinner, Wolfgirl."

"I told you before, I don't do stuff like that."

"Why is that?"

Taking another swallow, she tried, once more, to explain. "I've got medical school followed by a family medicine residency with a focus in women's health ahead of me. Managing that while trying to keep some man happy and content is, in my opinion, a lesson in insanity."

"Med students and residents don't have relationships?" he countered. "They don't marry, have children?"

"Not if they want to keep their heads on straight."

"Annie."

"Ronen," she returned his scoff. "I've seen too many relationships go down the toilet because the non-medical partner couldn't hold the relationship together all on their own. It can't be any different with cops. I understand civilian partners often have a very difficult time with isolation and lack of support."

"You're right," he replied. "But the ones who want it bad enough, however, adapt and make compromises."

Annie was almost saddened with his nonchalant response. The man had no clue. "There are no compromises, no adaptations when it comes to the intrigue and glamour of medicine. Might as well use a squirt gun to bring down a Scud missile." She struggled to a standing position. "And don't get me going on the issue of children."

"Why is that?"

"First of all, I'm not parent material. You said yourself a child deserves a mother's full-time attention, not some sleep-deprived zombie who has to focus all her energy on lab results, x-ray reports and EKG tracings plus all the other crap that goes into keeping her patients alive and healthy."

"You can't honestly believe it's like that in every situation, Annie. People who want it bad enough can—"

"Would you please shut up and listen to me?" she bellowed, all the time wondering why she bothered continuing. "I made the decision long ago never to marry, or have a child. It only makes sense that dating is out of the question."

"No mixed messages," he responded. "No harm, no foul."

"Hallelujah! You're finally getting it."

"But why can't you date until you've been accepted into med school?"

Wrong. He wasn't getting it at all. Typical male, she reminded herself. "I don't have time."

"Why is that?"

"Do they teach that in cop school?"

"Excuse me?"

"The 'why is that' response to every statement from the witness."

"Let me rephrase. Why don't you have time to date?"

"Medicine is like solving a puzzle. Why is this person sick; how long have they felt ill; what are the clues I need to look for? What steps should I take to solve the puzzle? I've never found anyone who excites me as much as solving medical puzzles. That's why I don't date."

"I understand all that," he said with a grand gesture. "It's no different than a fresh investigation." He waved one hand in the air. "Don't you get lonely? Don't you miss talking to someone other than patients?"

Loneliness couldn't figure into the equation; she wouldn't allow it. Besides, the man was denser than dirt. In a move intended to distract him from the worn-out subject of her personal views and choices, she said, "Looks like you've dug in for the duration here, so how about something to eat? I know a place that makes a pizza so terrific, it'll bring tears to those big-city eyes. Plus, they deliver."

"Pizza?" His face said he'd sooner eat dog food. "I just had it a month ago."

"Your willpower is amazing."

Annie made her way into the kitchen and popped a second beer before reaching for the receiver on the wall phone. "What do you like?"

"Nothing. Well... cheese is okay. As long as it's low-fat and non-dairy."

Annie shuddered at that particularly disgusting combination. "Gall bladder problems or lactose intolerance?"

"Both."

"Bummer." She reached for an alternative take-out menu taped to the message board over the phone. "How about Chinese instead?"

"Have you ever counted the fat grams in that stuff?"

She smiled into the receiver. "Don't worry, Cap. I'll take good care of your gall bladder." *And your irritable bowel.*

Soo-Ling's in Oneonta was her favorite place for Chinese take-out. The person who answered the phone, a frequent flyer at Urgent

Care, promised delivery within the hour—while also assuring Annie the delivery person would take the beer currently cooling in her refrigerator to tonight's team party at the VFW hall.

Annie entered the living room with another beer for the Captain and found him checking out her collection of wall posters. He turned just as she sank to the davenport and replaced the dripping ice pack on her knee. "How is it?"

"Hurts." She passed him the beer. "A little."

"Lovely shade. Goes well with your complexion."

"Thanks." She tucked the ice pack around the inflamed joint. "Bile-green is my signature color."

He gestured toward the posters of her favorite sports heroes hanging on the wall. Ronaldo, Cal Ripken, John Stockton from the Utah Jazz, and Wayne Gretsky. She called them her fan club. "Why the obsession with athletes?"

She rarely drank alcohol because even a little loosened her tongue. "On the wall, or the TV screen, they're safe and non-threatening."

"Is that why you won't go out with me?"

"It's not only you, Ronen. I won't go out with any man."

"Why is—nevermind."

Maybe he was trying. She'd give him points for that. "The men in Nohmensville aren't the type I'd choose to spend my off-duty time with."

"When I pulled you over this afternoon, you and your friends acted abnormally nervous for the circumstances."

Two beers might loosen her tongue. They'd never make her stupid. "Yeah, so?"

"I was wondering what caused that response."

Two beers, however, often unhinged the cover on her distrust of men in general, local police officers in particular. "You and I just spent an entire week examining morgue shots, discussing various methods of torture, and you still have no idea why my friends might be nervous after you flagged me down?"

Annie watched as Captain Marvel's shoulders went arrow-straight and his jaw hardened to granite. "You think I could—"

"Get a grip," she snapped. "Do you recall the location where you pulled me over?"

"Of course. It was at mile line marker number—"

She cut him off with a snap of her hand. "Not six feet from the shoulder of the road are woods so dense the sun can't get through the trees. How easy would it be for a cop—or someone posing as one—to distract a driver while his buddies rush out of the trees and ambush her?"

If his rock jaw got any tighter, he'd be risking multiple fractures. "I hope you've not shared those thoughts with anyone, Annie. Accusations like that can ruin a man's career, not to mention his reputation."

Refusing to be goaded, she asked, "Death doesn't ruin an innocent woman's life?"

"At this point in the investigation," he said tightly, as if he were trying to control himself. "There's nothing to tie local law enforcement to the women."

The stiff-necked, patronizing reaction annoyed her just enough to make her sneer, "Don't you mean NHI's?"

The change in him was instantaneous. He lunged out of the chair like he'd been shot out of a cannon. When he managed to speak, his voice was hoarse, shaking with anger. "Where did you hear that phrase?"

Clearly, this was not a man to piss off. "Around."

"I mean it, Annie. Is NHI something you heard in regard to the six women?" When she said nothing, he yelled, "Dammit, Annie! I can't do my job if you—"

It was the urgency, and the disgust, in his voice that turned the tide. "I have a friend, a social worker. She told me cops use the phrase when—"

"I know when they use it," he spat. "I know why, and it makes me sick. Would this friend talk to me? I have to know who would foster such contempt for human life to use such language."

"Does that mean it's an okay term—as long as your cronies don't use it in front of a civilian?"

"Listen to me!" Raking at his hair, Ronen sank down next to her on the davenport. "I apologize for raising my voice. NHI is a phrase so disgusting, so abhorrent, it should never be used, even thought, under any circumstances. Who is your friend? I'd like to talk to her."

So would I.

The last time she saw Barb was several days after Luba Sanko's death. Angry and frustrated, her friend was sloppy drunk and blaming herself as she packed for the move back to Albany. Though she tried her best, Annie couldn't talk Barb through her guilt—or out of moving.

Barb said she was getting out of Dodge, then promised it would be a cold day in hell before she returned. "I'll fix those bastards," she'd raged. "I've got proof."

Ronen took Annie's hand, bringing her back to the present. He worried a thumb over her knuckles. "The social worker. Was her name Barbara Thompson?"

"Yes, but—"

His previous outburst rang through her head. *Six women?*

Fear took a hot, greasy roll through her gut.

She'd not seen nor heard from Barbara in a couple of months. No letters, phone calls, not even a postcard. That in itself wasn't unusual, but the look on Ronen's face confirmed the hideous suspicion in her heart.

"You said six women. We only reviewed five files."

His hand covered hers in a tight grip. "We hadn't gotten to the last victim."

"Who is she?"

"Her body was found in early April. We believe she—"

Pushing him out of the way, Annie struggled to her feet. *"Who is number six?"*

"Barbara Thompson."

Five

Annie raged. Screamed. Howled like a wounded animal.

The last time Ronen heard sounds like that was after he had to tell Christopher his mother was dead. If he never heard them again, it would be too soon.

While he supported her head, she tossed the contents of her stomach into the commode, then managed to lose some more.

"I never cry," she informed him just before her stomach roiled again.

He was sure she didn't. Tough cookies like Annie Wolfe held their emotions inside—until death or something equally traumatic turned their world upside down. Offering her tissues, he murmured, "I know."

"What do you know," she growled, then vomited again.

Ronen rarely spoke of Lisa to anyone outside his immediate family. "My wife was killed by a drunk driver ten years ago."

Annie sat back on her haunches, staring a hole in his chest. "I'm sorry."

"It was a long time ago."

Without warning, her face turned as white as the bathroom tiles, then contorted in a rictus of pain. "Help me."

For the life of him, he couldn't figure out what she meant. "Help you what?"

"Stand, sit, lie down, I don't care!" she bellowed. "My knee can't take this position. Aw, Christ, if I've hurt it again, I—"

Ronen fell onto his buttocks, sitting spread-legged before pulling Annie into the cradle of his thighs. He hauled the trash basket in front of her face—just in case.

"There's nothing left to throw up," she mumbled. "I'm all right."

No. She wasn't. He knew, better than most, that Annie would never be the same again. Losing a best friend was as hard as losing a lover, a child, a parent. Knowing her friend had died in the same way as the other victims only intensified her feelings. "Sit here a minute, Ann. Catch your breath."

With a deep sigh, her back and shoulders fell back against his chest. The top of her head fitted perfectly in the notch between his chin and shoulder. Her hands fell to his legs where they kneaded the muscles beneath his slacks in a mindless ritual. "She saved my life."

Easing both arms around her, Ronen brushed his lips across her temple. Salt from her tears burned his tongue. "Tell me about the first time you met her."

Beneath his palms, the breath hitched in her chest. When she finally spoke, her voice carried the halting, uncertain sound of a frightened child.

"I was... panhandling outside the Port Authority in New York City. Barb was racing to catch a bus. She overheard this guy offer me food and a place to sleep."

Ronen's instinct was to hold her that much tighter. "How old were you?"

"Nine... ten maybe. She went at the guy like a crazy person, kicking and screaming, swinging her briefcase at him. I didn't know who to be more scared of, Barb or the chicken hawk."

Ronen shuddered. Barbara Thompson had every right to go after the predator who would have turned Annie out on the streets or used her in kiddie porn. "What happened then?"

The back of her head rubbed a spot on his chest; he felt her muscles gradually relax. The same dull sound he'd heard in a thousand victims' voices echoed in hers. The shock of sudden trauma carried a singular, one-of-a-kind note. "She took me home with her, fixed me something to eat, made me take a bath."

A brush of his fingertips swept damp strands of hair away from her cheek. "Can you tell me why you ran away in the first place?"

"Papa was going to sell me. I eavesdropped, heard him making a deal with one of his friends. Had to get away."

Bowing his head, he touched his cheek to hers and blinked back his own tears. "Of course you did."

"Barbara found me a place to stay, made me go to school. She saved my life." Annie stirred in his arms. "Did she look like the rest?"

Worse. Much, much worse. "Yes."

Fresh tears squeezed from beneath Annie's tightly closed eyelids, rolling uncontrollably down her cheeks. "Damn them."

"Only a few people in Albany know Barbara is dead. I have my reasons when I ask that you keep it between us."

"Okay." Turning to one side, she slid her arms around his waist, snuggling against him like a trusting child. "Ronen?"

"Hmm?"

"I don't want a lover."

"Okay."

"But I need a friend."

He touched her hair, stoking the silky length with shaky fingertips. "Understood."

"Will you be my friend?"

"Of course."

"Thanks." He could feel exhaustion's dead weight settle into Annie's limbs. "I need to sleep."

Ronen helped her to her feet, supporting her weight while she brushed her teeth. "I'm so tired," she whimpered as he bathed her face with warm water.

"You've had a rough day, slugger. Ready for bed?"

"You asked me that once before," she mumbled over a yawn. "Almost took you up on it."

"Is that so?" He slid one arm around her waist, taking the brunt of her weight as he helped her toward the door she indicated was her bedroom.

"Would have, if Stella hadn't stuck her big nose into it."

He decided it would be best to contemplate her confession at a later time. Inside her bedroom, Annie broke from his arm to limp toward a huge platform bed covered with plain white sheets. She crawled onto the mattress with a soft moan and immediately rolled to her side, curling into a ball like an exhausted kitten. Ronen took a lightweight blanket from the steamer trunk at the foot of the bed and tucked it around her body.

"Don't go," she sighed, fighting sleep. "Don't want to be alone."

"I'll stay," he promised. He would keep her safe from whatever was to come.

Annie was restless, couldn't seem to find a comfortable position as she twisted and rolled on the bed. In what appeared to be an automatic gesture, she reached for a small crystal unicorn that sat on the top of a crate beside the bed. She enclosed it in her fist, then drifted off with a deep sigh.

After she was finally relaxed, Ronen took the time to examine her bedroom. To his surprise, he found candles in a variety of shapes and sizes—some barely burned, others melted down to thin pools of wax. He smiled, and approved. Candles were one of his vices. Lots of candles, the bigger the better, in all colors and scents.

He also discovered a larger collection of crystal figures scattered across the top of a battered, lopsided dresser in the corner of the room. More crystals, strung with multi-colored ribbons, hung from suction cups in the turret window. The rays of the setting sun sent the figures winking in a kaleidoscope of rainbows and shimmering lights.

Ronen watched over Annie until he was certain she'd fallen into a deep sleep. Before he left the bedroom, he walked back to the window. A slight touch on a tiny angel sent it swirling into a dance of light. Who would have thought a woman whose kitchen looked like a food pantry for the homeless, whose living room resembled a sporting goods store, would sleep in a fairyland of whirling lights and rainbows?

As he closed the door to her apartment, a teenager flew up the stairs. The mouth-watering aroma of Chinese delicacies wafted from a bag in his arms. Despite his body's aversion to high-fat foods, Ronen's stomach growled. "I'll take that for you."

"This for Annie Wolfe," the almond-eyed boy said. "I drop off; pick up beer."

"Ms. Wolfe has taken ill. Let me pay you for the food. The beer is inside."

"Miz Annie okay?"

"She'll be fine."

The young man's smile beamed with pride. "Miz Annie knock the spit out of Walton today."

He'd almost forgotten the game and the powerful swat of her bat, her face glowing in triumph as the ball flew out of the park. "That she did."

"Miz Barbara left town," the teen said sadly. "We need Miz Annie. Very much."

~ * ~

Annie woke up to moonbeams dancing off the crystals in the window. She'd not slept so well, so deeply, in years.

Then it all came crashing back.

Barbara was dead.

The woman who'd saved her life and gave her friendship, asking nothing in return was dead. Beaten. Tortured like the rest.

She knew herself well enough to understand that if she allowed the tears that lurked just behind her eyelids to pour forth, they might not stop. Of all people, Barbara would understand why she wouldn't, couldn't, shed any more tears.

She could almost hear her friend's husky voice. *Get on with your life, kid. Don't screw this up.* What Barb meant by *this*, Annie would never know.

Then she remembered Ronen holding her in his arms, bathing her face after she threw up all over his shoes, supporting her while she brushed her teeth...

Like an attentive father.

Papa wanted to sell me. "Aw, crap!"

She'd never told anyone about her childhood, how she spent her days scrounging in garbage pails and dumpsters behind fast food joints with her brothers Tibby and Greg, lucky if they managed to salvage one meal a day.

At night, while Mama serviced the johns, she'd forced Annie to rifle their pants for money. That worked for a couple years, but when the men started looking closer at Annie than Bella, her mother put her out on the streets to work her magic fingers with less observant marks. Her father was fine with the change in status—as long as Annie pulled her fair share. He only had to lock her out once before she learned never to come home with less than a hundred in her pocket.

After some months of that, Gabor Lupo, known as Gabe the Wolf on the streets, realized there were men who would pay a helluva lot more than a C-note for his daughter's pre-pubescent body. The night Annie overheard him in an adjoining room making the deal to sell her, she took off, kept on running, and never looked back.

Relief was the only emotion she felt after she learned Gabe had been murdered in an upstate prison. Her mother was already dead of AIDS. In later years, she heard Tibby and Greg were killed during a turf war with one of the new Asian gangs.

At the tender age of seventeen, Annie came to realize that as the last surviving Lupo, she had two choices: carry on family tradition or make something of herself. Barb Thompson, as always, was there for her, helping Annie obtain her US citizenship, assisting her with the paperwork required to legally change her name to Annie Wolfe.

Tears blossomed anew when she recalled Ronen's care and comfort after she broke down from the news of Barb's death. Tears dried to dust when she remembered the disappointment on his face when she told him she'd never have children.

"Annie Wolfe, the former Illiana Lupo," she muttered, "product of a drugged-out whore and a scam artist, who'd as soon slit somebody's throat as look at them. Is that what the anal-retentive, picture-perfect Captain Marvel wants in a wife and mother of his children?"

The answer was as clear as the crystals dancing in the moonbeams. "Not in this lifetime."

Drawing in a deep, cleansing breath, she said out loud, "Good thing. I wouldn't know how to be a wife—or a mother."

Barbara Thompson was the only person who knew her background and that was only the bare essentials. Even John Latimer, her friend and mentor, didn't know the gory details. Annie preferred to keep it that way.

Until a sharp-eyed, smooth-talking cop caught her at a weak moment and—

As fast as her sore knee allowed, she crossed the hallway to Captain Marvel's apartment to demand he forget every stupid thing she'd said.

Chris opened the door to her knock. "Hey, Annie. How's it going?" His eyes went big as saucers. "Cool shirt."

She stared down at the black and red New York Ranger's hockey jersey signed by The Great One himself, Wayne Gretsky. "Thanks," she mumbled, giving the hem a hasty jerk. "Your dad here?"

Soft music flowed in an arc over the boy's shoulders. Something light and airy, with flutes and a harp, she thought, maybe a few clarinets.

"Come in," Chris invited. "He just got out of the shower."

Annie stepped into a living room that blatantly advertised the differences in their lifestyles. If her place looked like a locker room, Ronen's was a monk's cell. Barren and stark. Spartan. "I'll come back."

"He won't be long." Chris reached out, touched her arm. "Stay, Annie. Please." So like his father, she realized.

Annie paced the cell, touching the arm of a real leather recliner, passed by the matching couch that took up one end of the room. A spit-polished oak table in the far corner held a computer and all its shiny components along with files that profiled six dead women.

A collection of CD's, stacked in precise order next to the fancy laser printer, grabbed her attention. She examined each one, hoping to find something other than opera or the classics. While they'd worked at her place, Ronen insisted on having background music. The man's taste in *background* ran in the direction of big-busted women screeching their lungs out.

"Annie?" Chris called.

"Hmm?"

"I said, it's a blast working at Urgent Care."

Annie turned from the compact discs with a smile. John had kept her updated on Chris' progress over the past week. "Gifted," he'd said.

The smile died slowly when Ronen came out of the bathroom. Whether in full uniform, or a simple T-shirt and jeans, he still remained in control. His clear green gaze made a quick scan of her face and body. "How do you feel?"

Right now her emotions ranged high, far and wide, from anger to rage to heartache. She felt helpless, impotent—and hated it. Warring with the alphabet soup of feelings was the need to feel his arms around her once more. To bathe in the comfort of his strength and understanding.

And that, she hated more than the loss of control.

Needing someone, depending on anyone for comfort and support, was so foreign it was frightening. She hated this weakness in her. Hated Ronen for being there when she'd needed someone so desperately.

"I'm fine," she snapped. "Look, I want to know the details of—" She glanced at Chris, "—you know. I also want you to forget all the other garbage I told you. Before."

"Garbage? When was that?"

"Don't play word games, Captain."

With a light stroke of his fingertips, he ran a hand the length of her arm. "I'll tell you what I can."

It would be so easy to become lost in his touch. For a moment, she almost gave in. "Thanks."

Chris cleared his throat, loudly. "Guess maybe I'll take off. Go play in traffic. Boost an ATM or two."

"Be home by midnight," Ronen said absently. His fingers made a slow return to her elbow; his gaze felt like a caress against her face. "Warm enough?"

"I'm fine." At once breathing became a chore; concise thinking took a monumental effort. She thought she heard a door close.

Ronen walked to the bay window where the CD player rested on the sill, then returned to her side. Flutes and clarinet eased into a soft, sensual Brazilian samba. "What do you want to know?"

Understanding and compassion in his features gnawed at her insides. If she lost her composure again, relied on him again, she feared she might lose a vital part of herself. Annie had always taken pride in her inner strength, her survivor skills. She learned long ago to depend on no one, especially a man, particularly one who wore a badge with the same ease as a pair of faded jeans.

Swallowing all emotion, she forced calm into her voice. "I want to know about Barbara. How she died. Where she died." She forced air into her lungs. "I want to know why."

~ * ~

She looked so lost, so alone. Instinct suggested he offer a hug; common sense overruled that. Instead, Ronen brushed her hair back from her face.

Annie stiffened, looked ready to bolt. "This wasn't such a good idea."

His hand dropped. "Don't go. Please."

"What happened before—" She swallowed visibly. He could see her struggling, but could not help. Not yet. She had to get this out on her own. "I'm sorry I—"

"Sorry for what, Annie?"

"Everything."

One of the smartest career moves he ever made was to take a crisis intervention course offered by the counselors at Rochester's Rape Crisis Service. Those incredible women, who listened to and advocated for survivors of the most horrendous abuses he'd ever heard of, changed his life. And his way of thinking, as a man, as a cop.

They taught him how to listen, *really listen*, to victims. They also taught him to keep his mouth shut and let the survivors say as much, or as little, as they felt safe in saying.

When they're ready, the counselors said, they'll talk. They'll disclose to someone, eventually. If you're lucky, it'll be you. But be careful, they cautioned. What you hear might pull you under.

Don't push, don't force, don't coerce. Above all, they warned, be patient. It was ingrained in him now. He practiced what he'd been taught, so often that he did it now without thinking. When Annie was ready, she'd say more. The fact that she hadn't bolted out of the apartment meant he was building trust and confidence.

Ronen walked to the oak table to pull a manila folder from the center drawer, laid it open for her. "It's all here."

New York State Police Laboratory—Office of Coroner leaped off the page in bright, glaring letters. Her mouth tightened into a hard line; she stepped back.

"The details of Barbara's autopsy are there. Signature on her crime matches the others." He moved another step closer. "Are you sure you're ready for this, Ann?"

She swallowed hard, then scrubbed at her filling eyes. "Maybe I should wait," she mumbled. "For another time."

"In terms of the other reason you came," he said, moving carefully into her space, using the same tone he always took with victims. "As a cop, I hear many things. Most of it goes nowhere. No formal reports or memos to file."

Her beautiful eyes narrowed in doubt. "Bet you never forget them."

"There you have me." He tapped a finger on his temple and smiled. "Some stuff has been in here long enough to gather mold."

"I said some things before," she blurted after a moment of silence. "I'd just as soon you let them turn into penicillin."

"Done."

"Simple as that?"

"On one condition."

"Just like a cop," she muttered. "There's always a condition. Okay, what's the deal?"

"My mother always says to ease the soul we must nourish the body. Let me heat up that high-fat, high-cal Chinese feast you ordered before."

Annie's stomach responded with a loud gurgle. "Your mother is a smart woman. My place or yours?"

"My turf this time. Keys?"

He shagged the key ring she tossed him with a snazzy backhand catch. "Sit down, slugger. Rest your leg."

"You've got the moves of a ball player, Captain," she called out to him as he crossed to the door.

He turned. "A leftover from my misspent youth."

~ * ~

While she heated the food in his oversized microwave, Ronen set the kitchen table with place mats, plates and matching serving bowls, real silverware, and cloth napkins. Even before he poured ice water into leaded crystal goblets, Annie knew she was out of her league. One of her Loony Toons glasses, a plastic fork and the cardboard containers—eaten over the sink—was the norm for her.

"So, Captain," she asked over a mouthful of shrimp fried rice. "What made you want to become a cop?"

"It was that or juvie hall."

"You?"

"Me?" he mimicked, then grinned.

"I can't picture you breaking the rules. Any rules."

"I was well on my way to becoming a hard-core delinquent. My folks must have died twice fearing I'd spend my adult years at the ever charming Hotel Attica."

"What'd you do? Pop a 7-11?"

Munching a stalk of crisp broccoli, he said, "Drove the getaway car."

All she could do was sigh. "Ronen."

"My friends and I thought we were the coolest things since Jim Morrison and the Doors."

"Somehow I can't see you moving and grooving to 'Light my Fire', Cap."

"Long hair, tight jeans, leather jackets." His smile simmered warm and mellow in her belly. "We weren't real bright, but we were way cool."

"Until?"

"Somebody inside the 7-11 hit the alarm and all hell broke loose. I booked out of the parking lot, scared spitless, and collided with the unmarked cop car waiting around the corner."

"Were you hurt?"

"Not until I came nose to chest with a scowling, straight-arrow state trooper."

"How old were you?"

"Fourteen."

"Oh, boy."

"The trooper took me under his wing—so to speak—and adjusted my attitude, real quick. It took awhile, but I proved myself to him. When it came time, he helped me apply to the Troops. I'd probably be dead now if it wasn't for him."

Annie knew exactly what he was talking about. Without warning, a swell grief loomed. She battled it down.

"You okay?" he asked.

"Fine," she said. "I'm fine." And she was. For the moment.

~ * ~

"You wash dishes."

"Clean toilets, too."

The look on Annie's face was priceless. Ronen ignored the urge to haul her into his arms and soothe away her grief. Telling himself now was not the time, he maintained a safe distance, insisting she remain where she was with her leg elevated on a kitchen chair. "Humor me."

Ronen filled the dishpan with warm, sudsy water. "Your knee is of primary concern to me right now."

"My knee."

"There's nothing I'd like more than to see the Nuggets win the States next week. If only," he added as he rinsed plates and silverware, "to watch some beer-swilling doofus eat his words."

"Beer-swilling doofus," she mused. "There's so many around here to choose from, Captain. Could you enhance your description?"

"Name of Clyde something. He has a burping problem and compared you to his prize steer."

"Ah, yes. That would be Clyde of the Family Harbaugh." Her eyes danced at him over the rim of a glass of iced tea. "One of the town's leading citizens. Major gall bladder problem. The steer's name is Homer."

Suds drizzled down his arm to drip onto his bare feet. "He named a steer?"

It was good to hear her healthy giggle. "Clyde can't be bothered feeding and clothing his kids, but Homer is treated like a king. Heated stall, top-of-the-line feed, regular check-ups by Doc Holiday, the local vet."

Ronen stared at her. "You're kidding."

Raising a palm, she said, "Swear to God. The vet's name is Dr. Holiday; he named his practice The O.K. Corral."

He took a moment to digest all of this. "Is there a Mrs. Harbaugh?"

"Oh, sure. Polly and I see each other regularly."

"How does she feel about having a steer for a rival?"

Annie shrugged. "Since she's pregnant with number twelve, I'm sure Polly wishes Clyde would pay more attention to Homer. In her shoes, I know I would. But then, I prefer a man who has his own teeth and bathes on a regular basis. Go figure."

Taking a moment to run the tip of his tongue over his teeth, he said, "Twelve kids. Don't they practice—Uh, nevermind. It's none of my business."

"It will be when his oldest boy—that would be Clyde, Junior—gets into the homemade hooch his Grandpa Abner makes and starts shooting out streetlights with his thirty-ought-six."

"As long as he doesn't play 'Dueling Banjoes' while he's doing it."

She blinked, then said, "Not Junior. He's a Marilyn Manson fan."

After drying his hands, Ronen took a seat at the table. "Why, Annie?"

She stirred in her chair. "Why does Junior favor Marilyn Manson or why does his father take better care of his animals than his wife and kids?"

Tension paid a revisit to her body language the second he sat down. The best way to go, he figured, would be to keep her talking and distracted.

"Why would someone who dreams of medical school pick a patch of wilderness to live and work in that God himself has forgot about? Isn't it frustrating not to have the most up-to-date equipment and diagnostic tools for your patients?"

He thought about the sounds he'd *not* wakened to every morning since his arrival. "Doesn't the quiet drive you crazy?"

"I escaped the big city for fresh county air and a slower pace, Ronen. The challenge of treating patients without all the high-tech gadgets is incredible. Besides, how's a nuclear scanner going to help someone who can't afford medical insurance?"

He had to agree with her there. His father died because his insurance plan didn't cover all treatments needed to cure his prostate cancer.

"No," she said firmly, confidently. "This is where I belong. Where I'll return after I've finished my residency."

"To a town that has no concern for and displays outright prejudice toward the immigrants?"

"Not all of whom," she interrupted, reaching for the pitcher of iced tea, "are lily-white and pure as the driven snow. The petty crime rate in this town is out of sight. Some of the shopkeepers automatically blame the immigrants. Others regularly contribute to food and clothing drives for the children. And, I confess, some of the men at the compound scare me to death."

"Wolfgirl, scared?" he mused. "Who'd have thought?"

"I'm serious," she said. "There's no telling what some of those guys did for a living in their former homeland—and I don't want to be the one to find out."

There was no arguing with common sense. "What do you do when one of the scary ones gets sick?"

"I bring a chaperone into the exam room. Usually a very large male nurse or orderly. If I can't find a big guy, I ask Stella to come in. Nobody messes with her."

He smiled. "I bet they don't."

"In its own way a small town is exactly like a big city."

Sorely missing Rochester and all it had to offer, he snorted, "Hardly."

"Didn't something similar to this happen in Western New York in the early nineties—only on a larger scale? Close to twenty homeless women and prostitutes were murdered as I recall. No one did a thing until the press blew the cover off police inaction. True?"

The woman knew her history, unfortunately. "The police were acting but didn't let the community know for fear of inciting mass hysteria."

"But the citizens of Rochester, Captain," she pressed. "Did they care about dead prostitutes?"

He couldn't argue with the truth. "The murders happened in a rough part of the city—where good, honest folks rarely traveled."

"Except of course," she reminded him, "for the *good, honest men* who patronized the women."

"Where is this leading to, Annie?"

"Prejudice and bigotry exist everywhere," she responded. "Will it go away if I leave Nohmensville for good? No. Will things maybe get better for a few of the immigrant families if I return and treat them? I hope so."

"You're telling me if you complete med school and residency, you'll come back here—regardless."

"Regardless."

Wonderful.

"You look sick, Ronen. Is your gut acting up?"

"My gut, as you so elegantly call it, is fine." He came out of his chair with his hand extended. "Shall we retire to the drawing room, madam? I promise to limit conversation to less inflammatory topics."

"On one condition."

"That is?"

"No opera."

"Is there something wrong with the classics?"

She edged forward in her chair, giving him that clear-thinking, narrow-eyed stare. "For five terminally long evenings, I put up with the screeching of big-busted women till I swore if I heard one more fat lady sing, I'd grab your weapon and put us both out of our misery."

Biting the inside of his cheek, he asked, "You have an alternative suggestion?"

"Rusted Root."

Playing dumb, he lifted her into his arms. "Who?"

This time she didn't fight being in his arms. As she slid an arm around his neck he found her soft, pliant and almost cooperative. "Ever hear of Barenaked Ladies?"

"If they sing in the nude, I'd be more than interested."

"Jerk," she giggled. "How about Neil Diamond?"

"Now you're talking." The trip to his couch was too short. After reluctantly situating her on the cushions and elevating her leg, he dug through the closet, searching for ancient cassettes he'd packed only as an afterthought. Within seconds, the anthem of lovers everywhere, Diamond's "Play Me", filled the air.

Annie opened one eye, grinning lazily as he took a spot at the far end of the couch. "You continue to amaze me, Captain."

Somewhere between the song's provocative word play and the lush comfort of the over-stuffed couch, Annie felt another pillow slide beneath her knees, then her foot was taken by a pair of gentle hands. The words of the song symbolized the differences between her and this man. The sun and the moon, loneliness and need. And, finally, an invitation to play him. It felt right being here. With him.

No one ever told her about the wonders of a foot massage. No man had ever showered her with pleasure like this. When Ronen pressed the pad of his thumb into the ball of her foot, she almost came off the couch. A gasp, followed a drawn out sigh, escaped her chest. "If you stop, Marvelic, I'll shoot you."

"Can't have that," he murmured. His voice seemed to come from the end of a long tunnel. She didn't care.

His magical hands worked each individual toe, caressing the webbed spaces, then raising and gently pulling the length of each digit. It was so soothing, she felt her worries sweep away on the breath of a soft summer breeze.

"You're very tense, Annie."

"Please don't stop."

"No one's ever touched you like this?"

Only in her deepest, darkest dreams.

When he finished with the first foot, she boldly presented the second. "You have no idea how good this feels."

"I think I do."

The entire process began all over again. Working in silence, except for the moving words of Mr. Diamond, Ronen massaged the muscles and tendons of her foot and ankle like a master musician. Her legs went as limp as cooked spaghetti.

"I should go," she heard herself say after she heard a clock in another room chime eleven times. "Tell me to go."

"Do you want to leave?"

Wisdom and common sense reared their ugly heads. "I'm sure you have to be up early for work. You need your sleep."

"Not that much." His smooth, dreamy voice coiled her insides. "I'm starting a week of late tours at eight tomorrow night."

"Isn't that nice." She heard the gurgle in her voice and didn't give a damn. A bomb threat might force her to move; she doubted she had the strength. "I don't have to go in till noon."

His fingers worked the arch of her foot, pressing and stroking until every peripheral nerve ending communicated loud, clearly defined messages to the center of her pelvis. Need howled like a junkyard dog.

"Tell me about your work with torture victims."

"Now?" she wailed.

"I'm fascinated. Tell me about it. Please?"

Well, okay, she decided. As long as he didn't take his hands off her. "I needed something to fill my off-duty hours while I was in PA school. I first volunteered as an interpreter, later they trained me as a counselor."

"You're bilingual?"

"Quadrilingual if truth were told. Spanish, French, Hungarian and—"

Where was all this coming from? How did he pull personal things out of her with such ease? What was it about him that made her want to tell him everything?

"When you came to Nohmensville, you became involved with the immigrants."

"Yeah."

Long muscular fingers spread over the contoured muscles of her calves. "How often do you get out to see them?"

"Once a week, maybe more."

"What do you do there?"

With the deep, heaving sigh, Annie felt her blood pressure drop several more points. A hard, bounding pulse thrummed in her ears. "General health maintenance, well-baby checks, making sure immunizations are up to date, first aide, that kind of thing. Could we talk about something else?"

His hands initiated an exploration of the sensitive areas behind her knees. "What made you want to get involved with them?"

She opened her eyes to find a half-smile on his lips. Need continued to howl, issuing demands that no smart woman should ignore. Annie always considered herself a smart woman. She was ready—for anything he had in mind.

"They're poor, disenfranchised, sick, frightened. Someone has to stand for them."

The pressure behind her knee increased. "How well do you know them?"

"Pretty well."

"Any survivors of torture?"

"Ronen, they come from Bosnia, Cambodia and Romania, among other heavenly places. Of course they've been tortured."

"Do you know their names?"

"Duh. It helps to know your patient's name." Pressure turned to pain. "Hey! Cut that out!"

Eyes wide in innocence, he asked, "What's wrong?"

"You're cutting off the blood supply to my leg. Knock it off, Godammit."

"Sorry." His palm hovered over her shin. "I'm interested in what goes on out there. Eventually, I'll have to interview the survivors of the dead women. What's wrong with questions?"

Using her good leg to push him out of the way, she sat up, then swung both feet to the floor. So much for needs, arousal, and fulfillment. "When the 'questions' start sounding like an interrogation, Marvelic, sure as spit on a fastball, there's something wrong."

He came off the couch, Mr. Defensive Posture himself. "When I interrogate you, Annie, you'll know it."

She was angry enough—mostly at herself—to get in his face. As an extra, added attraction, she introduced a couple of pointed fingertips to his chest wall. "If you want to know something, Captain Marvel, ask me straight out. Don't bother with some half-assed attempt at seduction."

"Half-assed?"

Color spotted his cheeks. Once before she'd thought he wasn't someone to piss off. She was sure of it now.

When he looked at her, he was all cop. "How many of the immigrants are documented?"

Was this the real reason for him being assigned to Nohmensville? While he investigated the murders was it also a goal to nail a few illegals?

A conversation she'd overheard a couple days ago in Del Shea's What Knot Shoppe flashed through her mind.

She'd been standing in line at the check-out counter when two troopers from the Oneonta sub-station got in line behind her. One of them said, "You know what they called him up in Rochester, don't you?"

"Nope."

"The Coyote Hunter. Seems there was a major smuggling ring in the Rochester-Buffalo-Toronto corridor, bringing in Asian women from Canada in false bottoms of tractor trailers. Marvelic went under to nail the coyotes running them."

"No shit," the second one said.

At the mention of Ronen's name inside the quaint country shop, Annie's hearing went on full alert status. Smugglers. Aliens, she recalled thinking.

"Got them all," the first trooper declared. "Sent a whole bunch of bad guys to the joint."

"Undercover," the second one said. "Takes balls."

"Sure it does," came the response. "I just wonder what a big deal like him is doing down here."

Annie walked out of Del's, vowing to steer clear of Marvelic once the work on the files was finished—but then forget all about what she'd overheard. Until now.

If he thought she'd rat out her friends, he was in for a rude shock. "It's not my custom, nor is it my practice, to check for green cards or visas before I treat my patients, Marvelic."

"Maybe you should," he challenged. "Maybe one of the reasons why these women were so easily victimized was because of their immigration status."

"I don't understand." *Like hell she didn't.*

"Illegal aliens don't report crimes because they fear they'll be discovered, then deported."

"What exactly are you doing down here?" she demanded. "Solving murders or deporting a group of innocent victims?"

"For God's sake, Annie," he exploded. "Help me!"

Heart pounding, she bluffed. "I have no idea the immigration status of my patients. Or of my friends."

"You're a lousy liar, Ms. Wolfe."

"So arrest me."

Six

After twelve grueling hours in the Emergency Room, suturing drunks, delivering a set of twins too anxious to wait for the traditional labor room for their debut, and transferring an MVA victim to the closest trauma center, Annie prayed for the mercy of a tepid shower, crisp sheets, and eight hours of coma-like sleep. She put the Mustang on auto-pilot for the ride down I-88, heading for the shower, sheets, and sleep—in that order.

Other than making her arches scream like bandits, the busy shift accomplished one important goal: keeping her mind off Captain Marvel and last night's disaster.

Laying on his couch had felt so good, so right. Letting him rub her feet felt even better. So what if things got a little heavy, and her juices were flowing like the Chenango River? They were both consenting adults. For a few minutes, Marvelic hadn't stood a chance of sleeping alone.

Last night his touch soothed her, calmed her, and—for a few moments—made her forget. Until he changed from potential lover to grand inquisitor in the blink of an eye. How the hell would she know if any of the immigrants were in the States illegally? Why would she care? Abner Harbaugh sure as hell didn't. Employing illegals meant he could pay less money to have his crops harvested. It also meant he could treat them any way he chose, without fear of government sanctions.

Marvelic was right when he claimed no illegal would bitch if, or when, they were treated badly. No one knew better than she what illegals suffered, having spent her early years dodging INS agents. She, of all people, knew what it was to always be on guard, constantly looking over her shoulder for whatever or whomever might be around the next corner.

"Forget him, Wolfgirl," she grumbled out loud. "The man is a walking danger zone."

Lights from Nohmensville's all-night diner glowed like a beacon in the coal-black sky, immediately setting off a ferocious growl in her stomach. The clock on the Mustang's dash reminded her she'd not eaten in more than ten hours, just before she caught the first squalling twin.

If Pete Balkas was still on the grill at the Little Buda, she'd con him into fixing her a three egg omelet loaded with scallions, mushrooms and fresh chives. If she still had room after the omelet, she would treat herself with a serving of Marta Balkas' *saviako*, the best tasting pastry this side of Budapest.

A light misting rain began to fall just as she pulled into Little Buda's parking lot. It wasn't enough to bother with an umbrella. Still, a shiver raced down her back.

Head down, she pushed the door open. Her greeting for Pete and Marta died on her lips when a granite-hard arm grabbed her from behind. A bloody switchblade flashed across her visual field before finding a home in the skin beneath her ear. "Take it easy, lady and nobody gets hurt."

Shaking uncontrollably, Marta Balkas was using the cash register stand to hold herself upright. "Illiana, do not—"

"Give him what he wants," Annie said.

"I tell him, over and over," the woman wailed. "Petros, he take money to bank drop-box not one-quarter hour past."

The arm beneath Annie's ribs jerked upward, nearly cutting off her air. "Son of a bitch."

Stale beer, heavily accented with whiskey, only worsened the queasiness in her empty stomach. Boilermakers, she groaned, the worst kind of drunk. The knife point dug a little deeper beneath her ear. Something wet drizzled down her neck.

She forced calm into her voice. "Take my wallet. There's enough cash to get you on your way. If you let Marta go, I'll give you the pin number for my ATM card."

"Son of a bitch."

Her attention was drawn to a low moan coming from the far corner of the room. The gray-uniformed body of a State Trooper moved weakly, then slumped face down on the floor. Her heart stopped for a second. *Ronen.*

The tan Stetson fell from the trooper's head, revealing a thatch of dark brown hair. Her relief was short lived when she saw a crimson pool of blood spreading slowly from beneath his body. "I work in ER," she blurted. "Let me take a look at him."

"Son of a bitch."

"*Please*. If he dies, you'll be in a pack more trouble. If you let me help him, it'll go better for you."

"I... dunno."

"Tell me your name," she prompted.

"Jake."

With that, it became easier to breathe. "Jake, think about it. While Marta and I are taking care of the cop, you grab my wallet. The Mustang outside has a full tank of gas. There's a spare key under the floor mat. Take the car and go."

After shuffling his feet, but more important—lowering the knife—he stammered, "You p-p-promise?"

She handed him her wallet without comment. Jake took a step back. Behind them, the wall of windows exploded in a storm of glass. Annie went to the floor, shouting, "Marta, down!" then log-rolled across the room toward the fallen trooper.

Pounding feet blasted through the door. Shouts of "Put the knife down," came one on top of another. She crouched over the bleeding officer. She had a few supplies in her work bag, but nothing that would staunch this amount of blood. Panic threatened. Could she do this? What if his injuries were beyond her? What if—

Barb's voice intruded. *Save the what ifs, kid. This guy's dead if you don't do something.*

~ * ~

Ronen gave the computer screen a healthy swipe of his hand. Trying to sort through the morass of commands necessary to access information from the Veterans' Administration took more effort than accessing top-secret files from the CIA.

It wasn't like he could just prance into the local VFW and nose around, asking who was a member and who wasn't. The killers were probably all members in good standing. The kind who liked to hang around sharing war stories—literally.

"Regular salt of the earth types," he grumbled, then cursed when the whole damn machine crashed on him. "Shit!"

Shoving away from the desk, he turned to other, equally pressing issues. For answers, he looked to the second in command on the first platoon. "Where do we stand in Nohmensville?"

Night duty sergeant Rick Thurrell responded with a grin that resembled a kid waiting for seconds on his favorite dessert. "As of midnight tonight, the No Man's Land PD is defunct and the Gray Riders officially assume responsibility to protect and serve the good citizens of Nohmensville. Praise the Lord and pass the potatoes."

"Any word on the street about us taking over?"

"Zip. None. And nada."

"Excuse me?" Ronen asked, not really surprised. The entire town was sewn up tighter than his grandmother's corset.

Thurrell leaned back in his chair, picking absently at a loose thread on the cuff of his spanking-perfect uniform blouse. "Nobody's seen nothin'. Nobody knows nothin'. Nobody cares nothin'."

An obscene screech, like fingernails streaking down a blackboard, erupted from the radio. "Ten-thirteen. Repeat, ten-thirteen, officer down. Four-zero Maple Street, Nohmensville."

A second, more chilling, message came next. "Unknown number of hostages."

Ronen grabbed his hat, extra ammo, and Kevlar vest, then bolted for the door. He rode shotgun while Rick took the blue and gold unit down I-88 at speeds in excess of eighty.

"When was the last hostage scene around here?"

"Fall of '99," Thurrell said. "Old Man Harbaugh went on a toot, held a couple migrants for ransom till somebody brought him another bottle of hooch. That count?"

"Wonderful."

Ronen counted the days he had left in No Man's Land: three hundred and forty two.

By the time Rick pulled the unit into the parking lot of a small diner called Little Buda, the locals had it secured. Certain their offer of support would be declined, he and Rick crossed the parking lot. A lone red Mustang occupied the spot closest to the front door. Ronen's blood turned to ice when he saw the plate number.

Annie.

Glass crunched beneath their feet as they went through the door. "Don't ask," Rick warned. "You won't like the answer."

A man, spread-eagled on the floor, was surrounded by four uniformed officers, each had an automatic weapon pointed at his head.

"I need some help here."

Ronen followed the voice, found Annie in a far corner, scrambling around a body, aided by a woman dressed in black.

"We're kinda busy here, Wolfgirl," one of the locals said.

Ronen saw the blood-stained gray uniform and turned to Rick. "Radio for an ambulance, get the medical kit and blankets."

"I'm on it."

Two lunging steps put Ronen at Annie's side. "Tell me what to do."

"I need blankets, towels, and an ambulance."

Blood and gore splattered her clothes as her hands moved like wildfire over the trooper's body, voice cool and calm. Rick thrust a blanket into Ronen's hands. "Ambulance is on its way."

"Cover his legs, Captain," Annie said with a calm that awed him. How could she—?

"Marta?" she said. "Towels, please. Wet and dry."

The black-clad woman scuttled away. Seconds later, a pair of calloused hands reached over Ronen's shoulder and dropped dish towels on his thighs. "For Illiana."

Annie grabbed for them. "Help me get his shirt off."

Ronen split the tunic with one fast jerk and almost gagged when he saw what the shirt had covered. Annie never flinched, just started packing towels into an ugly, gaping wound that spanned the width of the officer's belly.

She took his hands, placed them on top of the towels. "Press here. Press hard."

"Aw, geez." More blood gushed from the wound, covering both of his hands to the wrist. An odor of copper filled his nostrils. He prayed he wouldn't pass out. More, he prayed he wouldn't throw up.

"Breathe through your mouth," Annie said, then called for more towels. "You'll get used to it."

He sincerely doubted that. "Yes, ma'am."

He packed fresh towels over the soaked ones and continued applying pressure on the wound. Through the bright spots that danced before his eyes, he could see Annie's sure, purposeful hands at work.

"Your knee holding up okay?"

That earned him a frosty glare. "It's fine. Where's the rig you promised?"

He heard the distant sounds of sirens. "On its way."

"That's good, 'cause we're losing him."

She stayed so calm, so controlled while issuing orders to raise the trooper's legs on an over-turned chair and cover him with more blankets. Her voice never wavered; she never whined. There wasn't a moment of hesitation. She knew what needed to be done, then did it.

Rick Thurrell reappeared at Ronen's side. "Damn. It's Joey Marks," he said, giving a name to the fallen officer. "They've got a baby due any day."

"Better find his wife," Annie said without looking up. "Get her to the ER in Oneonta."

"Will do." Rick stepped back from the action. Ronen heard him on the portable radio dispatching a unit to the Marks' home.

EMT's with a stretcher and rolling tackle box blew through the door. After one of them took over applying pressure on the wound, Ronen stepped back. With Annie calling the shots, he watched the team work like an efficient, well-oiled machine to save a man's life.

~ * ~

Through a one-way mirror, Ronen observed a Nohmensville police officer take Annie's statement. In another sixteen hours, this case would officially be his. Until that time he was present as a courtesy. Only to observe.

Observation didn't mean he couldn't form opinions. About Annie Wolfe, the woman, and the professional. About solid police work—the type he preferred to practice—not what was occurring on the other side of the glass.

"*Let's go through this one more time, Annie.*" Two cops had planted themselves across a standard-issue metal table from her. One took notes on a legal pad, offering no comment beyond an infrequent grunt. The second officer was clearly in charge.

"*You were on your way home from work when you just happened to stop at the Little Buda for a bite to eat. That's your story?*"

Ronen cringed, first at the investigator's tone of voice, second at the inference.

"*That is correct,*" she said.

"*Those the clothes you wore during the... encounter?*"

"*Yes.*"

He'd always figured witnesses deserved understanding mixed with an ounce of kindness, a cup of empathy, a pound of grace. This guy's style was several quarts low in each.

"*Perp says you offered him money, your car. That true?*"

Rick Thurrell appeared at Ronen's side, coffee in hand. "Settle down, Cap, before you bust an artery or something."

Ronen grabbed the cup and took a slug. "She saved a man's life, for Christ's sake. He's treating her like she's the next Lucrezia Borgia."

He kept his focus on Annie, saw the tremors in her upper body. Possibly it was because she was still wearing the blood-smeared clothes from the diner. More likely, it was because someone had turned the setting on the room's air conditioner to Frigid. It was an old trick—one he'd used himself—back when he was too stupid to know better.

"*He had a knife at my throat. I would have done anything, said anything, to get him out of there so I could—*"

"Yeah, I bet."

Shoulders hunched, Annie hugged her arms to her chest. The slight change in position afforded Ronen a better view of her neck, and the thick streak of dried blood beneath her ear. Somehow he sensed the blood hadn't come from Trooper Marks.

"How well do you know these two birds, Rick?"

Thurrell shrugged. "As well as anyone knows Raging Randy Terrance and Bozo the Claun."

"Where'd they study interrogation methods? Vlad the Impaler's School of Charm?"

"Work's for them, I guess. Bobby takes notes and grunts. Randy asks the questions and gets his rocks off."

"Every witness?" Ronen growled. "Or only the females?"

Rick snorted. "Welcome to No Man's Land, Captain."

"Any word on Marks?"

"Only that the docs on the Mercy Flight said if Annie hadn't been there and done what she did, we'd be planning a funeral."

Ronen sighed. For Annie's exceptional hands, steel trap mind, and her well-deserved aversion to local cops. She'd make a fine doctor. "Thanks."

"How long before you bust in there and play hero?"

Right then, Officer Terrance informed Annie she would have to take a polygraph. "*For the record. You understand.*"

He hurled the half-filled cup into the closest trash basket. "I don't know when I'll get back to the barracks. Leave me the unit."

Thurrell nodded. "I'll catch a ride with one of the guys."

Ronen entered the interrogation room, ready to kick ass. Blithely ignoring Terrance's growl of protest, he took the empty chair beside Annie. "Ms. Wolfe, I'm Captain Marvelic of the New York State Police Department. You look like you could use something warm."

With a slight nod, she accepted his jacket. "Captain."

There were many things he wanted to do. What he *had* to do was maintain the proper attitude. "They tell me Trooper Marks is holding his own."

She gave him a flick of a glance. "Appreciate the information, Captain."

He recognized sarcasm, heavily seasoned with the exhaustion that always followed an adrenaline high. Her slumping posture was a clear sign he needed to get her out of here. "Can we get you anything? Maybe a hot drink?"

"No. Thanks."

"Is there someone we could call, let them know you'll be late getting home?"

"No. Thanks."

"We doing just fine," Investigator Terrance sneered, the non-verbal message being: *until you horned in, city boy.* "Weren't we, Annie?"

She wrapped the jacket tighter around her body. "Peachy."

"I'm sure Ms. Wolfe would appreciate it if things moved along in a timely and efficient manner." Ronen glared a hole in Terrance's forehead, convinced the man had no clue—or simply didn't care—that his behavior was inappropriate.

"I know if I'd been taken hostage by an armed robber," he continued, putting a deliberate sneer in his voice, "had shards of glass raining down on my head while I was trying to save a man's life, I'd like to get home to a hot shower and a warm bed."

Officer Claun spoke for the first time. "Shoulda' said somethin', Wolfgirl. Randy woulda' stopped first thing you said somethin'."

Annie tucked her chin into the jacket's collar. "I'd like to get this over with. Do what you need to do so I can leave."

"I believe you mentioned a lie detector test, Officer Terrance?" Ronen asked.

The poster boy for police misconduct attempted to squirm out of his previous illegal threat. "Aw, Cap. She knows I was just jerking her chain. Doncha', Annie?"

"Sure."

"If that's all, gentlemen," Ronen said, gently urging her from the chair. "I'll see that Ms. Wolfe gets home safely. Have her statement ready for me first thing in the morning."

Terrance looked like he was about to pass a stone the size of a peach pit. "You can't take over my case!"

Ronen leaned over the table, came nose-to-nose with the red-faced, blustering man, and took great pains to speak softly and slowly. "Read the regs. Check with the mayor if you don't believe them, or me. Report. On my desk. Nine A.M."

"But—"

"Don't screw with me, Mr. Terrance. My mood is not the best right now."

~ * ~

Outside the station house, the rain had stopped; the sky was clear. Annie took several cleansing breaths, knowing full well nothing short of a Lysol shower would make her feel clean after dealing with Randy Terrance.

"How are you doing?" Marvelic came up beside her, hovering like some kind of concerned person.

Concern. Screw that.

"I'm fine."

Placing a hand at the small of her back, he directed her toward a patrol car. "I apologize for the way they treated you. Not all cops—"

Annie just kept on moving. Control was a fragile thing. She could feel it slipping with each tick of the clock. "Spare me, Captain."

"Terrance had no right to—"

This guy needed a maximum-strength reality check. "If you think that was the first time some cop tried to shake a female victim out of making a complaint or changing her story to make his job easier, think again."

After flipping the collar of the jacket up over her ears, she shoved her hands into the pockets to hide the shakes from his all-seeing gaze. "I've been jerked around by the best since I was old enough to pick a pocket or run a street scam. The NYPD blues make Randy Terrance look like chump change."

He held the cruiser's passenger door open, waited for her to belt up, then closed the door with a soft snick. He scooted around the hood, then took the driver's seat. "Mr. Terrance won't be running the town much longer."

"The lack of a badge won't stop him."

"I sensed that after watching him with you."

"Watched him? From where?"

"I was on the other side of the two-way mirror on the wall of the interrogation room."

Why wasn't she surprised? "Got yourself a first-hand look at the way things go in *No Man's Land*, didja?"

He tapped his fingers against the steering wheel, said tightly, "I repeat, I'm sorry."

Sorry didn't quite cut it. "Randy's a bully and a pig."

"Probably."

Probably? She nearly choked. Too many *suspects* had required evaluation in the ER after Terrance claimed they'd "resisted arrest". She'd seen too many facial and rib fractures, a result of their so-called resistance. And Terrance knew it. He'd put her through the wringer as a little reminder for what happened to uppity women who crossed the line.

The engine purred to life. She watched Ronen flip the heater switch to high. "Tell me when you're warm enough."

The last time she'd been warm enough was in her bathroom. When he held her in his arms after she'd barfed all over his shoes. Turning her face to the window, she blinked furiously. "You don't need to do this."

"What—driving you home?"

"Be supportive."

"Here I thought it was part of the job."

What happened next came with no warning signs, no auras, no lights flashing before her eyes. Emotion exploded in harsh, wracking sobs. Bringing her knees to her chest, she hung on for dear life and let loose. Then, Ronen was hauling her out of the harness, across the seat, and into his arms. One hand cradled her against his chest while the other rubbed her back with wide, sweeping strokes. "It's over, Annie. You're safe."

And she was. Safe. In his arms. Again.

"You rescued me," she blubbered. "No one's ever done that before."

"I'm so sorry."

That only brought on a fresh flood of tears. Oddly, crying didn't seem to bother him. He didn't tell her to stop, like most men would, because wailing women "tore them apart". He just let her carry on, ranting and raving like a mad woman. And continued to rock her.

She pulled back, staring at his shirt front. "I got it all wet," she murmured, smoothing her fingers over the cloth. "It's wrinkled."

"I don't care."

"I don't do crying."

"I understand."

"Blubbering because some bully got the better of me is a waste of time and energy."

"Wait a minute," he said, giving her a shake. "You've got a right to cry. For a lot of reasons. Hell, Annie, I got teary looking at the pictures of those women. I wanted to scream and holler with you for Barbara. What will it take before you'll weep for the losses you've suffered?"

"Never. Crying's for wimps and cowards."

"Sure as spit on a fastball, you're no wimp."

"Shut up, Marvelic."

One hand moved to cup the side of her face, then tip up her chin. "You have the most incredible eyes," he whispered, tracing a path across her brow with his lips. "I could fall into them and never need to leave."

Oh... dear, she thought frantically. *This is not—*

"And your hair," he said slowly. "It shimmers like black silk. I want to see it falling over my body like a velvet curtain."

She found herself staring at his mouth, the lips that quirked in a shy grin. She wanted that mouth. Now. "Thought I told you to shut up."

"Make me."

His mouth descended in maddeningly slow increments. She stretched to meet it. The slight brush of lips was electric, the taste exquisite. She needed more. Wanted—

A fury of bright stars slammed her eyelids. Headlights. She jumped out of his arms, scuttling to the far side of the seat. "Start the car."

"Annie—"

What had she done? If the driver of the other car saw them and reported Ronen necking in the unit—he could lose his rank. *He could lose everything*! "Start the god-damned car!"

"I'll take you home."

"Take me to the Little Buda. My car's there."

"Annie—"

"Do it. Now."

"Whatever you say."

"As long as you're being so agreeable," she sniped. "I'd ask one more thing."

"Of course, honey. Name it."

"Stay away from me."

Seven

For ten in the morning, John Latimer's office looked like Penn Station during rush hour. Ronen stood at the check-in desk, stetson in hand, waiting patiently for someone to take care of him.

A roar came from a back room. "I can't find my penis!"

Stella Grover's eyes rolled skyward as she handed Ronen a sheath of papers to fill out, then directed him to a chair in the waiting area before tackling her employer's emerging crisis. "Have we checked our briefs, Doctor?"

"I was practicing with it just a few minutes ago," he grumbled. "Now it's gone."

The white-haired Latimer poked his head through the window that separated the reception desk from the work area on the other side. "C'mon, Stella. I've got to be at the high school in fifteen minutes for the summer school biology class."

"So?" she retorted.

"The only reason half of those delinquents show up is to play with the pelvic models."

A middle-age woman seated beside Ronen sniffed loudly. "Ask me, the last thing our children need is plastic privates."

Feeling it best not to argue, he nodded. "Yes, ma'am."

The three page, single-spaced questionnaire asked for his medical history, and that of his parents and siblings. Diabetes—no.

Hypertension—no. Heart Disease—no. Cancer—yes. Mental Illness—lately he'd had reason to wonder about that.

Since the episode in his unit, Annie hung up every time he called, refused to come to the door when he knocked. Despite that, he continued his attempts to reach out to her. If that wasn't insanity, he didn't know what was.

"Ladies, I cannot do my job without my penis."

The ample form next to him jostled Ronen's hand as he tried to complete the last page of the questionnaire. "At his age," she huffed, "a body'd think he'd be done with all that nonsense."

If he was lucky enough to reach Latimer's age, with all his parts working, Ronen figured he'd be doing pretty good. "Yes, ma'am."

"Keep it in your pants," she announced abruptly. "It's what I always told my boys."

"Wise advice," Ronen murmured, concentrating on hereditary diseases.

Anticipating a physical exam was stressful enough. If John Latimer was leaving for the high school, who else was available to poke and prod at his body? Ask all sorts of intrusive questions? Being on the opposite side of an interrogation, no matter how well-intentioned the questions might be, was not something Ronen did on a regular basis.

His neighbor interrupted a vision filled with terror and trauma. "Told my girls to keep their legs crossed and their knees locked." She sat back proudly, arms folded across her ample bosom. "Don't you agree, officer?"

"Absolutely, ma'am." He completed the last portion of the sheet that detailed his sexual behaviors. As there was nothing to relate, that particular section didn't take long to complete. "Zippers in an upright, locked position. Knees tight enough to squeak."

Dr. Latimer stuck his head through the window again, nodding briefly at Ronen. His gaze landed on the woman seated beside him. "Sophie Jackson, that you?"

"Of course it's me, you old coot."

"Looking fit and sassy as usual," he replied. "One of the girls will be calling you shortly."

"Better be," she grumbled under her breath. "Been waiting nigh onto fifteen minutes."

Chimes over the entrance door sang merrily, admitting a young pregnant woman with toddlers hanging on each hand.

"Will you look at that," Mrs. Jackson sneered.

Dressed in the manner of Eastern Europe, the woman wore a cream-colored scarf covering her head from eyebrows to shoulders. The sleeves of her blouse went to her wrists; the hem of her skirt ended at mid-calf. With her hugely pregnant belly, solemn dark eyes, and slow pace, she looked exhausted. The temperature had rarely fallen below ninety this past week; Ronen's heart went out to her.

"Mrs. Dynic." John Latimer stepped into the waiting area, his manner gentle and concerned. "Bring the children this way."

Sophie Jackson rearranged her generous backside in the chair. "Ask me, it's *them* who need sex-ed. Look at her, bringing another brat into this world for our taxes to support."

Mrs. Jackson eyed Ronen's neatly pressed uniform from ankle to chin with a glow of maternal approval. "Weren't you the one directing traffic after church services this past weekend?"

It had been a pleasant way for him to spend the previous Sunday morning. Reminded him of when he was a kid. "Yes, ma'am."

"I hold no truck with those anarchy-ists who rant and rave against mixing church and state."

"No, ma'am."

Mrs. Jackson patted his arm. "Continue directing traffic after Sunday services, keep the town free of smut peddlers and perverts, I'll be happy."

"We'll do our best, ma'am."

"Mr. Marvel—" A voice stumbled over his name. "Ronen Marbel—I mean, Marvelisk."

Grateful for the interruption, he tipped his hat to Mrs. Jackson. "They're calling me."

A young woman in a nurse's uniform escorted him to the lab area where she took his height and weight, blood pressure, pulse, and temperature. From the corner of his eye, Ronen saw John Latimer pause in the corridor to speak to someone.

"What would I do without you?" the man wailed. "Come away with me, my little fuzz-flower. Be my love. Sip wine through a straw. Munch grapes from my tremulous fingers. Adjust my Depends."

Annie Wolfe's laugh brought Ronen to immediate attention. "Don't tempt me."

The nurse finished taking his pulse. "The room is ready, sir. Right this way."

Ronen reached panic level. "Wait, please. I specifically asked to be seen by Dr. Latimer. If he's leaving, who will—?"

"Not to worry," she said, leading him into an exam room. "We have several practitioners on duty today."

As long as it wasn't Annie, Ronen would have let Dracula examine him. Not that he didn't trust her skills. After seeing her in action with Trooper Marks, he would never doubt her abilities. He simply didn't think he would be able to control his bodily responses once she put her hands on him.

"Everything off, sir."

"Every... thing?" he gulped.

"Yes, sir." She gave his uniform a benign smile. "Would you like me to check your weapon at the desk?"

Actually, he preferred to keep it. Never knew when he'd need protection from some needle-wielding vampire. "Thanks, but it stays with me. One of the trooper rules."

"Whatever you say, sir." She checked her watch. "Shouldn't be too much longer."

The exam table was no different than any other, hard as concrete with stiff paper crinkling beneath his bare bottom. The room was the same: cold, utilitarian, and reeking of antiseptic. Covered by little more than a threadbare gown several sizes too small and a sheet over his legs, Ronen checked out the informational posters mounted on the walls advising the need for regular Pap smears, cholesterol checks, and HIV testing.

By his watch, he'd been waiting twenty minutes when the door burst open. "I'm sorry to have kept you waiting. We had a minor emergency."

Ronen looked up, found himself staring open-mouthed into Annie's big brown eyes. "The missing body part. I heard."

Hand extended, she rushed toward him. "Why are you here? Is something wrong? Are you sick?"

He wished he could be anywhere but here. Unfortunately, his commanding officer had other ideas. *I don't give a bat's ass how they do things in Rochester, Marvelic. Down here, I run a tight ship. You got two choices: get this physical—which is six months overdue—or don't come back.*

"I need a physical," he explained. "Major Valetta won't let me return to duty until the form is turned in."

"This is not a good idea," she blurted. "I—"

"Tell me about it. I made the appointment with Dr. Latimer; he's obviously tied up with other things."

"I'll ask one of the other clinicians to take you," she said quickly, then ducked out the door.

He barely had time to think over his options before Annie burst back in, slamming the door behind her. She looked frustrated—and more than a little peeved. "Not one of those miserable excuses for human beings would trade patients. Said they were busy. Said they shouldn't *interrupt the flow*." She ended her tirade with some rather inventive, under-her-breath cursing. "Someday, when they least expect it, I'll *interrupt their flows*."

"Can we just do it?" he asked, despising the whine in his voice.

Repulsion flooded her face. "I beg your pardon?"

"The physical, Annie. What did you think I meant?"

She straddled a rolling stool then duck-walked it to the end of the exam table. In faded jeans, tie-dyed T-shirt, and lab coat, she looked like a kid dressed up to play doctor. Strands of ebony hair had escaped from the thick knot on top of her head, coiling at the sides of her face and neck. Dark framed glasses could not obscure the bags beneath her eyes.

"Ronen—" she sighed; pleading filled her eyes. "It's not wise for me to examine you."

"Does this reluctance have something to do with the rule that a medical professional shouldn't treat someone with whom they are involved?"

"Exactly."

"Aside from that aborted kiss in my cruiser the other night," he offered blandly, "I wasn't aware you and I are involved. Am I wrong?"

She wouldn't have looked more shocked if he'd reached out and patted her supremely fine butt. "Of course not!"

"I don't like this any more than you do. Just give me the damn physical so I can get out of here."

"Someone else should do the exam," she repeated. "We'd both feel more comfortable."

"I have to have it today."

"I understand that, but couldn't you go back to work for a few hours? Stella would be happy to work you into a later appointment slot. If that doesn't work for your schedule, maybe you could come in tomorrow."

Rescheduling was out of the question. In less than two hours, he was scheduled to be on a conference call with agents from Immigration and the FBI's Violent Crime Unit. If he had to cancel the call because of a stupid physical, the delay could cause irreparable damage to the investigation.

"It's now or never, Annie. Unless—" Sometimes he was so good, he scared himself. "Unless you're chicken."

Narrowed brown eyes drilled a hole in his forehead. "Have you been experiencing delusional episodes, Captain?"

Damn, she was cute when she got snippy. "Not today."

She took a deep breath, let it out slowly. "Very well, let us begin." She came off the stool, moving to his right side. "Relax," she murmured. "This won't hurt a bit."

Hurting was the last thing on his mind.

Starting at the top of his head she probed his scalp, felt behind and beneath his ears, palpated his jaw with firm, competent hands. "Are you taking any medications? Even those purchased over the counter?"

His bones slowly turned to butter with each stroke of her fingers.

"Meds, Captain?" she repeated.

"What? Oh." Concentrate, he ordered his brain. How could a man think at a time like this? "Just vitamin and mineral supplements. That's all."

She pressed gently over his eyebrows, cheekbones, and nose. "Any tobacco, alcohol, or recreational drug use?"

"No."

"Ever?"

"Years ago, when I was young and stupid."

One of those eye scope things appeared in her hand. "Look at the wall behind my shoulder, please." Leaning close, she shined the light into his eyes. The outer edge of her breast brushed against his arm. Butter turned to cast-iron in body parts other than bones.

"Looks good," she chirped, slipping the instrument into her pocket. "Tell me what the sign behind me says."

He read it and, given the circumstances, didn't find the idea one bit humorous. "We don't need to chat about Viagra. Thanks anyway."

She made notes on the chart. "Are you sexually active?"

Two can play this game, he decided. "Nah. I usually lay there, let the girl do all the work."

After checking his ears and palpating his neck with quick, practiced motions, she lowered his gown to mid-chest. "Breathe deeply, evenly." She ran a stethoscope over his chest. "Let me do the work."

How could he breathe deep when it took all his concentration to avoid imminent climax?

Then he smelled her perfume.

"Our heart rate is slightly increased, Mr. Marvelic." He could see her struggling to control the expression on her face. If she burst out laughing, he'd pull his weapon. "Should we do an EKG—or are we feeling a tad stressed today?"

"You have no idea."

Her mouth cracked, briefly, then went back to the standard professional countenance. "Let's switch to another body system. Lay back, please."

She flipped up the bottom of the table to support his out-stretched legs. Then, damned if she didn't start running her hands from his ankles to his knees in slow, firm motions. Slender fingers pressed the backs of his knees before tracing the length of his calves to the inside of his ankles and the top of his feet. He nearly choked.

When sanity returned, barely, he asked, "What are you doing?"

"Checking your peripheral pulses. Has no one ever done it for you before?"

"Not like that."

"Your feet and lower legs have good blood supply," she said in a reassuring tone. "The pulses are what we call bounding. If you choose, we can dispense with checking the femorals."

"Where do you—how do you check for those?"

"By palpating your groin."

He choked. "No, thank you."

"Very well. Let us proceed with the abdominal exam."

"Aw, geez." That needle-wielding vampire was looking real good right now.

Fingertips pressed, palpated, and tapped his belly. She explained everything as she went, asked him about the pain he experienced after eating spicy or high-fat meals. As she probed, examined, and questioned, the sheet moved lower; his anxiety went off the scale.

"Do you perform self exams?" she asked, in the same tone one might use to ask if he brushed his teeth regularly.

"Exams on what?"

"Your testicles, Mr. Marvelic. Do you examine them on a regular basis? If not, I'd be happy to show you how to do it."

Fun time was over. "Having a good time, aren't you?"

"Smashing."

Without missing a beat, she had him sit up and began to put him through his paces, asking him to close his eyes, then touch his nose with a fingertip, flex his forearms and raise his legs against resistance.

"I've neglected to ask about life experiences." His teeth gnashed; his fists clenched. This prim, professional manner was going to drive him up a wall. "Did you serve in the military?"

"Marines," he growled, wanting desperately to choke the grin off her face. "Four years. Beirut and Guantanamo."

"One of a few good men. Higher education?"

"BS in Criminal Justice."

"B. S. Appropriate, given your line of work. Any hobbies?"

"Collecting hard-core porn, reading back issues of "Satanic Gazette", and running guns for the PLO."

"A well-rounded individual," she murmured, turning to the counter behind her. "We're almost done."

Thank you, God.

The snapping of a rubber glove and a squirting sound didn't set off alarm bells. They should have. Physician's Assistant Wolfe faced him with a placid, professional expression. "Assume the position, Mr. Marvelic."

~ * ~

After sending Captain Marvel off with reqs for lab work and samples of meds for his irritable gut, Annie took his file, and those of the other patients she'd seen during morning office hours, into the lunch room to dictate her notes. She was annoyed with herself for allowing Ronen to goad her into doing something inappropriate, then for teasing him unmercifully.

He definitely doesn't need Viagra.

In order to dictate a thorough, concise note, she flipped through his chart, scratching down reminders on the note pad next to her hand. *Marines. Guantanamo. Beirut.*

It was an epiphany. Complete with bells, whistles and sirens.

If she'd thought to ask Ronen about military service, how many other patients in John's practice had been asked the same question?

"Southeast Asia, Central America, late seventies to early eighties," she mused out loud. "That means I should look for any male between the ages of—" After doing some quick math, Annie headed for the front desk.

Ronen's warning to stay out of the investigation didn't mean squat. "He can't tell me what to do. Besides, I'm not going into bars; I'm sitting right here." The more she excused her actions, the faster excitement thrummed across both temples.

"I have every right to review charts for... quality assurance purposes," she reasoned, bolstering a defense should Captain Marvel wig out after discovering she'd ignored his warnings. "I'm just doing my job."

Stella was more than happy to pull the records of every male patient between the ages of forty-five and sixty-five, insisting that Annie leave the charts in the break room after she finished. Since Stella managed the office record room with the efficiency of a drill sergeant, Annie gladly accepted her help.

There were more records than she'd expected, but once she got a system going, it didn't take long to plow through the pile of charts for the information. Nohmensville and the surrounding area, it turned out, was home to a number of veterans with extensive military backgrounds, including Vietnam. Several had remained on as advisors to the military long after that nasty little war was over.

A few, residents at a local nursing home, were immediately discarded. And she was rather surprised to discover that John Latimer, a local minister, the mayor, and Jim Valetta had served in either Korea or 'Nam.

But only one man served tours in Vietnam *and* Central America: Randall James Terrance.

"Bingo."

An hour later, John Latimer found Annie in the break room, munching on apple sections between note dictations. He pulled a no-cal, no-caffeine soda from the refrigerator. "How'd it go with Renate Dynic?"

"If we're lucky, it's only pregnancy induced hypertension. I explained the possibility of toxemia, drew stat lab work, and convinced her she needed to be admitted for observation. Stella drove her to the hospital."

"Good. Her kids were looking a might peaked. What's the scoop with them?"

"Dehydration and pneumonia. I admitted them all under your service and wrote the usual orders. Husband's not too thrilled with me; I told him to go pound salt."

John drained the soda in three swallows, then reached for the uneaten wedges of her apple. "Works for me."

The man's zero tolerance for fools, and other types of abusive males, was only one of the reasons why Annie adored John. "Renate told me there's a whole slew of sick kids at the compound. I'll take the Drug Bus out there this afternoon, see what I can do."

"Make sure you're home by dark. Don't stop for anyone on the way. Call me before you leave the compound."

"Yes, Daddy."

"You wish." After polishing off the apple slices, he washed his hands at the sink. "The Lone Ranger left here with a clean bill of health?"

"Other than a quirky gut and a nasty family history for prostate cancer, he's as healthy as a horse," she replied without thinking, then made the stupid mistake of trying to cover her blunder. "Lone Ranger? I don't know what you're talking about."

"I got eyes, little girl. That man makes you nervous."

"What he makes me, Doctor, is mad."

John leaned against the counter. "When Molly was alive, she said the same thing about me."

"You volunteering my services to help Captain Marvel on the serial murder investigation didn't help matters. Remind me to pay you back sometime."

"Serial murders?" he exploded. "Christ on a cookie sheet!"

"More than two bodies with the same MO and signature." She'd picked up a few phrases from Mr. Hot Shot Investigator. "We call them serials."

"A word of advice?"

If John Latimer told her to jump over the moon, she'd do it. "Of course."

"You need to be focusing on the SU interview, not a man."

"The only man I'd ever consider focusing on is you," she teased. "But, have you forgotten the championship game?"

"Screw softball. The interview is more important. Dave Murray will put you through your paces. You set for him?"

She'd never be "set" for an interview with the Dean of Admissions for SU's Medical College. Just thinking about what one of the most highly respected medical educators in the nation might ask had her ready to jump out of her skin. "I hope so."

"What are you wearing?"

"Since when did you become a fashion consultant?"

"Trust me, Wolfgirl. Dave Murray likes a woman in a dress."

Annie came out of her chair with a shriek. "Are you out of your mind? The day I try to influence my admission to medical school by wearing some sleazy, low-necked dress with a hem up to my ass is the day I hang up my suture scissors! If that's what SU is looking for, I'm not it."

"Get off your feminist horse, Wolfgirl," Latimer barked. "There's not enough room for both of us. Wear a loose-fitting dress, very sedate and proper, and you'll have Murray eating out of your hand. Oh—and put on a pair of pumps. Dave's a sucker for a woman in heels."

"John, this isn't right. It isn't fair."

"Wake up and smell the coffee, little girl. Of course it's not right—and rarely is life fair, as you well know. Applying to med school is like crossing the DMZ. You dress for battle, make sure you're fully armed, and take no prisoners."

"John."

Latimer reached out a gnarled hand to draw her into his arms. "Do it, little girl. You'll be that much closer to achieving your dream of becoming a doctor—and fulfilling mine."

"Yours? I don't understand."

"After a residency in family medicine, a sub-specialty in women's health, you'll come back and take over the practice."

Every drop of blood went straight to her feet. "You can't be serious. John, you can't just hand over this office to me."

"Why not? It's mine; I can do anything I want with it."

"Yes, but—*give it to me?*" she gulped. "Oh, John." Tears loomed dangerously close. "I don't know what to say."

Putting her at arms' length, he tipped her chin up, forcing her to look at him. "You are the daughter Molly and I never had. She would want you to take over my patients because you deserve it and she trusted you—and because she loved you as much as I do."

He wiggled the finger beneath her chin. "Of course, Molly never coached you in softball, so her feelings were probably a tad warped."

Annie lurched for the door. "I... uh, need to go."

John sighed. "With a prostate the size of a baseball, I often feel the same way. So while you're off bawling somewhere, I'll look over your assessment and plan on—what'd you call him?"

"Captain Marvel," she blubbered, then raced out the door.

Eight

"What the hell is a Drug Bus?" Ronen swore. "And where the hell did she take it?"

He'd been looking for Annie all afternoon, to thank her for giving him the physical—and to ask a favor. Couldn't she stay in one place for more than five minutes? Not Wolfgirl.

"Places to go, things to do," he snarled. "I'd give her something to do. If I could get her to sit still long enough."

The guy behind the counter at Gill's All-Rite Pharmacy told him Annie'd come in within the past hour, stocking up supplies for the Drug Bus. After that, she was headed to Urgent Care.

That meant another trip across town only to have his son tell him she'd come in, pulled drugs and sterile solutions from the shelves, then left.

"For where?" he barked.

Chris' hesitation only added to Ronen's agitation. "Her mood is not the best, Dad. It's not like I needed my head ripped off at the shoulders. Know what I mean?"

Unfortunately, he did. "Save yourself a lot of aggravation, son. Enter the priesthood."

"Right, Dad."

John Latimer was the one who finally told Ronen where she'd gone, then gave him directions to the workers' compound at Abner Harbaugh's place.

"Workers' compound, my ass," Ronen muttered as he looked for landmarks on the road. "Migrant labor is migrant labor. Fancying it up with socialist phrasing doesn't change what it is. Shacks are shacks. Filth is filth. And Annie is—" He drew in a heavy breath. "Annie."

Once he was outside the town limits, he had to admit the countryside was beautiful. Rolling farmlands and lush, verdant forests were picture-perfect settings for an artist's canvas or a photographer's knowing eye. When fall arrived and the leaves turned, the colors would probably knock out a man's eye.

Man, he missed Rochester. The Planetarium and Strong Museum. The funky Park Avenue restaurants and quirky artisan shops of the Corn Hill district. Worst of all, he was going to lose out on the entire concert season at the Eastman Theater. "All because I had to play Captain Marvel, solve the problems in No Man's Land."

The Bronco hit another rut in the unpaved road. He felt his left kidney jolt into his spleen. "Kiss this crap good-bye."

He checked the odometer. According to Latimer's directions—if the man was experiencing a lucid moment when he wrote them down—the right-hand turn after the big red barn with the rusting combine out front was the one to take for the workers' compound.

"Latimer forgot to mention the road would go from regular pavement to a sea of gravel and hard-packed mud."

The right-hand turn, after what Ronen hoped to hell was a combine, brought the Bronco to an electronic gate. One which, under different circumstances, would hold coils of razor wire at the top. "What the hell?" he yelped. "Is this a farm or a prison?"

Former Nohmensville police officer Robert Claun sauntered out of the guard's box, approaching the Bronco at a sloth's pace. "You here on official business or's this a social call?"

"I'm here, Mr. Claun. The reason is not your concern."

Cocking a hip, splaying beefy fingers over the love handles at his waist, he challenged, "Mr. H. know you're comin'?"

The man's aggressive posturing didn't impress Ronen. Neither did the Glock holstered beneath his armpit. "My impression has been this is a farming operation, not a prison."

"The boss likes me to know everything that goes on during my shift." Claun smirked. "Everything, city boy."

"I'm thrilled you've found employment to suit your talents, Mr. Claun. Manure and mucklands seem consistent with your philosophy of life. Has Annie Wolfe been through here?"

"About an hour ago. Somethin' about sick brats. Why?"

"Official business."

Claun pressed the remote control in his hand. The gate swung open with a soft whir. "Straight ahead for the main house."

"If I want the workers' compound?"

He barely twitched. "First right. Can't miss it."

As he drove through the gate, Ronen checked the rear-view mirror. Bozo was raising a portable radio to his mouth. "Why am I not surprised?"

After bouncing down a long, unpaved, organ-jolting goat trail, he finally found a row of whitewashed bungalows. An ancient hearse, painted in eye-popping psychedelic colors, was parked at the end of the row. "The Drug Bus," he said, not at all surprised.

After pulling in next to the hearse, a group of kids ran out from behind the largest of the buildings. They stopped short, carefully watching his every move as he exited the Bronco.

A baby propped on one hip, Annie joined the kids. "Why are you here?"

She'd changed into faded jeans, old work boots and a T-shirt that proclaimed: *A Woman Needs a Man Like a Rhino Needs an Uzi.* A stethoscope hung from her neck. Dark-framed glasses, the same ones she'd worn earlier in the day, insisted on sliding down her nose no matter how many times she pushed them back.

He took one step forward. The compound wasn't as bad as he'd imagined; it wasn't a piece of heaven, either. A pervasive odor of rot hung in the air. Other than the brief drizzle the night of Annie's interrogation by Randy Terrance, it hadn't rained in weeks, yet the compound gave off a feeling of perpetual dampness. It smelled of mold and something... not quite dead. It was dark, dismal, and perfectly hideous.

How can she work here? How can she expose herself to this?

"What do you want, Ronen?"

The children surrounded Annie in a protective circle, letting him know he'd have to go through them to get to her. "I need a favor."

She leaned over the shoulder of the child standing in front of her. In soft, reassuring tones, she spoke in a language other than English. The boy asked something; she responded. The words, the phrasing, stirred something deep in his memory. After a moment, a mental picture of his parents' home came to mind. The kids, some of them anyway, were Romanian.

"What sort of favor?" she asked after the boy took off.

"I need to interview the victims' survivors. Would you help me? Please, Annie. It's important."

"One condition."

The FBI contact had been emphatic on two points: speak to the survivors as soon as possible and identify any locals who'd served time in 'Nam or Central America.

"Anything," he promised. "As long as you'll interpret."

"No questions about their immigration status."

"That's the last thing I care about."

One perfectly arched brow raised in doubt. "Oh, really, Mr. Coyote Hunter?"

"Ann," he started, then sighed in defeat. She'd never believe him unless—

"If it starts to look like I'm checking papers, I promise, you can burn every CD I own."

"Even the screeching fat ladies?"

"I'll strike the first match."

He could see hesitation on her face. More so, he watched the wheels turning in her steel-trap mind. She murmured a few words to the rest of the kids, patting the shoulders of those closest to her. They scattered in ten different directions while the baby in her arms gnawed on the stethoscope tubing.

"What did you tell them?"

"That you're my intended. The parents will want to check you out."

"A pretty tall tale, Wolfgirl."

She shrugged. "Whatever works."

"You consider yourself one of them?"

Pride stiffened her voice as well as her shoulders. "At least you had the sense not to come in uniform."

"Jesus, Ann. I'm not here to frighten—or deport—anyone."

The men approached first, followed by the adolescent males. Annie's description was right on target. From the looks of a few, Ronen wouldn't want to meet them in any kind of alley, dark or otherwise.

The women, some with babies in their arms, and older girls hung back, keeping a wary distance. Not all were East European. Some were Asian, a few appeared to be Hispanic. One man, whom all seemed to defer to, took his place at Annie's side. The remaining males fanned out behind them, farming tools held at parade rest. A united front.

He was glad Annie was here. Without her, speaking to these people would be impossible. He needed her presence.

Who was he kidding? He needed her for more than a presence.

She murmured something to the head man. A broken-tooth grin ignited his coarse, dark features. He stepped forward, extending an incredibly filthy hand. "How did you do, sir?"

Staring at the hand, Ronen cringed. "I—"

"Take his hand," Annie said in a sweet, lover-like tone. "Or I'll break each of your fingers after we're alone."

One of the girls giggled, then covered her mouth with her hand. A couple of the boys shared grunts of approval. Ronen suspected they understood English better than they let on.

"I do well, sir." He took the leader's hand. "Ronen Mikhail Marvelic."

Huge smiles erupted throughout the crowd. "Romanian! Ah, ah! Welcome, welcome."

Singly, the men came forward, reciting their name and country of origin. The adolescent males followed, each posturing in his own way, some aggressively, others less so.

The women proved more reticent. After a bit of prompting from Annie, and the sharing of knowing glances and smug giggles between themselves, the women came forward. Throughout all of the introductions, Ronen became aware of the change in Annie's posture, a softening around her eyes, a relaxation in her body language.

When a shyly smiling girl tugged on her hand, Annie said, "Ronen, this is Danuta Sanko, Luba's sister. She helped Maria Salvado in the School of Light, and currently is my number one helper in the dispensary." Sweeping an arm around the girl's shoulder, Annie hugged her. "Isn't that right, *mi pey*?"

An adoring light shone in Danuta's young eyes. "I like helping you, Illiana."

"And I like having you help me. Please take Mr. Marvelic into the dispensary while I speak with your parents."

Ronen followed Danuta into a small whitewashed hut that stood at a distance from the others. An exam table and well-stocked glass-front cabinet, both sparkling clean, surprised him. But then, he should have known better. Annie might not demand the most modern in equipment; she would expect everything be kept spotless.

Crisp, folded sheets were stacked neatly on a three-tiered cart. Cloth gowns filled the second shelf. The corner of the room was taken up by a refrigerator. A length of chain, each link thick as a man's finger, criss-crossed the surface and was secured with a heavy-duty padlock.

Danuta straightened the stack of sheets, making sure they lined up in precise order. "I clean every day, the way Illiana expects."

"You do a good job, Danuta," he responded, unable to take his eyes off the padlocked refrigerator.

The girl must have seen where his gaze was trained. "We lock to protect supplies from thieves."

"It must be difficult having to live like this."

"Is better than what we came from."

"Where is that?"

"Kosovo."

Annie came through the door, escorting two anxious looking adults and a sullen teenage boy. A baby of about ten months, if Ronen's guess was accurate, bounced in the woman's arms and gave the stranger in his world a drooling, toothless grin.

"Ronen," Annie said, "may I introduce Luba Sanko's parents and her brother Viktor."

He shook each hand as it was offered. Annie murmured something, the Sankos immediately relaxed. The boy was another story. If anything, the slope of his shoulders raised; the glower on his face hardened to a defiant stare.

"I'm sorry for your sadness," Ronen began.

Clutching the squirming baby to her chest, Mrs. Sanko touched her husband's arm, whispered a few words. Both looked to Annie who responded with a lengthy explanation.

After some time, the father nodded. "Da. With you we will speak. Illiana's betrothed is to give trust."

Illiana. He recalled Marta Balkas calling Annie by that name, as had Danuta. He tested it on his tongue, and found it lyrical, as well as perfect. *Illiana.* Beautiful name for a beautiful woman.

Mr. Sanko took a chair, motioning to his wife to sit beside him. Annie sat next to the wife while Viktor and Danuta moved to stand behind their parents.

Ronen brought a stool around to face them. "Please tell me about your daughter."

The Sankos each stiffened. Ronen persisted, softening his voice even more. "What did she dream of? What made her smile? What made her fear?"

He saw Annie's eyes blur as she covered Mrs. Sanko's hand with hers. The catch in her voice became more pronounced the longer she translated.

Looking directly at the mother, Ronen asked, "If you could use one word, how would you describe Luba?"

Mrs. Sanko listened attentively, then paused to calm the squirming baby. Danuta reached for it, but he or she wanted nothing to do with its sister. He, or she, wanted only Ronen. His heart melted. "May I hold the child?"

The parents looked to Annie. She cleared her throat, then nodded. To Ronen's delight, the baby lunged into his out-stretched hands. "Hello, my love," he said softly, cuddling the child to his chest. "Aren't you wonderful?"

The baby grabbed onto his nose with a shout of glee. Ronen returned the laugh, and knew at once how much he'd missed holding a baby in his arms.

~ * ~

Stella Grover met Annie at the front door of the mansion with a few direct orders. "Shower. Change. Join me in the gazebo."

After the day she'd put in, Annie doubted she had the strength for polite conversation. Thinking took priority. She needed to work through everything she'd witnessed over the past several hours.

Captain Marvel had lived up to his nickname. He was truly marvelous with the Sankos and the other survivors who still lived in the compound. His gentleness and sensitivity with all of them was wrenching. Mrs. Sanko's response to his request to describe Luba in one word ripped through Annie's heart so fast, she'd lost her breath for a moment.

When the grieving mother replied, "Sunshine", Ronen bowed his head for a moment, then said, "I know what it is to have the darkness claim the day. I am sorry for your loss."

The look on Marvel's face when Nadja Sanko lunged into his arms was enough to destroy every reservation she'd held about him—as a cop, as a man.

Why couldn't the police have behaved like that when she'd needed it?

Because none of them was Captain Marvel, dummy.

Damn, she had enough conflicting feelings as it was. With the med school interview little more than twenty-four hours away, she needed to be clear thinking, not distracted by some guy who sent her into cardiac standstill every time he looked at her.

"I know where you've been, missy," Stella accused. "Taking care of *those* people again. Don't think I'll let you traipse through my home without first disinfecting. Lord knows what kind of lethal germs are lurking around that camp."

"I'd hardly classify dehydration and pneumonia as lethal."

Annie sighed, knowing full well if she hadn't started treatment on a couple of the kids, the situation might have deteriorated into something really serious. Man, she was tired of fighting deprivation and bigotry.

Stella's breath came out on a huff. "It's a beautiful night, Wolfgirl. Too beautiful to waste cooped up in that locker room you call an apartment."

"I'm sure you're about to offer an alternative."

"Hot fudge sundaes in the gazebo. Go on now," Stella directed, more gently this time. "Shower and change. If you're not out back in fifteen minutes, I'll come looking for you."

Because the woman was quite capable of carrying out her threat, and because she'd not indulged in one of Stella's luscious desserts in much too long, Annie caved in. Maybe hot fudge topped with a heavy dollop of whipped cream was just what she needed to get Captain Marvel out of her head. "I've got ball practice in the morning, a three hour drive to Syracuse after that," she cautioned, "so I can't stay long."

"Long enough to relax you into a good night's sleep."

Fourteen minutes later, after a refreshing shower, Annie took the path through the carefully manicured flower garden, ending her journey at the lattice-walled structure at the rear of the grounds. Stella's description was more than accurate. It truly was a gorgeous night, with a mirror-smooth sky dusted with a sprinkling of diamond-bright stars. Each gem twinkled an invitation to dream—or make a wish. Mourning doves called out a plaintive song. Owls hooted an isolated refrain. From the octagonal structure mellow jazz competed with the birds' songs.

"Uh oh. Stella's in a mood."

Henry Grover had been dead a little over eighteen months. When Stella was feeling particularly lonely, she played jazz, ate gigantic hot fudge sundaes, and reminisced. Annie couldn't ignore the woman's need for company. She'd opened her home, made her feel welcome in a strange town, mothered her when she needed it, nagged her when she didn't. Annie owed it to Stella to be there for her.

As she approached the gazebo, she could see a flicker of candlelight. She's *really* in a mood.

Mentally preparing herself for a later evening than she would have liked, Annie took the three steps up into the gazebo. She started to say something, then looked up. Her landlady wasn't playing jazz, nor had she lighted a zillion candles.

And she certainly wasn't drizzling steaming hot fudge over mounds of vanilla ice cream, topping it all off generous scoops of whipped cream. *Well, dammit all.*

"Hey, slugger. Just in time."

"Where's Stella?"

"On a date."

"Tell me another fairy story, Marvelic. Stella doesn't date. She's in mourning."

With a shrug of those immense shoulders, he sprinkled chopped nuts over the whipped cream. "Didn't look too mournful to me when John Latimer picked her up for bingo at the VFW."

Holding out a bowl whose contents made her mouth water, he used that devil's voice to coax her. "Take this before it melts all over my hands."

Annie forced the mental image created by his invitation out of her mind, focusing instead on a second bowl piled equally high with ice cream, fudge sauce and whipped topping. "With your lactose intolerance, Captain, you're going to eat that?"

"Someone wrote me prescriptions today to combat my little problem."

"Lucky you."

"Lighten up, Annie. Enjoy the night, the music, the chocolate." Ronen glanced at the bowl in his hand. "On second thought, Chris might be interested. Let me call him."

"I like your kid, Marvelic," she said, grabbing the bowl from his hand. "But not enough to share hot fudge with him."

She took a seat on the bench and dug in like an addict too long without a fix. Savoring the rush of hormones triggered by the hot fudge, Annie slowed down. Make the most of the moment, she told herself as the combination of flavors caressed her tongue, stimulated her taste buds, sated her appetite. "Man, this is better than sex."

Ronen pulled seat cushions to the wood-planked floor, sat with his back against the curved bench, stretching his legs out in front of him. He licked the spoon clean with a slow grin. "Must be you haven't had sex recently."

She thought about that one. "Doesn't mean I don't remember what it's like." She went back to her bowl. "Trust me, Captain. Hot fudge is better."

"Must be you've never had great sex." He licked the spoon a second time.

"Another truth-ism," she admitted.

"Care to give it a shot?"

She nearly inhaled a salted peanut. "With you?"

"You needn't sound so appalled. I know how to do it."

"I'm not appalled. I'm—" This was rapidly getting out of hand. "What's the name of the artist—the music, I mean. Aw, hell, Marvelic, I didn't think you listened to anything other than long-hair stuff."

His shoulder brushed the outside of her arm. "I admit this guy's got long hair. And underneath the hat he never seems to be without, he's probably bald as a billiard cue. But," he sighed, "he's from Rochester, so I buy all his stuff."

If he tongued that damn spoon one more time, she'd yank it out of his hand and beat him to death with it. "The name?"

"Chuck Mangione. The song is called *Doin' Everything With You*. Like it?"

Like it? She adored it. "It's... okay."

"Liar." He set his bowl aside, then quick as a snake, snatched her onto his lap. "You do that a lot."

When her brain finally got around to sending a message to her vocal cords, she croaked, "Do what a lot?"

"Lie when you get jammed."

"Jammed? Me?"

His smile melted something deep inside her. It would be so simple, so easy to stay right here. Enjoying the sparkling sky, the night fragrances, the oak-hewed arms circling her waist and back. She looked into his dancing eyes and found herself wishing for things too impossible to consider.

"Missed some." His tongue teased the edge of her lower lip.

"What?" If she turned, just a fraction of an inch, she could have what she'd wanted from the moment he asked for help at the compound. Correction—from the moment he promised she could burn his CD's if he screwed up.

A long finger turned her face that fraction. "You taste good, slugger. Real good."

"So do you," she blurted. "No lie."

Lips brushed hers as lightly as a butterfly's. "Prove it."

It would take an act of congress before she would admit she wanted his mouth on hers and... everywhere else on her body.

Grinning again, he brushed his lips over hers. "Chicken?"

"A man uses that line on me once, pal. Then I retaliate."

"Really."

Grabbing the sides of his gorgeous face, she brought the tip of his nose to hers. "Yeah, really."

Kissing Ronen Marvelic, she discovered, was an experience. After one taste, she knew it was everything she'd ever wanted from a man. Captain Marvel tasted the way he smelled. Clean, strong, healthy.

"More," he groaned. "Christ, Annie. Give me more."

She eased her arms around his neck. Nibbling, tasting, urging his tongue into her mouth. A flash of heat exploded in her belly. Her nipples pouted, itching for his touch. His hand spread over her hip, squeezed the upper part of her thigh, moving in slow, teasing circles toward—

"*Dad!*"

At that moment, Annie could have strangled Christopher Marvelic without blinking an eye. If PMS worked as a defense for homicide, she figured *kissus interruptus* must be equally as valid.

"Dad, you've got a phone call," the boy yelled out from the darkened back yard.

With an ugly curse, Ronen came to his feet. "This better be good."

Annie sprang to her feet just as Chris thundered up the steps of the gazebo. "It's Aunt Rachel. Hey, Annie, how's it going?"

Ronen glanced at her. "I have to take it, Ann."

"Of course you do." Noting that the sundaes were now a disgusting mass of brown and white swirls that threatened to spill over the edges of the bowls and drip onto the wood floor, she said, "I'll clean up this mess."

He approached, one hand out. If he touched her, she didn't know what— "Take the call."

"Wait for me?" When she didn't respond, because she couldn't, he murmured, "Please."

Lifting her chin, Annie looked at him straight on. "Take the call, Ronen."

"I'll be back."

Using the time alone, Annie thought over her options as she stacked the dishes and silverware. She'd always considered ambivalence to be deadly for a healthy state of mind. There was, in her opinion, nothing worse than being unable to make up one's mind, particularly for someone used to making quick, often life and death decisions.

"He's terrific," she reasoned out loud. "With a great kid and a wonderful manner with victims and families." She refused to think about how well he kissed, and the way he had of looking at her that made her toenails melt.

"It can't work—not with your track record," she told herself. "And certainly not with med school—if you're lucky—ahead of you."

Then she remembered him standing there. Ice cream melting over his hands, grinning like a kid, and calling her 'slugger'.

Rather than standing around, she loaded a tray she found tucked beneath one of the benches, with the dirty dishes and leftover dessert ingredients, and headed into the house.

Stella Grover's kitchen was a study in sixties chic with avocado appliances and shag carpeting, anti-war posters on the walls, and love beads dangling from the door frames. While running a sinkful of suds, she continued her litany of reasons to keep a distance from him.

"Mr. Perfect," she muttered. "He'd drive me crazy inside a week with those starched shirts, ruthlessly knotted ties and spit-shined shoes, not to mention that rigid spine and tight-assed walk. And if he thinks I'd tolerate opera, he needs to get a life."

~ * ~

Ronen didn't really expect to find Annie still in the gazebo. On the off chance she remained in one place for longer than five minutes, he returned to the structure after taking the call from his sister.

"Surprised?"

All remains of the sundaes were gone. Most of the candles had gutted themselves out in rivers of scented wax. Chuck Mangione was well into *Bellavia*. Something was different. Her face—her body language. Resolve was the only word that worked.

"Truth?"

"I expect nothing less, Captain."

The warm, willing woman who'd melted in his arms a few moments ago was gone. In her place was the earnest, focused professional. He joined her on the plank floor, scooting a patterned cushion next to hers. Their elbows touched, briefly, then separated. "The responsibility you bestow on me is awesome, Ms. Wolfe."

"It's time, Ronen."

"Time?"

"I want to know why Barbara's death forced the state police to become involved in this mess."

This wasn't what he'd expected. It certainly wasn't what he'd hoped for while his sister bent his ear long distance. Then, maybe he had been waiting for it all along. Annie had needed time to absorb the shock of her friend's death, time to mourn, to say good-bye before she could hear the details.

With all his heart he wished he could shield her from what she wanted to know, cushion the truth to make it a little more palatable. Murder was never palatable, he reminded himself. And Annie Wolfe was the toughest woman he'd ever met. If anyone could handle it, it was her.

"Barb wasn't only a social worker."

"Of course she wasn't *only* a social worker. She was part saint, part rescuer, part advocate. Tell me something I don't know."

This was going to hurt, he was sure of it. "Barbara was an undercover agent with Immigration and Naturalization. She used her training as a social worker for her cover."

Moonlight poured over Annie's beautiful face; in it he could see the effects of the truth. Her fingers knitted so tightly the knuckles turned white. Her voice quieted to a low hum. "How long was she with them?"

"Twenty years, maybe more. Barbara heard about the women dying and asked to be assigned down here."

"Twenty years," she croaked, looking around as if she was checking for eavesdroppers. Her voice tightened. "Isn't that a hoot? The social worker who saved my life turns out to be someone who could have—"

Interest sparked, he pressed. "Someone who could have what, Annie?"

She shook her head. "Doesn't matter. Not anymore. It's enough that Barb is dead because of me."

"Honey, nothing could be further—"

The pained resignation on her face nearly broke his heart. "Might as well have swung the bat myself."

Blood turned to ice in his veins. They'd discussed many things about the case as they reviewed the photos. Choice of weapons wasn't one of them. "What makes you think the weapon was a bat?"

Throwing her head back, she swiped at the tears staining her cheeks. Her voice cracked. "Ronen, please. I've worked ER's for a long time. I saw the bodies up close, studied the photos with you. It doesn't take a Dr. Quincy to figure out the women were used for batting practice."

While gross in the extreme, the description was more than accurate. "There's no way you caused Barbara's death."

"Yes. I did."

"All right then," he reasoned. "Tell me how you did it."

"I—" she started, then stopped to take a deep breath. "I wasn't looking for her to come down here, though God knows the immigrants were in desperate need of a good social worker."

Annie paused for a moment. "Undercover with the INS. Never once in all the time we were together did I think she could have sent me—"

"Sent you where, honey?"

"Doesn't matter," she responded quickly. "I was tired of feeling alone, sick of thinking I was the only one who cared about dead women. After Maria Salvado's death, I heard one of the cops say one dead hooker was one less working girl they had to worry about. His partner agreed with him. It was like they were cleaning the streets of unsightly trash. I was sick to death of it, Ronen! Don't you understand? I had to talk to someone."

So she called on the first and only person who treated her as someone with value, someone worthwhile. The person who saved Annie from a parent *who planned to sell her.*

"Of course you did," he murmured, taking her stiff body into his arms. "Barbara listened to you."

"You don't know that," she wailed.

"I know she convinced her superiors to let her come down here and look into things."

"And that got her dead! *I got her dead.*"

"Annie, stop it!" he repeated. "Barb knew what she was getting into when she asked for the assignment. Every undercover agent knows the risks. She took those risks because she cared about the women. She cared about you."

She tilted her head back, looking at him with big, blurry eyes. "What made you blow into town, going where no investigator had gone before?"

Folding her tighter in his arms, he kept his tone neutral. "Barb e-mailed photographs of Luba Sanko's body to Albany along with her theory about the *piñata* signatures on the other victims. An INS agent and a BCI investigator from the Troops were on their way down here to connect with her but she never showed at the meet. Her body was found two days later in an adjoining county."

"But the victim profiles don't match," Annie insisted. "Barb had a mouth as big as all outdoors; she wasn't afraid to get in anyone's face. If she saw incompetence she would use whatever it took to—"

He watched her turn white as death, felt her limbs vibrate beneath his hands, heard the anguished moan. "Oh, God."

Alarmed, he demanded, "What is it? Honey, you're shaking like a leaf."

"Nothing. It's nothing," she croaked. "Tell me the rest."

Nothing? Bull. Shit. Annie was hiding something.

"Ronen, didn't you hear me? What happened then?"

"Immigration pushed the governor to intervene and send in the Troops. I was chosen."

"What will you do now?"

"The police reports have disappeared. No one can find them. All I have are the autopsy protocols from Dr. Moran."

"Not much to go on."

"We've got a sizable population of easy victims, killers who are either protected by very powerful people or just plain lucky, a town with a clearly defined class lines who doesn't give a damn who dies as long as—"

"It's not one of their own," she finished.

Nine

For the sake of one of the Bronco's passengers, Ronen kept all profane comments to himself, and instead offered a malevolent growl at yet another street sign which announced, *One Way Only*.

"Something wrong, dearie?" Stella Grover trilled.

"When did they make Adams Street one-way?"

He'd been touring the University Section for a good twenty minutes, searching for Annie. Sometime in the last twenty years the powers that be had completely changed traffic patterns in this part of the city. He thought he might go nuts before he found his way to Upstate Medical Center. "Dammit, I'll never find her in time for the game."

Stella reached over to pat his hand. "You'll find her, Ronen. Land's sake, the game can't start without Wolfgirl."

As a favor, he'd given his landlady a ride to the big game. "Gotta see my girls whup the pants off the Lowville Lions," she'd claimed. "From warm-ups to the victory dance."

Stella's car was "feeling poorly"—or so she said. He figured the lonely widow was reluctant to make the three hour drive to Syracuse by herself. Secretly, he found it a wise choice, having witnessed the woman's driving skills—or lack thereof—as she tore around town in the salmon-colored Caddie, blithely ignoring traffic signals and speed limits.

"I wonder where she could be." Stella toyed with the rope of beads hanging from her neck. "Are you sure John said she'd be in front of the hospital?"

"That's what he told me," Ronen grumbled. "She called him on his cell phone; said she couldn't find a cab to bring her to the stadium; asked if someone could come get her. Since I was born and raised here, I made the dumbest mistake of my life when I volunteered to fetch her."

Listening to himself, he almost cringed. *Fetch.* For God's sake, he was beginning to sound like a hick.

"We'll find her," Stella said confidently.

"Dad, stop!" Chris yelped from the back seat. "I see her."

"Where?" All he saw was a long-legged girl in a navy-blue dress and straw hat standing on the corner of Adams Street and Irving Avenue. "That's not Annie, son."

"Trust me, Dad. That's her." Chris hung out the window. "Wolfgirl, over here!"

Ronen's jaw nearly hit the steering wheel when he saw Annie loping toward the Bronco. "Hey, kid," she huffed. "Thanks for rescuing me."

If he wasn't feeling like a fool over getting lost, Ronen might have smiled. *Annie Wolfe in a dress. Will wonders never cease.*

A big grin creased her face as she leaped into the back seat. "Hey, guys."

Something was different about her, Ronen decided. Her eyes shone like the weight of the world had been lifted from her shoulders. That beautiful face glowed with... a kind of triumph. Excitement radiated off her perfect body in near-palpable waves.

Stella turned halfway in the seat. "John sent your bag so you could change on the way to the game, dearie. How are you feeling? How's the knee? Ready to kick some Lowville butt?"

"Head 'em up and move 'em out," Annie crowed. "I got places to go, things to do."

Was she ready? She'd never been so ready in all her life. Still high from the interview with Dr. Murray, she could almost forgive the scowl on Ronen's face. The only thing that would beat this already fabulous day would be for the Nuggets to be crowned state champs.

"Hand me the bag, Chris."

Raising the hem of the navy dress Stella had loaned her to wear for the interview, she was going to shed all remnants of *girl stuff* and get on with the business of playing softball.

Then she realized who was in the back seat with her. And exactly what she was about to do. "Hold that thought, kid. Ronen, pull over."

He braked to a stop on a tree-lined street in front of one of the many three-story Victorians common to the sprawling SU campus. Students, loaded down with backpacks, browsed among sidewalk displays of rugs, posters, and jewelry. Delivery trucks and hospital courtesy vans barreled down the narrow street like the original kings of the road.

"Dammit," Ronen growled when a linen supply truck narrowly missed his bumper. "What is it now, Wolfgirl? We're already late."

Dramatic eye movements accentuated her fast-paced delivery. "I'm in a dress and... other stuff. Do you want your son back here while I change?"

Nuts. "Chris," he muttered. "Trade places with Mrs. G."

The boy blushed clear to his earlobes. "Sure, Dad." Thrusting the athletic bag into Annie's hands, Chris bailed out the door like the devil himself was on his butt.

"Ah, Ronen," Stella offered doubtfully. "I'll never be able to make it into the backseat. Without a running board, you'll have to give me a big boost up."

"Yeah, okay. Give me a second."

Next thing Annie knew, Chris was in the driver's seat and Captain Marvel was climbing in beside her. "Go," he ordered the boy. "And keep your eyes on the road."

"You do the same, pal," Annie informed her new seat-mate.

"Fair's fair, slugger. You've seen me naked."

Stella chuckled. "About time, if you ask me."

The car swerved. Chris made a gagging sound. "Eeeyeww! I don't want to know about it, don't even want to think about it."

"I gave your father a physical exam, Christopher," Annie explained with a side glance for Ronen. "Against my better judgment."

"You loved every minute of it. Admit it."

The more she yanked on the stockings Stella had lent her, the worse they snagged on the stupid garter belt. "I'd sooner kiss a snake."

He handed her the athletic bag. "That could be arranged."

As Chris took the narrow one-way streets through campus, following signs for Coyne Stadium, Annie ditched her clothes one piece at a time—tried to anyway.

"You in a dress," Ronen murmured. "Never thought I'd see the day."

"You'll see more than that if I can't get these stockings unhooked. Stella," she yelped, "how do I get these damn things off?"

"Like this." Ronen reached beneath the hem of the dress to deftly unsnap the garters with quick flicking motions of both thumbs. His hands felt wonderful on her skin. Heat shot up her legs as his fingers slowly peeled away the hosiery.

If her heart beat any faster, she'd need a Coronary Care Unit. "Multi-talented man," she wheezed.

"Years of practice."

"Why am I not surprised?" The garter belt was the next item to go. In her rush to get out of it, it rolled and tangled into a tight, constricting band at the tops of her thighs. "Dammit!"

Ronen pushed her to her back, looming over her with an evil grin on his face. "Are you out of your mind?" she hissed. "Your son is in the front seat!"

"You'd prefer it was him doing this?" Bunching the dress around her waist, he slid both hands beneath the waistband of her boxers. "PAC-Man?"

The restrictive band of elastic was threatening to cut off the circulation to her lower limbs. "Shut up and get this damn thing off me!"

"Yes, ma'am."

"If I ever get my hands on the man who invented this instrument of torture, I'll slice off his—"

A shout of laughter from the driver's seat cut off the rest of her threat. "Keep on driving, Chris," she ordered, then glowered at Ronen. "You have something to say?"

"Speaking from a male point of view," he said, giving the rose-embroidered garter dangling from his hand a wistful look, "I'd nominate the inventor for sainthood."

She sat up to pull white athletic socks up her calves, followed them with red stirrup socks. "Another thing I'm not surprised at you being the Poster boy for Male Chauvinists of America."

He had the uniform pants ready for her. "Nice tattoo, Wolfgirl."

"Thanks." The tight-fitting pants were a struggle under the best of circumstances. The confines of a bench seat called for a double-jointed contortionist.

"*Vinnie's Place*," he murmured. "You two close, personal friends?"

She could hardly deny the large red heart tattooed on one thigh with Vincenzo Morbello's first name and ownership inscribed inside. At the time, having a guy's name permanently inked onto her body, it seemed like a fun thing to do.

Of course, in those days being hammered out of her gourd made lots of things seem like fun. Sometimes she marveled that she'd managed to avoid cirrhosis of the liver.

Not that she'd share any of that information with Captain Marvel. Mr. Straight Arrow with an ass so tight it squeaked. "Very close," she said. "Very personal."

"So where's Vinnie now? Don't see him hanging around, staking a claim on you."

If he looked any more smug, she'd pop him one in the chops just for the hell of it. She'd not seen nor heard from Vinnie in close to ten years. That didn't mean she'd failed to keep track of a few of her *close, personal friends*. "We lost touch after he relocated to Sing Sing."

"On which side of the bars?"

"Give me a break, Marvelic," she said, grabbing the Nuggets jersey from his hand. "I got a game to think about."

And she did, sort of. Anything to divert her thoughts from the feel of his hands on her skin. The rough edges of his fingertips, the gentleness with which he drew the stockings from her legs, the—

She pulled the dress over her head, pleased that she'd chosen to wear a sports bra—to make changing easier. "If you expected something from Victoria's Secret, you're out of luck."

"I'd never be so foolish. Shoes?"

"Thanks." She slipped into the spikes, tightening the laces with quick, jerky movements. "This is not how I planned for things to go today."

After the shoes, she addressed the issue of hair. The topknot loosened beneath her fingers, falling heavily around her shoulders. If Ronen's breathing took a slight hitch in regularity, she could ignore it. With quick, practiced motions, she braided the thick mass under control, then threaded it through the opening in the back of the cap.

Unable to resist the opportunity, she leaned forward to ask over Chris' shoulder, "Are we there yet, Daddy?"

"Hold your horses." Chris pulled the Bronco into Coyne's massive parking lot, put it into Park, then turned his head. A bright, teasing grin lighted his face. "Knock their socks off."

She was beginning to care too much for this kid. That meant she'd have to be careful for the rest of the summer. Emotional ties were something she couldn't afford. "I'll do my best," she said gruffly, searching the bag for her good luck charm. Couldn't play good ball without her lucky unicorn in her pants pocket.

After bouncing out of the back seat and heading across the asphalt pavement, Ronen's yell brought her up short. "Slugger!"

She turned to find him leaning out the window of the Bronco. Aw, hell. The horn on the piece of crystal jabbed her palm. Impulse sent her racing back to him. "Here." She closed his fingers around the crystal piece. "Keep this safe for me."

He lightly touched her chin with his fist. "Hit one for me."

Aw, hell! The grin was too good to ignore. She planted a loud, wet kiss on his mouth. "See you later, Cap."

~ * ~

"Sorry about the game, Annie."

Chris looked so forlorn, she felt compelled to slip an arm around his waist. "Thanks. We did our best, but they outplayed us. Maybe next year."

With a sudden glow in her heart, she recalled the day's other events. There would be no "next year" for her. Wolfgirl was hanging up her cleats, effective today.

Stella Grover's place was festooned with balloons, ribbons and banners congratulating the champions. Too bad this year's champs lived at the opposite end of the state.

Sensing a presence at her side, she looked up into Ronen's smiling face. He'd cheered his heart out during the game, never giving up—even after it became abundantly clear the Nuggets were seriously outclassed by the Lowville team. Having him there for her felt good. Real good.

He handed her a glass of beer. "No remarks about sissies, Wolfgirl. Drink and enjoy."

"I'll do just that." His mouth drew her gaze like a magnet; she recalled the kiss in the gazebo. How much she'd wanted it. If she drank anymore beer, she might be enticed to repeat it. Ronen Marvelic looked thoroughly enticing tonight.

Kathy Baker swayed by with a tray of drinks in her hand. Annie slid the filled glass onto it. The catcher gave her a glazed look. "I'm bombed, Wolfgirl. Gotta go home. Can I leave my car here?"

"You gonna be okay to walk home alone, Kath?"

"I'm fine," she slurred. "Can I borrow a sweater or something? Somebody spilled their drink all over my shirt."

"Sure thing. Stella keeps a pile of jackets and sweaters by the back door."

Baker surprised Annie by kissing her cheek. "Sorry about blowing the game."

Annie took her by the shoulders, gave her a shake. "Coulda happened to anybody. Go home, sleep it off. Things'll look different in the morning."

"I sure as shit hope so."

The catcher wandered off as music from the 50's and 60's started blasting from the stereo. The dining room floor was cleared for dancing. Stella and John Latimer launched into a nimble jitterbug, proving that age does not always impact on one's ability to move with the groove. The third base-person and her date appeared to be doing a version of the Funky Chicken. Either that or both suffered from some sort of seizure disorder.

"Rockin' Robin" ended with a flourish. An old, achingly romantic tune by Johnny Mathis came on—to the collective moans and groans from enthusiastic party-goers.

Ronen touched her hand. "Shall we?"

"You mean dance?" she squeaked.

"I've been told I'm pretty good at it."

He was better than pretty good. Dancing with Ronen Marvelic was like nothing she'd ever experienced. His movements were smooth and fluid, enticing her body closer with a touch at the small of her back. Annie loved to dance slow; she rarely had the time, energy, or the right partner. Opportunity was something that never occurred in No Man's Land where the good old boys considered dancing to be something relegated to wusses. To her, slow dancing was the closest thing to sex while remaining fully clothed and in an upright position.

"For a team who lost the big game today," he murmured, "spirits are pretty high. I expected a wake."

Annie felt too relaxed, and too good to debate post-game mortality and morbidity. "It's softball," she sighed, resting her head on his shoulder. "Not life and death."

"Funny, I didn't expect you to feel that way."

Long, powerful legs spun her in a slow circle; she could go on like this forever. In his arms, feeling him move against her. "What did you expect?"

"Intensity, single-minded focus, passion."

The man knew her better than she realized. "I'd say your assessment is reasonably accurate."

The devil's voice asked in a slow, measured croon, "Are you intense and passionate about everything you do?"

"It's the only way to fly, pal."

The great Mathis continued to weave a magic spell about this being a lovely way to spend an evening. If this one evening was never to be repeated, Annie knew she would remember it for the rest of her life.

Ronen moved her in another slow circle, increasing his hold on her waist. "I've always considered it essential that to make love properly, one must be intense, passionate, single-minded, and focused."

As they turned, her thigh brushed against his groin. If memory for signs of male arousal served correct, he was as focused as she. "I couldn't agree more."

"Really?"

Pulling back, she looked him straight in the eye. "Shall I show you?"

"Why don't we show each other?"

The decision had been coming for a long time. Probably from the first day she met him. She was too tired—and way too horny—to dissect her ambivalence any longer. "Before we do, there's one tiny thing we need to get straight."

A long finger traced her lips. "I have protection."

"That's good, but I meant something else."

"Okay," he sighed. "Lay it on me."

"I expect you to do half the work."

~ * ~

It was slow, methodical, patient. Individualized to her needs. "Tell me what you like, what you want."

"Everything," she whispered, opening her arms in invitation. "Anything."

He brought her to her knees, breast to chest. The strength in his arms, in his hands, as their palms touched and fingers linked, was hypnotizing. That a man so big, so strong, could be gentle at the same time surprised her. And he was so warm.

An evening breeze drifted through the open turret window, cooling her overheated body. The night sky, ink-black and filled with a thousand stars, enveloped her in a blanket of needs, desires, wanting. If the stars seemed to sparkle that much brighter, they only added to the magic Ronen created with a look, a slow smile, a touch.

Wrapping her hair in his fist, he brought her neck closer, giving his mouth access to the pulse pounding just below her ear. While his hands explored her from neck to hips, he learned what pleased her, what satisfied her, declaring his need by identifying hers.

She touched him. "Tell me what you like, what you want."

A hum tumbled from his lips as he eased her onto her back. Leaning back on his haunches, his broad chest and torso filled her vision. It was the most erotic thing she'd ever seen. Proudly erect, he looked like a Greek god, all-powerful, all-encompassing.

Her knees fell over his legs as he knelt over her. Warm, smooth palms eased the length of her inner thighs. The touch of his knuckles on the tender skin sent her bucking off the mattress. With a shake of his head, he soothed her with a warm caress on her belly.

He cupped her, felt her response flooding his fingers. She went over the edge with a soft wail. "More," he demanded.

"Ronen, please." She tugged on his arms, pulling him to her.

"Again." He used his mouth, fingers and hands on her, working her to achieve what he wanted. "Now."

The strength of her reaction robbed her of breath. That he could bring her so far, so fast a second time, humbled her.

Then he came to her. Into her arms. Into her body. She held him, absorbed his tremors, hushed his shout of release with a kiss. As they drifted off, arms and legs still entangled, she murmured his name.

"Cut the Captain Marvel stuff, okay, honey?"

"Not what I said," she gurgled.

Her laugh had him ready all over again. With a grunt, he rolled to his back. Brushing damp strands of hair from her sweet, cherished face, he asked, "Then what did you call me?"

"Captain Marvelous."

~ * ~

Morning came too soon. Annie wasn't ready to face him in the bright light of day. Not after all they'd done to and for each other in the dark of night—not once but several times.

It wasn't because of embarrassment or shame. Sex between two healthy, consenting adults wasn't something to be ashamed of. Rarely had she felt so healthy, so consenting, so adult.

With a glance at the empty side of her bed, she wondered what he was feeling. Maybe he needed a little time, some space to get his thoughts in order. That was okay. Time and space was exactly what she needed.

Another need demanded immediate attention. Coffee. After stumbling out of the bed, she threw on a ratty T-shirt and a pair of Tweety-bird boxers. After several gallons of caffeine, she'd load her body into the shower and soak till her skin pruned.

Annie came up short in the kitchen doorway. An outrageously gorgeous man with broad shoulders and warm green eyes sat at her table, eating cereal, drinking something a sickening pink color—and reading the Wall Street Journal. "Oh. You're here. In my kitchen."

"Good morning."

Not only did he look rested and relaxed, he smelled of her soap and shampoo. No! She would not entertain visions of him standing in her shower while water sheeted over his body.

"Sleep well?"

Never at her best on any morning, particularly this one, she snarled, "What?"

"Did you sleep well?"

Having to share her kitchen so early in the morning, after a night to end all nights, didn't help her prickly mood—or negate the need for time and space. "Coffee. I need coffee."

While the pot brewed, she took a seat opposite him at the rickety table. A plate of bagels and a pot of vegetable cream cheese occupied the majority of the scratched surface. "Where did this come from?"

"Oneonta has a great bagel shop," he offered in a bright tone that only further incited her irritation. "Twenty different varieties. I figured you deserve something other than peanut butter and moldy toast."

"My bread's moldy?"

"You could corner the market on penicillin, Ms. Wolfe."

"Sorry."

"Shall I toast one for you?" His hand hovered over the selection. "We have poppyseed, sesame, onion and pumpernickel."

"You don't have to—"

He raised her hand to his lips, kissed the center of her palm. And never taking those warm eyes off hers, he murmured, "Yeah, I do."

Whoa. The first jolt of caffeine took the edge off her jangled nerves. A second cup settled them, almost. The third cup had her ready for anything.

Anything did not include banging knees or bumping elbows with him over her impossibly small table, in her incredibly cluttered kitchen. *How will I get all this stuff to Syracuse?*

"I'd like to compliment you on your choice of bathroom decor."

That stopped her for a moment. Until she remembered it was her habit to rotate the posters of the Orioles' Cal Ripken, Jr., Brazil's soccer star, Ronaldo, and John Stockton of the Utah Jazz every so often, giving each of them a new outlook on life. Biting into a delicious, crisp bagel, she recalled whom she'd recently rotated into the spot on the back of her bathroom door.

"You follow golf?"

"No. But I helped provide undercover security for the Ryder Cup when it came to Rochester a couple years back."

Stomach filled and nerves settled, she felt more in control. "I always felt golf was dumb, tracking a stupid little ball through sand traps and water hazards and lugging a bag of clubs that must weigh a ton. That was before I watched TV coverage of the Concorde landing in Rochester and saw this divinely gorgeous man walk off the plane. Nick Faldo, they said his name was. I decided maybe golf deserved further consideration, so his poster joined the rest of the fan club."

"Annie, I want to talk."

"About what?" As if she didn't know.

"Last night."

Oh, baby, here it comes. It was fun; it was nice; I'll call you. Which was okay with her. She felt the same way. Sort of.

Then he looked at her. And smiled.

Ah, hell, she didn't know how she felt. "What about it?"

"I don't want things to end here."

A hunk of bagel caught in her throat. After a healthy, upper-airway-clearing hack, she said, "Ronen, you know I'm not in a position to make a commitment. I've told you this time and again. Last night was fun, great actually, but—"

"I'm not asking for orange blossoms and bird seed," he interrupted. "I simply want to spend more time with you."

More time? Impossible. "Ronen, I'm leaving town at the end of the summer."

He looked like she'd kicked him. "Leaving? Where?"

"Syracuse."

"Is that all?" He sat back with a relieved sigh. "That's only three hours away. I thought you meant out of state."

"Ronen, yesterday—" Excitement, borne from relief, bubbled to the surface all over again. "I was offered a spot in the fall class at the med school. Ronen, I'm in! I'm going to be a doctor!"

There. She'd said it out loud. For the first time. He was the first to know. She wanted to pound her bare feet into the linoleum in an elbow-waving, knee-knocking dance of joy.

"You did it," he mumbled.

Annie reached across the table, covering his hand in a tight squeeze. "*Please* be happy for me. This is what I've worked for all my life. It's all I've ever wanted."

"But... what about a home and family? What about kids?"

Was he nuts? Had he not been listening? "The rules haven't changed. Med school will be tough enough. I told you before," she said firmly, as the resolute look on his face shattered her heart into tiny pieces. *Ka-chink.* "No ties. No family and certainly no kids."

"I see." He checked his watch. "I have to get to work. Can I see you later?"

"Sure," she mumbled, more than a little irritated with his lukewarm response to what she considered earth-shaking news. Why didn't Mr. Ambition understand a woman could have goals, could have a passion for helping people, and still be a worthwhile person? "I don't like the way I'm feeling right now, Ronen."

"How are you feeling?"

"Like you're blowing me off; like what I want and need isn't important."

"Annie, you'll be a wonderful doctor. I'm glad for you."

His mouth said one thing, his eyes another.

"You're not listening. I wonder now if you ever listened."

He rose from the table, took her into his arms, stared into her eyes. "I don't have time for long, drawn-out discussions, slugger, but I will offer a compromise."

"Like what?" If he tried to con her back into bed, she'd grab his weapon and shoot him. Right between the legs.

"If I promise not to use the R or F words ever again, will you consider spending time with me until you leave for Syracuse?"

"R or F?"

"Relationship. Family."

"Oh." She considered his offer for all of two seconds. "You won't bitch, whine, or moan if I have to work a double shift?"

"Promise on my Captain Marvel decoder ring."

She laughed in spite of herself. "You won't get all bitchy and moody if I'm too tired to go out?"

"Ann. Where would we go?"

"I hear shooting rats at the town dump is the current rage."

"Please."

"What time do you expect to be home tonight?"

"Eight." He leaned down and kissed her. Hard. Then kissed her again. "Make that six."

Sliding her arms around his neck, she kissed him back. Harder. "I'll make dinner for us."

"You cook?"

"In addition to maintaining the health care needs of the entire community, yes, Captain, I cook. Sort of. What would you like to eat?"

"You."

Ten

If one word described his day, it would be *bitch*.

Because of cutbacks, or so he was told, all VA computers would continue to be shut down—temporarily, he was assured. So, until Congress got its act together and restored funding, information on vets who separated from active service prior to 1985 would not be accessible for several weeks. At the earliest. Ronen's response colored the air blue.

On the outside chance that Annie was correct about local cops being involved in the deaths, he attempted to run down Randy Terrance and Bobbie Claun's employment history prior to coming on the Job with the Nohmensville force—and was told personnel files for all town employees, past and present, were sealed. The air in the office went from blue to purple.

And the hits just kept on coming.

Long about three o'clock, Sophie Jackson and her posse paid him a visit. By the time they left his office, if he'd been into bubble baths, he would have begged Calgon to take him away from the *joys* of small town life.

Having Annie greet him at her door, wearing little more than a smile and a shirt which demanded a full pardon for Reilly Stuart Cameron, a Syracuse woman wrongly imprisoned for murder, made the whole rotten day worthwhile.

"Hey, slugger. How's tricks?"

"Not too bad, big guy. By the grocery bags beneath your eyes and the droop in your posture, it looks like yours could have been better. Steel rod in your spine experiencing a bit of structural fatigue?"

Throughout the seemingly endless day, his thoughts centered on only one thing: when he could be alone with Annie so he could take her in his arms and blot out all the crap that went along with enforcing the law in No Man's Land.

He'd bet Wyatt Earp didn't have half this trouble when he took over Tombstone. Then, Wyatt didn't have to contend with bureaucratic red tape, budget-challenged computer systems and... Sophie Jackson.

"It's a war out there, Wolfgirl. An all-out assault on the guys in the white hats."

"Let me guess. The formidable Mrs. Jackson and her band of merry-makers paid you a visit."

"You're amazing."

"They want you to shut down all the gin joints in town so their husbands will come home at a decent hour *or* they want you to do something about the trash littering the town's streets and roads."

"Close enough," he grumbled, pulling her onto his lap for a nuzzle.

"So, what'd you tell Sophie and company?"

Man, she smelled good. "That closing down bars isn't in my job description, but cleaning up the streets and roads was a great idea. In their presence, I gave the sheriff's office a call, asked them to send a work crew over."

"Oh, dear." Clearing her throat several times didn't erase the twinkle in her dark eyes. "Sophie no doubt looked at you like you'd made personal body noises in the middle of church services."

The woman knew her townspeople well. "The venerable Miz Jackson demanded to know the meaning of 'work crew'."

"And?"

"After I explained clean-up would be performed by prisoners, I thought she'd have a cow there on the spot."

Annie made a choking sound. "Wait," she said, touching her temple with an index finger. "I'm trying to conjure a mental picture of the delivery."

"Very funny."

"More like disgusting."

"Sophie stormed out of my office under full sail with the rest of the clucking hens bringing up the rear. I tell you, Annie, it's a jungle."

Slipping her arms around his neck, she crooned, "Poor baby. Shall I rub those big, broad shoulders?"

"The entire back, if you don't mind."

Much to his dismay, she jumped off his lap, moved behind him and proceeded to loosen his tie and unbutton his shirt. Those incredible hands attacked each one of his aching muscles until he was lulled into a pile of dough.

When he was finally able to entertain a coherent thought, Ronen recalled something she'd said a couple times. "What do you mean when you say I've got a steel rod in my spine?"

Bending over, she gave his earlobe a nip. "After years of observing Troopers' perfect posture, I've often wondered if you guys—and women, of course—have a steel rod surgically implanted in your spines."

She crossed her arms over his chest, enclosing him in a fragrant embrace. "I mean, do they line you up and zap one of those babies into you as you walk off the stage at graduation?"

"Annie."

"I'm serious." She whipped the shirt off his arms with the ease of a strip-tease artist. Her hands were like cotton sheets, so soft and cool on his over-heated skin. He couldn't summon the strength, much less the willpower, to suppress the groan that left his chest.

"I've watched you guys walk," she claimed. "All straight-legged and tight-bunned."

"Annie."

"Do they make you take strutting lessons like models? Grade you on your runway performance?" She traced a pointed tongue down the side of his neck. "Do you practice in full uniform or in regulation

Trooper undies? I'd like to see that," she chortled, reaching for the buckle on his belt. "A Trooper in his undies."

He wanted to laugh so bad. "Annie."

"Do they mandate the style?" she continued. "Like *only* boxers or *only* jockeys? And how do they make sure one of you doesn't sneak in a pair of electric-blue bikinis? Does the morning uniform inspection include making everyone drop their pants? My word, Ronen, if they check your undies, you'd have cause for a sexual harassment suit."

"Annie."

There was no stopping her. But as long as she kept her hands in their current location, examining his boxers for thread count or flaws in structure and design, she could recite the Bill of Rights for all he cared.

"We could do a calendar as a fund-raiser," she proposed. "I bet there's a whole herd of horny women out there willing to lay out some major bucks for a cop calendar. Would you pose for Mr. April, Captain Marvel—that being my birthday month and all?"

"I don't pose for pictures, in any style of dress."

"Bummer. I'd be first in line to get a picture of you nude. Especially if you felt like you do now."

"Annie!" He yanked her hands out of his pants, then stood.

"What? What?" she shrieked as he hoisted her over his shoulder, heading for the bedroom. "I haven't made the bed!"

"Think I care if you've got clean sheets?" He dumped her on the bed, then ripped off the rest of his uniform. "It's your turn for a complete physical exam."

"*All right*! Where do you want to start?"

"I trust you'll tell me if I'm not being *thorough* enough?"

"Absolutely." She moaned when he found her wet and warm, and very swollen. "Oh, yeah. You bet."

"Let us begin." He straddled her thighs, then ran a broad palm from throat to pubis. "Are you sexually active?"

She laughed, then showed him.

~ * ~

Such a beautiful man, Annie thought as she watched Ronen sleep. A contented smile soothed his usually serious features. She smiled, too. Captain Marvel's version of a physical exam might not meet her professional standards; it more than met her personal ones.

She snuggled into what few pillows were left on the bed and grinned. Yessir, the Captain fulfilled her personal standards, real well. Gonna put him in the Sexiest Man Hall of Fame. Right up there with Harrison Ford, Sean Connery, and... Tommy Lee Jones.

Ronen's hand shot out, splaying over her fanny to draw her against his chest. "Not again, honey. I'm bushed."

To lay in this man's arms, absorbing his warmth, came as a treat. To be comforted by his touch, protected by his strength, was a precious gift. If this lasted for the rest of her life—

The rest of her life.

"Now there's a scary thought," she grumbled, forcing herself to leave the bed. "Up and at 'em, Wolfgirl."

A tepid shower eased the stiffness from her joints, soothed aches in other, more private, areas.

Captain Marvelous.

Never in her wildest dreams did she imagine she would become involved with a cop. Any cop. From childhood, she'd been taught the police were to be kept at a distance, treated with respect so as not to arouse suspicion, but *never* trusted.

Along came Marvelic with the fabulous body, beatific smile, and integrity up to his eyebrows. A shudder claimed her when gentle hands took her from behind and proceeded to inflame her body all over again. "Ronen."

"You were expecting the garbage man?"

"Nah. Tuesday's his day."

Lips nuzzled her neck. Fingers stroked her breasts, gently tugged on her nipples. "Who's got the other days of the week?"

It was the steam that made it so difficult to breathe—or so she told herself. "No one that I recall."

He spun her around. "Good. I want them all."

An erection of fierce proportions intruded between her thighs. "Captain," she squealed as he lifted, then filled her. "We have to stop meeting like this."

"Not yet."

~ * ~

"Okay, pal. Do not come out of there until you are fully and completely dressed."

Feeling like a million bucks, Ronen stood next to her bed, tugging on his pants. "I love it when you take command."

"I mean it," she called from another room. "The human body requires more than sexual release to maintain proper homeostasis."

"Oh, yeah?" He put a deliberate swagger into what she called his tight-bunned, straight-legged walk before entering the kitchen. "I don't have the first clue about homeowhatsis. If it's kinky, I'm all for it."

She glanced up from the stove. It pleased him to see her jaw drop. True to form, Annie's recovery was instantaneous. "Did we forget our shirt, Captain?"

"Next you'll say I have to put on shoes."

"Pants, shirt, and tie will suffice," she offered primly, giving whatever was simmering in the pot a stir.

"The tie? Annie, give me a break."

"Purple turns me on."

Storing that one away for future reference, he mused, "What about the Stetson?"

"We'll do a Naked Except For The Hat scene another time."

"Would you wear a nurse's cap and stethoscope?"

"Anything else?"

He grinned, then grabbed her. "Nope, that'll be enough."

"Such a romantic," she claimed, feigning a swoon.

"I could be," he murmured against the sweet smelling skin of her neck. "If you'd let me."

She immediately stiffened. If he hadn't tightened his arms, she would have pulled away. Common sense, plus basic survival instincts, mandated a change in tactics.

"I'd like to stop by the VFW tonight, check out who's who. Would you help me out, introduce me to whomever's there?"

"Why would you want to go there—" A teasing light came back into her eyes; pliancy returned to her limbs. "I get it. You want me to be your beard."

"One of the first things I noticed about you, Ms. Wolfe, is your mental quickness."

"Members' pictures hang on a wall across from the dance floor. We'll be in and out, twenty minutes max."

"Good. PBS radio starts broadcasting *Carmen* from the Met tonight at nine. I'd hate to miss it."

"I'm sure," she replied, spooning whatever she'd made into a waiting bowl. "While you're yawning yourself into a coma, I'll catch the ball game."

"Who's playing—or doesn't it matter?"

"Of course it matters! The O's are taking on the Yanks at Camden Yards. Should be a good one."

Knowing how Annie could get during *a good one*, he said, "We'll toss for who wears the ear phones."

"Deal. And Captain?"

"Yes?"

"Don't expect Mr. Diamond or Mr. Mathis for this evening's musical entertainment. It's C & W all the way."

Oh, God. "Country and Western? You mean there's a dance tonight?"

Plunking the bowl into his hands, she offered him a snappy grin. "Once a month, starts at seven, just like clockwork."

"I could go another time."

"Don't like crowds, Cap?"

"That's not it at all," he said, carrying through on his revised tactical maneuver. "I don't want to cause you any... discomfort over being seen with me in public."

"Don't flatter yourself, Marvelic."

~ * ~

"Discomfort, my butt," Annie snarled. "He wouldn't know *discomfort* if it came up and bit him on the ass."

Stella Grover offered her another glass of watered-down fruit punch. "Having a good time, dearie?"

"Peachy. Just peachy."

What was supposed to have been "twenty minutes max" was now well into hour number two. Captain Marvel, the beau of the ball, appeared to be having himself a high old time. Every woman in the joint was lining up to take a turn on the dance floor with *Twinkle Toes*.

"He's a marvelous dancer," Stella sighed with a nod for Ronen and his current partner.

Annie gave the pair a sour look. "A regular Fred Astaire." Sophie Jackson, resplendent in printed polyester, giggled like a coy schoolgirl while "Fred" led her through the intricate steps of a cha-cha.

Purple was not her color, Annie decided. The knit material clung to Sophie's curves like shrink wrap. The worst, the absolute worst, were the platter-size daisies that plastered each of Sophie's massive buttocks like giant targets. For one insane moment, Annie fantasized about walking up and jabbing the yellow bull's-eyes with a sharp instrument—just to measure how much hot air might be released.

The way her luck was running tonight, the entire building might implode.

At that precise moment, Ronen flashed her a questioning look. Ignoring the urge to respond with a digital gesture, Annie made a beeline for the ladies' room while Willie Nelson began a twanging lament about someone always on his mind.

Man, could she sympathize with old Willie. Ronen Marvelic had occupied her mind, and her body, for days. No matter what she did, no matter how hard she tried, nothing erased him from every conscious thought. And preoccupation was so ugly, not to mention pathetic.

If there was one thing Annie Wolfe was not—it was pathetic.

Of course it helped, she acknowledged when she found the bathroom empty, that no one in town knew she and Fred had been carrying on like two teenagers turned loose in a sex shop.

She entered the first stall and closed the door. Yep, she decided, after what they'd done to and with each other over the past twenty-four hours, they were lucky one of them hadn't popped a disc or ruptured a few vital tendons. Never again would she view her kitchen table in quite the same way.

Or the couch, shower, and the spot on the living room wall just beneath the poster of the now-retired Cal Ripken.

Play time was over, she promised as she left the bathroom and made her way toward the exit door. She'd walk home, give her overworked brain a chance to clear. Marvelic wouldn't even know she'd left. Probably wouldn't care. The toad.

With escape only steps away, a belligerent voice snapped her back to reality. "Where you going?"

A beefy hand gripped her arm hard. Streaks of fire bulleted all the way to her shoulder. Glancing up at the hand's owner, she said, "Get a life, Terrance."

"Got one," he claimed, digging harder into the soft tissue above her elbow. "Dance with me."

Steeling herself against the noxious stench of his cologne, she forced herself to lean closer. "Drop your hand," she said, "or I'll drop you."

For the sake of any onlookers, she was sure, Terrance's grin turned sheepish. His feigned innocence only firmed up her stand. "You still ticked about that bit after the Little Buda heist, Annie? I was only doing my job."

She didn't have time for his brand of crap. "What exactly is your job these days, Randy? Besides strutting around old man Harbaugh's place, swinging your big—nightstick?"

The vise tightened. Agony seared a new path from her shoulder to the nape of her neck, and threatened to blow off the top of her skull. On principle alone, Annie refused to back down.

"I know what you been doin' with Marvelic," Terrance warned. "I was you, I'd watch my butt."

"Yours is tough to miss, Randy. It being such a wide load and all."

A plethoric hue suffused Terrance's features. Annie braced for a fist in the face. *Ronen, where are you when I need you?*

"Hi, guys." Bobbie Claun, reeking of stale beer and fried onions, joined the fray. "Watcha doin'?"

"Wolfgirl thinks she's too good to dance with me," Randy sneered, yanking once again on her arm. "Whaddya say we teach her a lesson, Bobbie?"

"Dancing's for wusses." Claun's sour breath could bring down a rampaging rhino. "Thought we were gonna play poker."

Something like fear flickered in Terrance's eyes. "Mind your own business, Annie," he warned, then dropped her arm.

"Or what?" Angered, she turned and got in his face. "Gonna do me like Barb Thompson?"

Bobbie Claun blanched, staring at her with wide, frightened eyes. "What're you talking about?" When Annie ignored him, he turned on Randy. "What's she talkin' about?"

~ * ~

Her threat to Terrance almost stopped Ronen's heart. If there hadn't been a crowd, he would have strangled her on the spot, then hidden the body where no one would ever find it. He knew all the tricks, all the ways to avoid detection. *It could be done.*

Since he had an audience—granted it consisted of two lowlife idiots—the best he could do was slide his hand beneath Annie's braid and give the back of her neck a squeeze. He hoped she understood the warning gesture and kept her mouth shut. "Mr. Claun, Mr. Terrance. You're both members of this organization?"

"Well, well," Claun belched. "If it ain't Studly DoRight of the New York State Mounted Patrol."

Terrance hoisted his pants up over a sagging gut. "Something wrong with being a vet, Marvelic?"

"Of course not," Ronen responded evenly. "I'm a veteran myself."

"Of what?" Claun jeered. "Shore Patrol?"

"Something like that."

"We was just havin' a friendly conversation with Wolfgirl," Claun muttered. "That against the law, Stud—I mean—Dudley?"

"Shut up, Bobbie," Terrance barked. He turned to Annie. "I'm keeping an eye on you. And your friends. Best remember what I said."

Annie fluttered her lashes. "With every breath I take, Randy."

Ronen waited for the two men to saunter off before taking her arm. "Are you out of your mind?"

"No." She jerked away from him. "Are you?"

"Not another word, Annie. Not one." Over her clear objections, he directed her out the door and across the parking lot, a firm hand at her back. He waited until they were inside the Bronco before exploding—and hoped volume alone would prove his point.

"What possessed you to taunt Terrance and Claun like that? If you're not insane, you certainly have a death wish."

"Randy's jerked my chain once too often," she spat, squaring her shoulders against the back of the seat. "It was my turn to jerk him back."

The Bronco's engine purred to life. "Why not hand him an engraved invitation to shut you up permanently?"

That got her attention. "I beg your pardon?"

"Don't give me that innocent look," he growled as he pulled out of the parking lot onto Elm Street. "Sonofabitch, Annie! You announced to him and that jerk-off Claun that you know Barbara Thompson's dead!"

"I lost my temper," she stammered. "If it makes you feel—"

"I don't want to hear it!" He turned the corner onto Main, barely missing the bumper on a four-by-four parked in front of the Lay Back And Enjoy saloon.

"Civilians," he sneered. "As if I needed, wanted, or asked for help in this mess. So what does Valletta dump on me? A smart-ass with a short fuse who thinks nothing of shooting off her mouth at the slightest provocation."

She stared at him, jaw open, and for one of the few times in recent memory silent. Yup, he had her attention.

"Give a civilian a taste of the inside scoop," he ranted, "and all of a sudden they think they're the next best thing to Batman and Robin. Getting in the way, going off half-cocked, talking to the wrong people, putting not only themselves but everyone else in danger." He took his eyes off the road for a second to offer her a glare. "How could you be so stupid?"

"Until tonight, Captain," she replied coldly, "I don't recall shooting off my mouth to anyone. In fact, until tonight I wasn't aware I'd been dumped on you. You have a problem with being *dumped on*, talk to Jim Valletta—not me."

At the corner of Main and Oak, Ronen had reached his limit. He brought the Bronco to an abrupt stop, then faced her. The glow from a nearby street lamp illuminated her face. Without warning, a haze, like a veil of gauze, blurred his vision.

It wasn't Annie he was staring at, but Ted Collins' widow, face bloated and streaked with tears as she screamed accusations at him. Ted's death was his fault, he'd known that from the beginning. Just as he knew, now, that it would be his fault if something happened to Annie. Once again, Captain Marvel lost control of an investigation case because of a civilian's big mouth.

The vision dissolved with a shake of his head and with it came recognition of the cause of his rage. Fear. For Annie. For himself.

For long seconds, she said nothing. Accusation filled her eyes, and made the silence, cut only after he restarted the engine and proceeded home, that much worse. He had to make it better, had to make her understand. Forgiveness, he hoped, might follow. As soon as he pulled into the mansion's parking lot and put the Bronco in Park, Annie jerked open her door.

"I didn't ask to become involved in 'this mess'—as you so eloquently described it," she said with quiet determination. "I never wanted anything to do with you, Marvelic. I still don't."

"Ann, honey. Let me explain."

"I'm not finished!"

"I want to apolo—"

"Save it for someone who cares." She leaped out of the Bronco, slammed the door, then stuck her head through the open window. "Know what else, *Captain Marvel*? You are an incredibly lousy dancer."

Eleven

The seventh body was discovered the next day, face down in the muck of Harbaugh Enterprises' east potato field. Rick Thurrell was waiting when Ronen arrived at the scene. "Acting coroner's on his way."

From a distance Ronen recognized several men and women from the immigrant compound. Huddled together on the opposite side of the access road, fear and anxiety hovered over them in a thick cloud. "Who discovered the body?"

Rick jerked his chin toward the workers. "It took awhile for one of the men to find help."

"Better find Annie," Ronen sighed. "She'll make taking their statements easier."

He moved to the edge of the dump site, Rick trailing behind him. "Cap," he said cautiously. Ahead of them, two troopers were cordoning off the area with crime scene tape. "Better hold off on that for the moment."

Ronen glanced over his shoulder. "Think I haven't seen a DB before?"

"Not like this one."

Ronen glanced down at the body.

And wished he hadn't.

The nude corpse was covered with all manner of debris. All he saw was the long black hair. Matted with blood and dirt, it fell in thick ropes over her neck and shoulders. Her hands, nails broken and bloody, were tied at the small of her back. Deep purple bruising circled the base of each thumb.

A Nuggets jacket, emblazoned with "Wolfgirl" across the shoulders, partially covered the corpse's buttocks. With the legs posed in a position suggesting sexual assault, Ronen had to wonder if the jacket was afterthought—or a message.

Pain seared a hard, fast path beneath his breastbone. He rubbed a fist over his chest and recalled how he left things with Annie last night. Later, he'd heard a mixture of sounds coming from her apartment during the intermission of *Carmen*. The roar of cheering crowds, her shouts of encouragement to someone named Cal. Had she left her place after the game and...?

Swallowing his fear, Ronen prayed like he hadn't in years. *Please, God. Not again.*

He straightened, made himself turn back to the tortured remains in front of him. "Notify Valetta and the DA."

"Will do." Thurrell strode off, cell phone in hand.

One of the troops involved with cordoning off the area approached. "What next, Cap?"

"Who called it in?" Ronen said, struggling to keep his voice under control.

The trooper jerked a thumb over his shoulder. "Guy's over there."

Ronen looked toward the access road. Randy Terrance leaned against the side of a panel van, an ugly smirk on his fat face.

Gonna do me like you did Barb Thompson?

It took all Ronen's self-discipline to remain focused, in control. "When?"

"Thirty minutes, give or take," the troop responded. "Said he was making rounds when one of the workers flagged him down. He's the, uh, chief of security for—"

"I know who Mr. Terrance is," Ronen clipped. "Any vehicles seen entering or leaving the area since you've been on scene, Trooper—" He checked the name badge pinned above the man's breast pocket. "—Dolan?"

"No one, sir."

"Thank you. Have you started the log?"

Dolan tapped a finger against the posse box in his hand. "Yes, sir, right here."

"Thank you. Any other vics?"

Dolan gave a start. "Don't think so, sir."

"Guess you'd better check to make sure, trooper."

"Yes, sir." Dolan turned on one heel and stalked off.

Rick joined Ronen next to the body, handing him a pair of latex gloves. They squatted down to get a better look. "DA and the Major are on their way," he said. "I pulled the crime scene kit from my unit and asked two of the boys to canvass the area. They'll start interviews."

"Appreciate it," Ronen gritted, barely able to keep a lid on his roiling gut. *Please. Please. Please.*

A rusted-out four-by-four screeched to a halt in a blaze of dust. An overweight, slovenly dressed young man with a camera slung around his neck tumbled out of the truck. "Heard it on my scanner," he huffed. "Got here soon as I could."

Ronen looked up at him. "Who are you?"

"Clyde Harbaugh. Most folks call me Junior 'cause I'm named after my daddy." The young man's broad grin showed a mouthful of ill-kept teeth, plenty of gum, and a truck-load of enthusiasm. "I do gofer work over at the Clarion. Take pictures and stuff. Guys around here call me for all their crime scenes."

Ah, yes, Ronen thought, the Marilyn Manson fan who shoots out streetlights when he's got his load on. He recalled the night he and Annie shared Chinese take-out, the way her eyes danced as she described the locals, and their idiosyncrasies.

Emotion threatened to overwhelm him. *Please, God. Don't let it be her.*

He redirected his attention to the body. "Make sure you get shots of everything: hands, wrists, shoulders, and the angle of her legs. All views. Understand?"

"This is lucky seven for me, Cap. I know what to do."

No matter what Ronen told himself, he could not see beyond the matted hair and blood-smeared legs. Control danced just out of reach. Fear threatened to rip his composure, as well as his heart, to shreds.

The gofer scuttled around the corpse, snapping the Canon LX, and making cooing noises like he was taking shots of a favorite wrestling hero.

Ronen was aware the county crime lab had lost its funding two years before, leaving local law enforcement to rely on trained volunteers to get the scut work done at crime scenes. By the looks of this bird, they had themselves a winner.

The guy whistled a merry tune as he took posterior shots of the body from every angle. Probably, Ronen reminded himself, it was the excitement of being one of the key players at a major crime scene. Maybe it was nerves. Whichever, the victim deserved more respect.

Seemingly unaffected by the carnage at his feet, Junior Harbaugh paused in his whistling. "Looks like the others, Cap. Trick gone bad, you think?"

Somehow, Ronen managed not to grab the little twerp by the throat and choke the snot out of him. "Excuse me?"

"You know. A hooker, a john," the gap-toothed kid said. "Things got rough. She said no; he said tough and popped her."

Two things prevented Junior Harbaugh's premature demise: Rick Thurrell's hand on Ronen's arm and the arrival of yet another vehicle.

John Latimer emerged from a dust covered Taurus. The hem of a wrinkled lab coat flapped around his baggy slacks. Abrupt and impatient as always, he barked, "You boys mind telling me what's so all-fired important that couldn't wait for me to finish making rounds?"

"John—" Ronen began, hand out in a gesture of support.

The physician brushed him aside with a grunt before pulling a pair of gloves from his pocket. As he squatted over the body, John's color immediately turned paste-gray. "My sweet Lord." He fell to his knees. Sweat beaded his forehead. Breath rattled in his chest.

Alarmed at the man's pallor, Ronen asked, "Are you all right? Should I call for someone else?"

"There is no one else," John growled, shaking off Ronen's hand. "Damned ME ran off to Alaska. I said I'd take over coroner duties till they could appoint a new one. If that wimp Moran had done his goddamned job in the first goddamned place, she'd be alive today." Each word seemed to sap his strength a little more. "May God damn him and everyone else in... this... god... damned... town." He straightened with agonizing slowness. "I don't need to state the obvious. Roll her over."

Nudging Ronen to one side, Rick Thurrell motioned to Trooper Dolan. "Give me a hand."

Not sure he was ready for this, Ronen struggled to maintain a pose of authority. It was that—or go mad. He stepped to one side while Rick and Dolan turned the body over. Relief that came with recognition of the woman's face brought tears to his eyes.

Thank you, thank you, thank you.

"Thank you, thank you, thank you," John Latimer said out loud.

"Rick," Ronen barked. "Find Annie Wolfe. We'll need her to interpret when we take statements from the laborers."

"Do my best, Cap."

John Latimer turned to Ronen, the square back in his shoulders, the bite back in his voice. "Can't spend all day around here. I'm late for rounds." His pale blue gaze, lighted with a zealot's purpose, examined Ronen's face. "You boys need anything, that's where I'll be. Don't be afraid to call."

"Yes, sir." Ronen watched the aging man walk toward his car. Despite his gruff posture, John moved with a halting, almost defeated slump in his shoulders. Each step looked like it might be his last. Ronen motioned to the closest trooper. "Follow Dr. Latimer back to the hospital. Make sure he gets there safely."

"Yessir."

Ronen turned back to the body with a heaviness in his chest. Rarely, in all his years working undercover or profiling violent criminals, had he seen such malice perpetrated against another human being. Livid purple bruising covered her arms from elbows to shoulders. Her chest and belly looked like they'd been painted with three inch black bands. Someone had used her for a punching bag—or batting practice.

Junior Harbaugh's assumption was on target. In death, Kathy Baker looked exactly like the other victims.

Why does she have Annie's jacket?

Then he remembered the party after the Lowville game. More than a little tipsy, Kathy hadn't wanted to drive, but needed something warm to put on for the walk home. There was little doubt now. She'd been abducted after she left the party. *Wearing Annie's jacket.*

With nothing more to do for the Nuggets' catcher, except find her killer, he growled, "Get pictures of her thumbs before we bag her hands, Junior."

"Bag her hands, Cap? Uhm, sure... if that's what you want. I got some zip-locks in my camera case."

Ronen kept his response clipped and short. "Paper."

"But Randy always said plastic was fine."

"That's why Mr. Terrance is now walking tours of duty in a manure patch, Mr. Harbaugh. Trooper Dolan?" he bellowed.

"Yes, sir?"

"Take over here. Sergeant Thurrell has paper bags in his kit. Make sure you secure them well above her wrists."

While Junior took additional photos of Kathy's hands, Ronen stepped away from the scene to phone Annie at her apartment. When he got no response beyond the recorded message on her answering machine, he dialed the crime lab in Albany. The head technician came on the line just as Dolan began to bag the hands. "Hey, Marv! What's shakin'?"

Because he was describing the scene to the tech, Ronen missed the beginning of the exchange between Dolan and Harbaugh. Until he heard the trooper's snort of disgust. "Guess he's too busy to listen to us peons, Junior."

"Big city," the gofer commiserated. "Ain't he the one?"

Ronen clicked off the phone. "She's going to the state lab in Albany."

Dolan gaped at him. "We can do her here, Cap. That's where the rest of them were—"

"And that's only one reason why we're up to our asses in alligators, Mr. Dolan," Ronen said quietly, fixing him with a freezing glare. "She's going to the state capitol. If you have to drive the damn wagon yourself, make it happen. Ms. Baker's body will be delivered in Albany within two hours. Understand?"

The trooper blushed clear to the tips of his jug-handle ears. "Yessir. Whatever you say, sir."

~ * ~

Things had moved at a steady clip throughout the shift. Annie hadn't felt harried, nor was she bored out of her gourd. There was enough time to speak at length with each patient and organize a treatment plan in an individualized manner—but not enough downtime to think about Captain Marvel and all the crap he'd spouted last night.

She liked and respected the staff who were on duty. Head Nurse Joe Murphy was always right there, anticipating every medication and treatment order before the words left her mouth. ER tech Amy Hudzinski responded with her usual practiced efficiency. Together, the three of them clicked like the gears on a fine-tuned engine.

"Any physician, stat to the Emergency Room... Annie Wolfe, stat to the ER, please."

Annie was just coming off the elevator from the cafeteria when the page sounded a second time. She took off at a run. As she blew through the back doors to the ER, a trooper, aided by Joe and Amy, was lifting an old man from a wheelchair to a gurney. Even from a distance she could see the patient looked ready to crash.

She moved fast to the stretcher. "What's up?"

John Latimer took her hand in a weak grip, closed his eyes and grunted, "Chest... pain. Help... me."

~ * ~

Ronen trudged the length of the mansion's parking lot on legs that felt like they were dragging forty pound weights. Stella Grover pulled the pink Caddie into her parking spot and tooted her horn. She joined him on the sidewalk.

"My land, Ronen! What has this town come to?"

"I don't know, Mrs. Grover. I surely don't."

"Heard you on the radio on my way to my DAR meeting. You sounded so... important," she twittered, "so official. Why, my friends busted a gusset after I told them you're my tenant."

"Thanks," he murmured absently. He had to find Annie. Needed to touch her. Hold her in his arms.

"Imagine that," Stella offered over her shoulder as she mounted the porch steps. "Crime Stoppers offering a reward for a bunch of no-account immigrant trash. Not that the Baker girl wasn't sweet," Stella hastened to add. "Her mouth ran faster than a whippoorwill's ass, but that poor child worked her fingers to the bone at Harbaugh Enterprises. Never harmed a soul—except for blowing the big game, of course."

For the sake of positive landlord-tenant relations, not to mention those between law enforcement and the community, Ronen kept silent about the woman's skewed values. "I'm looking for Annie. She upstairs?"

"Mercy, no! She's putting in an extra shift at the hospital in Oneonta." Stella peered over the rims of her rhinestone-studded glasses. "The price those movers quoted that child to ship her things to Syracuse is nothing short of highway robbery. You should do something about it, Ronen."

Arrest the movers or lock her in his bedroom? he wondered. Given his present mood, both options were right up his alley. Glancing up at the turret window, he gave out another heavy sigh. After the day he put in, he'd give a king's ransom for eight hours of uninterrupted sleep. He'd have to go without Annie's arms around him through the night.

He wasn't ready to do that. After today, he would never be ready.

"I'm heading to the hospital, then to the barracks, Mrs. Grover. When Chris gets home, tell him to call me there."

Ronen took the thirty minute drive to Oneonta, fear and guilt weighing heavily on his heart. He had to make Annie see that they belonged together. He wanted more kids—with her. Wanted to hold a baby in his arms—their baby. He'd make her understand she could do babies, then do med school.

~ * ~

"You look worse than the pus we drained out of that gomer's chest this morning."

Annie arched a brow at Joe Murphy. "Who needs enemies with friends like you?"

"Just stating the facts, ma'am. Figured you'd be pitching a tent in the CCU. Wear out your welcome up there already?"

"If I had to listen to those damn monitors and alarms for one more second, I was going to rip someone's throat out," she promised. "Starting with that idiot of a charge nurse."

Joe grunted. "Wanda the Whiner. She would've lasted ten seconds in Desert Storm, less than that in 'Nam. If the docs didn't kill her first, the patients would have."

Joe's round, placid face belied his background as a career Army nurse. He'd served tours in heavy combat areas, starting in Vietnam and ending with Desert Storm, before retiring. Along with the excitability quotient of a bag of cement, he possessed the skills and temperament of a battle surgeon. A few hours ago, she'd trusted him with John Latimer's life—and knew whatever she said would stay between them.

"I'm going to lose him, Joe. That happens, I'm hanging up med school."

"If that's fear talking, shut the hell up."

"It's not knowing what I'm doing talking," she admitted.

"I was under the impression that was the whole purpose of you becoming a doctor. So you could learn all that doctor stuff, save lives, play God."

If ever she needed a boot in the butt, she knew right where to come.

"If John gets wind you're thinking of giving up, we sure as hell will lose him." Joe plucked grapes from a bowl on the table, probably leftovers from someone's lunch. "Don't come crying to me when the old man comes back to haunt you."

A thundercloud of guilt hovered over Annie's shoulders. "I should have seen this coming. He's working too hard, doesn't take his meds or watch his diet."

"Bullshit," Joe muttered. "John was dancing up a storm with Stella Grover at the VFW last night, having the time of his life." He reached across the battered table in the staff lounge to grab her hands. "The old man is spending his last years the way he wants, Annie. Who are you to tell him otherwise?"

Part of what Joe said was true. Despite John's brutal schedule and lousy diet, he'd been looking and acting more spry, more happy, in the last few months than she'd ever seen him. Who was she to dictate to him how to live his life?

"Can I ask a favor?" Joe began. "Get you thinking about something other than the original grumpy old man?"

"Ask anything you want. Don't expect a positive response."

"Hockey pre-season starts next week. Take practices for me."

"Are you nuts?"

"Did I forget to say please?"

"Joe, with all the free time I have, I'm just sitting around waiting for the blood to clot in my ass."

"Really?" He wiggled his eyebrows in a *Magnum PI* leer. "Better let me take a look at that, honey."

"In your dreams, Mr. Murphy," she replied sweetly. "For your information, when I'm not searching the Syracuse want ads for an apartment, I'm working double shifts, trying to pack all my junk and praying the movers won't charge me both arms and a leg to ship it all."

"It's only temporary, Annie, until I find someone to fill the slot permanently."

"I haven't got time."

"Think about it. With the Sanko kid coming on board, the team could take the state finals this year."

"Viktor went out for the team? Good. It'll help him work out his aggression."

The eyes of the hospital's chief hockey fanatic danced. "You should see him take a shots on goal, Annie. Only thing I know with that kind of punch is a scud missile."

"Read my lips, Joe." She leaned into his smiling face. "I. Can't. Do. It."

He came back with a salary figure that made her eyes swim. "You aren't serious."

"As serious as drug-resistant TB. The town is counting on this year's team, Annie."

She did some quick figuring in her head. The money was enough to cover her moving expenses plus the security deposit on an apartment. Her financial worries would be over—for the moment. She wouldn't need to work extra shifts. That would free up time so she could keep a closer eye on John. "Could I get paid in advance?"

Joe's hand, the size of a bear's paw, waved blithely. "We'll work something out."

"Three weeks is all I've got."

The grin he gave her was triumphant. "Three weeks of Annie Wolfe is better than six months of Gretsky."

"I doubt that."

"So, is it a deal?"

"The only thing holding it up would be if John—"

Amy Hudzinski blew in the door. "You guys won't believe what's going on out there."

Annie immediately came to her feet, ready to fight another battle in the war against disease, trauma and death.

"Not the ER, Wolfgirl," Amy advised as she flipped on the portable TV in the corner of the room. After fiddling with the knobs, she announced, "Here we go."

"*In a follow-up to today's tragedy in Nohmensville, we bring you a report from—*"

"Tragedy?" Annie yelped. "What the hell are they talking about?"

The camera focused on a reporter, standing in front of the atrium of the county courthouse. As he recapped a press conference held within the past hour, Annie's pulse thundered. Film footage moved on to show Ronen, in full uniform, walking up to a bank of microphones, flanked by the county prosecutor and the mayor of Nohmensville. After finishing what sounded like a prepared statement, reporters barraged him with questions.

Annie paid strict attention to his face. He looked exhausted, and frustrated. Images of last night's argument flashed through her head. She needed to call him, had to know how he was doing. She *must* see him.

"Kathy Baker," Amy moaned after the news piece concluded. "We were all together the other night at your place, Annie, after the game. How could something like this happen?"

A sense of dread washed over her. Images of Randy Terrance's leering face, the painful grip on her arm. Her stupid challenge. *Gonna do me like you did Barb?* "Did the reporter say how long she'd been dead?"

"Waiting on the results of the post," Joe mumbled. "Christ almighty, I hope this forces the troopers to get off their asses and do something."

"Crime Stoppers is involved," Amy said. "That's some big bucks for tips leading to an arrest."

Annie shared the doubt in Amy's voice. Just then, the door opened. Ronen entered, looking like the wrath of God. She stood, crossed the room, and walked into his arms. He felt so good. So strong. So perfect.

His lips pressed into the soft spot beneath her ear. He inhaled her fresh, unique scent. After hours of worrying, he finally had her in his arms, soaking up the comfort of her body against his. And almost wept in relief. "Jesus, I thought it was you."

"I'm here," Annie murmured. "Safe and sound." She took his face between her palms. "I'm so sorry for last night."

"Annie, I never for a second believed you—"

"Hush," she said. "I know you didn't."

Every bone in his body screamed for the mercy of a long soak in a tub. His jaw ached from clenching it so hard during the press conference. Now that first-hand proof of Annie's safety was in his arms, the aches and screams lessened; tension slowly drifted from his neck and shoulders.

It could have been her laying in that field.

Tears welled for what he could have lost. Instinct took over. He couldn't hold her tight enough, would never be able to get deep enough into her arms.

"Ronen, ease up. I'm okay."

His arms loosened. "Sorry. I just—" He peeled his gaze from her beautiful face to stare at their two curious onlookers. "Do you mind?"

"Not at all." The man wearing the satisfied smile grabbed the hand of the goggle-eyed woman standing beside him. "About those policies and procedures that need review, Amy."

"Now?" she wailed. "I'm on break. Why can't I stay?"

"Hudzinski?" Annie pulled her face away from Ronen's chest. "Get lost."

After the pair of grinning staff left the room, Annie led Ronen to the couch. "You look awful."

"I've had better days." What he needed to make the ugliness disappear was to keep her close. "Come pamper me, Annie Wolfe."

Her hands moved over his back and shoulders, reinforcing the message that she was strong, and warm, and alive. "Can you tell me about it?"

"Worse than the others." Guilt rose like a demon, taunting him for the relief he'd felt when he'd recognized Kathy's face. He'd deal with guilt later—as he had—in his own way. "Until we turned her over, I thought it was you."

"Why?"

"Your Nuggets jacket partially covered her body. I think she was grabbed sometime after she left the team party." He paused, then added, "It looks like she might have been raped."

"Aw, Christ."

Ronen clasped her hand to his chest. "I believe you were the target, Ann. In the dark, with your jacket on, the killers mistook Kathy for you."

Annie went very still. "Don't say anymore. I haven't got time for this."

"Make time."

"Don't tell me what to do, Marvelic."

The abrupt change in her manner triggered a memory. "The night you and I were in the gazebo, talking about Barbara, you started to say something, then stopped. What was it?"

"Nothing," she spat. "Not important."

He'd had enough. Up to his eyeballs enough. "Cut the crap, Annie."

"What crap?"

"You've tapped danced, played dodgeball, and exercised any number of evasions since the first night we worked on the files. What do you know? Don't even think about putting me off."

"Captain Marvel is willing to accept something from a civilian without proof? Let me mark this in my calendar."

"Annie, I'm in so far over my head, I'll take anything I can get. Tell me what you suspect. Then tell me what you know."

She came off his lap, moving to the other side of the room. The silence was broken only by overhead pages for the nursing supervisor and maintenance. "Luba Sanko was brought into the ER in full arrest," she said with a heaving sigh. "We couldn't save her."

"I figured that. Something else must have happened."

"John talked to the parents; he made me take the cops."

"And?"

"There were three of them." She glanced around the room as if she was seeing it for the first time. "They were here, in this room. Barb, Randy Terrance, Bozo the Claun, and—" Her eyes closed briefly. "A trooper. I don't know his name."

When Ronen considered the missing files, all the brick walls he'd come up against time and again, it made sense that someone on the inside was keeping him off-center.

A trooper. Shit. "Go on."

"Before I barged in," she said, "I eavesdropped through the door and heard Barb telling Randy if he didn't do something, she knew someone who would. That's when I walked in."

"And?"

"Randy tried his usual bullshit cons. When that didn't work, he warned us not to tell him how to do his job."

"And?"

"Ronen, don't you see?"

"No!" He exploded to his feet. "All I see is a bully who likes to push the buttons of strong, independent women. That doesn't make him a killer."

"Does it make a difference that he served time in Vietnam and Central America?"

"How do you know that?" Fear for Annie's safety flowered once again. Then came rage. He closed in on her, clamped his hands over her shoulders. "I warned you, Ann."

"You told me not to check out the bars. I didn't."

Several deep breaths later, he gritted his teeth, then asked, "Okay, what did you *check out*?"

"Patient records at John's office. It was right there in black and white. Randy did three tours in 'Nam."

"Along with a million other guys."

Shaking off his hands, she spun on one heel and came at him like a terrier after a rat. "Excuse me, sir, a *million other guys* did not spend three years in Southeast Asia because of the cool weather and fabulous scenery. They stayed because they liked the work. *Liked* it!"

Ronen took a mental step backward. A civilian had uncovered more about Terrance than he'd been able to. Maybe that's what was pissing him off. "It's not enough to tie him to murder."

"He spent time in El Salvador during the Reagan years," she added. "And he likes to beat up suspects."

"You got all this from looking at an office record?"

"Everything except beating people up. I've seen the results of Randy's interrogation techniques with my own eyes."

"Does anyone know you checked his records?"

"Stella pulled the files for me and put them away once I was finished with them."

"Them?" he croaked. Annie was in this deep enough to bury them both if they weren't careful. "How many constitutes 'them'?"

"Seven, maybe eight."

After muttering a few favored curses, he asked, "Who?"

"A few don't count because they're too ill to get out of bed much less inflict the damage I saw on the bodies."

Godammit, he'd get to the bottom of her snooping once and for all. After that, he'd lock her in a closet. "Who, Annie?"

"John Latimer and one of the local clergy," she sighed. "Jim Valetta and a couple of the Harbaughs. Clyde, Senior, was terminated from the service for—I forget the term—it sounded like he was unfit for duty."

"Must run in the family," he mumbled, unable to force the picture of Junior Harbaugh scampering around Kathy Baker's body out of his head.

Something was there, *right there*, pulling at his gut, begging for him to choose the winning door.

"Look," she said, "I have to get back to the patients."

"I'm putting a twenty-four hour guard on you."

"I can't have armed guards following me around. Not now."

"I don't understand. What else is going on?"

"John was brought in a few hours ago with a coronary. He's upstairs in CCU. The first week to ten days are critical to his survival."

"I still don't understand."

"It's a medical thing. The damaged heart muscle gives off enzymes that can be measured in the blood—" She shook her head. "Nevermind. Just know that John needs close observation for the next seven days."

Seven. Where had he heard—?

It wasn't Junior Harbaugh's face dancing through his head this time. It was his voice. *This is lucky seven for me, Cap.*

The connection was stunning in its simplicity.

"Yess!" He wanted to howl in triumph. "I need a phone." He grabbed Annie by the shoulders. "Have I told you how wonderful you are?"

"Not recently," she drolled. "Can you tell me why you look ready to jump out of your skivvies?"

"Actually, I can't. The important thing is, we finally got a break. I have to leave. You know Rick Thurrell, right?"

"Sure. He was with you at the Little Buda."

"I'll have him come over here, stick by your side."

"Plain clothes, please."

"What?"

"Ask him to wear regular clothes. I don't want the staff or patients asking a lot of questions."

Relieved that she'd consented so easily to the guard, Ronen hauled her up onto her toes, then kissed her till she melted against him.

"Thanks for letting me take care of you."

Twelve

"You've got yourself some trouble, Mr. Harbaugh."

After arresting Junior, Ronen personally delivered him to the county lockup for overnight consideration of his errant ways. Little more than twelve hours later, he found himself paying a second visit to the jail, hoping to shake the little twerp into giving up his partners.

Supported by his shark-faced attorney, Junior sneered, "Lawyer says I don't have to say nothin'."

"Absolutely correct, Mr. Harbaugh," Ronen said. "You have the right to remain silent."

He fanned out a packet of photographs, some confiscated from Junior's desk at the Clarion, others from a bulletin board in his bedroom. "Perhaps these might convince you of the wisdom of avoiding twenty-five to life in a maximum security cage."

Junior gave the pictures short consideration. "So I'm into S and M. It's legal."

Ronen wanted to punch him. "Several townspeople have already identified some of the women in these photographs, Mr. Harbaugh. Women who later turned up dead." He shoved the least offensive shot of Luba Sanko's battered body in Junior's face. "You would have me and your attorney believe a fifteen year-old child willingly posed for this?"

"Just having some fun," the gofer mumbled.

"Let's talk about that. The fun, I mean."

"You have no proof my client took these photographs—or that he had anything to do with the deaths," the attorney challenged.

Ronen shook his head, all for show, then struck fast and hard. "What was that you said yesterday, Junior? Kathy Baker was lucky six for you. That right?"

"Don't—" the lawyer interjected.

"Nope," the little creep drawled, leaning back in the molded plastic chair, and wearing a contented smirk on his face. "I said seven. Lucky seven."

Leaning on his palms, Ronen looked across the table at the attorney, his voice serpent cool. "Until this moment, counselor, only five homicides have been confirmed. Interesting that your client just admitted Kathy Baker is number seven. How do you suppose that came to be?"

The lawyer didn't turn a hair. "I need to confer with my client in private."

"Good choice." Ronen straightened to his full height. "The DA will be presenting to the Grand Jury within the week." As he headed for the door, he glanced back at the now quaking Junior Harbaugh. "This could be the county's first death penalty case."

Satisfied he'd made his point, Ronen left Junior and his attorney huddling like hamsters. The DA was young but with a fair amount of experience with major felonies. Ronen trusted him to demand names, ranks and serial numbers on the big fish—the ones who tied the ropes and swung the bats—before making any deals with a minnow like Junior Harbaugh.

Jim Valetta met him in the hallway. "Anything?"

"Not yet."

"You show them the pictures?"

"Blown up to enhance every bruise, wound and bite mark."

"And?"

"Junior said he was having himself some fun."

"Pervert," Valetta muttered. "You'd think his lawyer would have him singing the SODDI blues."

"Right now Junior's got his own version of Some Other Dude Did It." Ronen continued down the hallway toward the door leading to the parking lot. "I'm going to Oneonta General to check on Annie and John Latimer. If you need me, call me there."

~ * ~

"You're going to what?" Ronen lowered his head to his hands. "One of these days, Annie, you will tempt me to take a leap off the nearest bridge."

It was now day three of what the hospital staff termed "Annie Watch". The subject of said watch was hanging on to her temper by her toenails. "Don't start with me, Captain."

"I'll start anything I want," he grumbled, taking a vacant chair in the physician's charting room. "You finally agreed to police protection, but insisted they be in street clothes with weapons concealed."

"I did not need," she reminded him for the eight thousandth time, "staff or patients asking why uniformed cops are on me like ants on honey. As it is, my serum paranoia level has risen to toxic range."

"Then," he countered, "you dictated the officers couldn't be inside the ER proper to maintain eyes-on contact."

No matter how thin Annie's patience was wearing, she was determined not to turn bitchy. Ronen had enough to worry about without her smart mouth. Besides, bitchy took too much energy.

"Have to admit, Captain," she said, turning her chair to face his exhausted green eyes, "whomever you picked to guard me is blending very well. I can't tell the cops from the ER's frequent flyers."

He smiled, sort of. "Glad to be of service, Ms. Wolfe." He covered one of her hands with his. "I mean that."

"I sense a 'but' is about to be delivered."

"Not exactly. I'm concerned that you're exhausting yourself by spending what little free time you have at the bedside of an unconscious man."

There was nothing else she could do for John. His lab work and EKG's showed he wasn't any worse—but he wasn't getting any better either. He looked old and pathetic laying there in the bed. Thinner, grayer, defeated. Annie wouldn't leave him. Couldn't leave him.

"What if John wakes up and I'm not there?" *What if he dies and I'm not there?*

"Then why take on the responsibility of running hockey practices? Won't that keep you away from John even more?"

Translation: won't that keep you away from me even more?

My, my, my, she thought, *the man could whine with the best.* "I recall a promise you made not so long ago."

"What, when, and where?"

"My kitchen, the morning after—" Heat rose from her middle with the simple memory of how perfect he looked on that gorgeous sunny day. "In exchange for my continuing to see you, you said you wouldn't bitch, moan, or groan when I had to work."

"Lacing on a pair of skates and zinging hockey pucks across a sheet of ice is not work!"

"Tell that to the New York Rangers. Besides, you know I'm running practices because I need the money."

"I told you I'd pay your moving expenses, Annie."

"And I recall refusing."

"Why is it so hard to accept anything from another person?"

Payback is usually more than I can afford.

She turned to the next patient chart. "Because it is."

"You owe me, Annie."

How lame. "Owe you what?"

"Quiet time, together, alone. Music, food, candlelight."

He stood, reached out to pull her from her chair. His strong hands covered her shoulders. Heat flared instantly. "Do you know how long it's been since we've been... together?"

Down to the hour, minute and second. "Yes."

"Let's do something tonight."

The suggestion was tempting. "As soon as practice is over, I'll come back here to check on John, then—" Her gaze went to the calendar tacked on the wall behind him. "Shoot. I'm on duty in the ER at Margaretville tonight."

At least he waited to slam the charting room door shut before he started bellowing. "Margaretville is forty minutes from here!"

"So?"

"You're exhausted, Ann. You haven't slept in days and—"

"I can't get out of it, Ronen. It's not fair to the staff or the patients."

He loomed over her, anger and frustration simmering in his eyes. "When are things going to the get fair for me? What do I have to do to get your undivided attention? Have a coronary? Blow an ulcer? Come at you swinging a hockey stick?"

By sheer strength of will, Annie contained her temper. "Don't whine, Ronen. It doesn't become you."

He looked ready to choke. "I never whine."

"That's an awfully good imitation, sir."

"Shut up. Just shut up."

"I think that's wise. Who'll be on me for practice?"

He smiled for the first time. Only it wasn't his usual smile. This one was pure evil. "Me. And I plan to make every second absolute torture."

As only he could, she knew. "Big talker."

"What time does it start?"

"Four o'clock."

Ronen checked his watch. "Not enough time to go home, change, and get back here. Guess you'll have to tolerate the grays, Wolfgirl, weapon and all." He gave her a hard, smacking kiss before turning to saunter out the door. "I'll be in the cafeteria when you're ready."

Savoring the arrow-straight back and smooth, long-legged stride, Annie watched Ronen leave the ER. She sighed once before returning to the chart.

A hand on her shoulder interrupted her plans to work up the patient in Treatment Room A for Legionella. "Girlfriend," Amy Hudzinski trilled. "If you give up those buns of brass for med school, you are worse than crazy."

"Could be," Annie murmured, with one last look at the departing brass body part.

"You gonna be a doctor?"

A new team member entered the fray, complete with squeaking wheely bucket and industrial size mop.

Rachel Floyd, the new housekeeper assigned to the ER, fitted in well with the rest of the staff. After only a few days exposure, the young red-haired woman was trading smart remarks with the best of them. "Think you could do something about my face?"

For days, Annie had tried her best to avoid staring at the vicious scar that contorted the left side of Rachel's face. It wasn't horror that captured her attention, but professional curiosity. Somebody had botched the repair. Medical malpractice-type botch.

"I know someone in New York City who's worked miracles with torture victims," she said. "I could give her a call—if you're willing to give it a shot."

She knew very well anyone with such an obvious deformity would jump at the chance to look more normal. Unfortunately, someone who worked at the low-paying job of a hospital housekeeper would be deterred by the cost. Even with the surgeon waving his or her fee, the added hospital costs associated with extensive plastic surgery repairs would be out of sight.

"Nah, thanks anyway," Rachel said. "No sense in wasting good money on something that can't be made any better than it already is. I can see and talk and chew. What more do I need?"

"Must have been a man who fed you that little fairy story," Amy groused.

The mop bucket gave out a terminal shriek of protest. Rachel still had some kinks to iron out in the area of keeping her equipment under control. "Ain't a man out there who don't think he knows what's best for a woman. Pond scum," she grumbled with a hard jerk on the bucket's handle. "All of them."

Amy hooted. "Not all of them. Take Captain Marvel for example."

The housekeeper leaned on the mop, an expression of serious contemplation on her ravaged face. "It's the good looking ones a girl's got to be careful of. Bet Mr. Buns is the opera type. Bore a woman to an early death."

Not the worst way to go, Annie thought.

"Give me a man who appreciates jazz," Rachel announced, swinging back into the rhythm of scrubbing muck-splattered floors. "Now that'd be someone worth trying on for size. If you get my drift."

"Johnny Mathis does it for me," Amy chimed in. "That man's voice twists my panties."

Wasn't that a charming picture, Annie decided. To get her panties off, Captain Marvelous only had to look at her. Mathis was good. Not as good as Ronen.

"Why is that trooper always here anyways?" Rachel asked. "And those jerks out in the waiting room. May be dressed like rednecks, but they're cops all the same. I can smell one a mile away."

Amy's sigh was dramatic in the extreme. "The good captain can't stay away from Wolfgirl. Unfortunately, our Annie doesn't appreciate a man with a tight tush, killer green eyes, and all his own teeth."

Rachel sniffed. "Some of us need to raise our standards."

"Can't get any higher than that," Amy asserted.

"Stick to your guns, Annie," the housekeeper advised. "Don't let some Pepsodent smile in a uniform change your mind."

"I'm trying," Annie said. She really was trying. It just took so much effort, and she was so tired.

"I been watching you. You're going to be a great doc. Take it from me," she said with a gesture for her scars. "Seen them all and heard them all. Ain't a one of them who can hold a candle to you."

The support, from out of nowhere, was just what Annie needed to shore up her flagging spirits. "Thanks, Rach."

She finished writing orders on Treatment A, then came to her feet. "I have a hot date with a bunch of adolescent hockey players. If the buns of brass come back, tell him I went to the john."

As she made her way to the staff bathroom, Annie thought she smelled Ronen's aftershave. The clean citrus fragrance made her think of his threat to make every second of this afternoon's practice absolute torture. "Won't take much," she muttered.

Her hand was on the bathroom doorknob when she was grabbed from behind and hauled into a nearby broom closet. Annie fought like a demon, kicking and gouging—until she smelled citrus again.

Hands pulled her against a hard chest, mashing her nose into a rigidly knotted tie and an expanse of lemon scented skin. She pulled away from Ronen's seeking mouth. "How dare you pull a stunt like this? I ought to kick you in the—"

The threat was abruptly terminated by a knee-knocking kiss. "Sorry. Wasn't thinking." He kissed her again. "Shit, I haven't had a lucid thought in days."

"Is that so?" For some bizarre reason, the thought of Captain Marvelous losing control pleased her to no end.

"I meant what I said before," he promised, then slid his mouth down what little skin was exposed by the vee-neck of her scrub shirt.

Annie's eyes crossed. Twice. "What was that?"

"Being alone with you." His voice dropped to a low, melting croon. "Doing things I've only read about in books."

It didn't take much to conjure a few interesting mental pictures, all of which featured him naked and aroused to mythic proportions. "Care to elaborate—"

His hands were performing the most intricate exam on her costo-vertebral angles. "Use your imagination."

"I am." His CV angles weren't shabby in the least.

He tongued each breast through the scrub top. "You've got too many clothes on."

The *latissimus dorsi* muscles beneath her hands went into spasm. Annie longed for more time to indulge all her senses, feeling and tasting his skin minus the layers of material.

"Jesus, Annie, touch me." He turned her in a half-circle and pinned her against the door before sliding between her thighs. Heat burned a path from her knees to deep in the center of her pelvis. She could feel herself swelling, liquefying. His hands slid beneath her scrub top to roam and tease. Slowly, the top rose, taking the sports bra with it.

His mouth was descending when the doorknob rammed her spine. A muttered profanity from the other side of the door followed. Annie stumbled; if Ronen hadn't caught her, she would have fallen face first into a scrub bucket.

The light switch clicked on. Not only was Annie nearly blinded, but the yelped, "What the hell?" nearly deafened her.

Rachel Floyd squeezed herself, the mop and the bucket into the tiny closet, shut the door behind her, then glowered at the two of them. "Real professional, folks."

"Do you mind?" Ronen clipped.

"Going off duty; gotta put my stuff away," the housekeeper said. "I was you two, I'd find someplace else to do that kind of stuff." She gave Ronen a head to toes perusal. "Not just your buns that're made of brass, fella."

~ * ~

"The hockey team is doing real well," Annie murmured in that soft croon she always used when she sat at John's bedside. Orienting him, she called it. Quiet and matter-of-fact, as if he could hear everything she was saying. Ronen wondered if she would speak to him that way if he were ever is a position similar to John's.

Of course she would. She treated all patients like gold.

She treated him as an afterthought.

"The hospital's been inundated with flowers and plants and balloons." She reached over to smooth back a lock of John's silver hair. "Christopher helped me deliver the flowers to the OB floor and the balloons to pedes. We took the plants to Molly's grave. I didn't think you'd mind." Her voice started to crack.

Ronen touched her shoulder. "Let me take you home."

Annie glanced over her shoulder at him as if he was a minor annoyance. A pesky mosquito. "In a minute."

She'd said that ten minutes ago.

Annie squeezed John's lifeless hand. Bent over it to give his fingers a kiss. "Wake up, John," she said, more directive this time. "Open your eyes and talk to me. I need your thoughts on a couple of patients. I need to know how you'd handle the problems."

In recent days, Ronen listened to all the advice John's doctors had given Annie. Lab work and EKG's were looking good, they said. John's body was healing itself. He would wake up when his body was ready. Until then, they reinforced, she needed to be patient.

Unfortunately, Annie was a few pints low on patience right now, even lower on rest and relaxation. If she didn't slow down and take eight straight hours off, Ronen feared she might collapse.

"This isn't helping him or you, Ann."

"Look, pal, take your stop watch outside. Supervise the nurses pushing pills. I'll leave when I'm damned good and ready."

Which couldn't be too soon for him. The smells alone were enough to gag a maggot. The human body might be a miracle, but the odors from secretions it gave off made him nauseous. Nothing, however, came close to the eye-watering *eau de disinfectant.*

The smells were one thing; the Spike Jones concert outside the door was worse. A piece of hospital machinery gave out a spine-breaking howl. "Turn the wheels the other way, Rachel!" a voice yelled over the screeching din.

"I'm trying. The bucket won't cooperate."

Between the smells and the noise, if he didn't get out of here soon, Ronen was going to lose it. "I'm taking a walk," he muttered. "You'll be safe enough here. Don't go anywhere until I'm back."

"Pay no attention to him, John" Annie offered blithely. "Captain Marvelous has some idiotic idea that I might be in danger." She glared at Ronen over her shoulder. "He doesn't need to hear this."

"Why don't you say that a little louder? Maybe put it over the PA system? Let everyone in the hospital know what's going on."

"Bite me, Marvelic."

"I'm afraid of catching something."

"Christ Almighty. What does a man have to do to get some rest in this joint?"

Ronen stared at the man laying on the bed, certain he was hearing things. Annie yelped, "John?"

"Is there a fourth person in the room?"

For all John's bitching and moaning, Ronen felt his heart swell in relief.

"You're awake!" Annie crowed, taking the old man's hand again. She bowed her head to the mattress, bawling like a baby. "Thank you, God. Thank you, thank you, thank you."

Not sure what to do, Ronen said, "Let me get one of the nurses." He leaned around Annie to touch John's hand. "Welcome back to the living, my friend."

"No need to call one of those harpies," Latimer grumped. "Let them figure things out for themselves."

"John," Annie admonished. "They need to notify your doctor."

"So he can poke and prod some more? Treat me like an object instead of a person? Bullshit."

"John—"

"And don't think I'm not aware of how much time you've been spending here, little girl. Marvelic, take her home, put her to bed."

A nurse entered the room to perform one of those regular hourly checks on the monitors attached to John's chest. "We're awake, I see."

"I am, don't know about you," he muttered, then closed his eyes. "Get out of here, Annie."

"Not yet," she said. "I need to make sure this isn't a figment of my imagination."

John opened his eyes to stare directly at the hovering nurse. "If she's not out of here by the time I count to three, tie her down and give her a high colonic."

The nurse hooted. "He's awake."

"Sharp observation," John grumbled, then closed his eyes with a grown. "Bunch of harpies."

Annie conceded. "Okay, I'll go—for now." She leaned over to kiss his weathered cheek. "I'll be back, old man."

"Not too soon," he muttered over a yawn. "What does a man have to do to get some sleep around this joint?"

~ * ~

"I'm a little tired," Annie admitted as she sank onto her bed. The slur of exhaustion in her voice was unmistakable.

"Can't imagine why," Ronen mused.

She squirmed, then fidgeted some more, unable to find a comfortable position. Never had she hurt in so many places at one time. Her lower back ached like a sore tooth. Her arms felt like lead. To even think about raising a hand to rub at the stabbing pain over her eyebrow took Herculean effort.

"Wake me in two hours. I've got—" What did she have? She couldn't remember where she was supposed to be later on, but knew it had to be important.

"Two hours," he murmured in that soft, silky tone she'd missed so much over the madness of the past five days. "Whatever you say,

Ann." He pulled off her sneakers and socks. "After a nap, you'll be ready to fight the next battle."

"Fine." One syllable words were all she could manage at the moment. Now, if she could find a comfortable position.

Her scrub pants and shirt slid off her body beneath his magic fingers. "You need rest and a well-balanced meal, Annie. While hope does not soar that you'll do what I suggest; I can always dream."

"Right."

A lightweight blanket fell over her body, covering her from chin to toes. "You've not been doing yourself or John any good by running yourself ragged. I don't care what the damn movers charge. Take it from me, money isn't everything."

"Nope."

"What if you collapsed? Who would sit with John? Who would drive the ICU nurses nuts? Who would keep that adolescent herd of hormones-on-blades in check?"

"You."

She stuck out a hand, searching for the unicorn that held permanent residence on the nightstand. The crystal figurine always comforted her, helped her to fall asleep. Clutching it in her fingers, she let out a deep, cleansing sigh.

It wasn't enough. Not nearly enough. She knew he was standing there, watching her. She could smell him. "Ronen?"

His lips touched her forehead. "Hmm?"

"Maybe sex would help."

"Sorry, I'm not into making love with dead bodies."

"Then... could you hold me until I fall asleep?"

The mattress dipped. His arms came around her chest and belly, holding her against his body. That wonderful, comforting chest. His breath stirred her hair. "Sleep, baby."

"I will. Now."

~ * ~

Ronen didn't leave her immediately. Couldn't leave her. He understood that. Not now, not ever. She was dead weight in his arms. He didn't care.

They both needed rest. They both needed a lot of things. Top on the list was to solve the murders so he could get on to more important matters of convincing Annie to accept him as a permanent part of her life.

Small town life was beginning to grow on him. He made his rounds faithfully every morning, chatting up store owners and customers. Folks were beginning to open up to him. The Jackson's were celebrating a new grandbaby. Mrs. Sanko was expecting again. Abner Harbaugh was thinking of expanding his operation into the next county—if he could find a parcel of land at a price he was willing to pay.

The townspeople trusted Ronen with the small stuff, but not what he was after. Not the big stuff. No one speculated, in his presence anyway, on Junior Harbaugh's arrest and subsequent confinement in the county jail. After viewing the photographs at the Preliminary Hearing, the judge refused to set bail.

Junior's attorney wisely requested his client be kept in solitary confinement. The longer the gofer stayed in jail, Ronen knew, the higher his friends' anxiety would rise over the potential of Junior running his mouth. As they might try to silence him in one fashion or another, solitary was the safest place for the little mutt.

Annie sighed, then burrowed deeper into his arms. Nuzzling the back of her neck, Ronen inhaled the scent of lilacs and felt a smile ease the tense muscles of his face and jaw. For a few hours, he put the case aside and enjoyed the feel of Annie Wolfe in his arms.

Until blood-curdling screams brought him straight up in bed.

Thirteen

"Tee bore, run!" Annie screamed. Her voice dropped to a low, keening wail. "Let me out, Greg. Please." She thrashed wildly, striking out at whomever or whatever held her prisoner. "Aaarrghh! Let... me... out!"

Ronen caught her fist in one hand, then deflected a boney knee before it ended all hopes for more children. "Annie," he said, taking pains to keep his voice low and calm. "Wake up, honey."

Even though her eyes opened, he understood immediately she wasn't looking at him, but a terror only she could see.

"Please," she whimpered. "No more."

"No more," he whispered.

With that simple promise, she rolled to one side, curling into a tight, impervious ball.

As soon as he was assured hers was a deep, natural sleep, Ronen left the bed. In deference to the relentless heat wave, the only clothes he could tolerate were a pair of cut-off shorts. After a quick search and destroy mission on both his and Annie's refrigerators, he pulled together a semblance of dinner. When Annie woke, she'd need nourishment.

It would be a long night, he vowed. And nothing would stop him from learning what was behind the nightmare he'd witnessed.

~ * ~

Annie woke slowly, brought to a fully wakeful state by the delicious smell of grilling meat—along with clear, convincing messages from her bladder.

On her way to the bathroom, she glanced at the digital clock on her dresser, and stopped dead in her tracks. Five o'clock!

Hockey practice started an hour ago. Disappointment in the kids' eyes would hurt more than any snotty comments from Joe Murphy who'd probably want to kill her.

Out of sheer bodily need, she hit the bathroom before facing a greater, more dangerous opponent: Ronen, the only person to witness one of her nightmares.

Captain Marvelous was laying in wait when she walked out of the bathroom. "We need to talk."

"I'm late for practice," she said, looking him straight in the eye. "Because you didn't wake me up."

"Joe filled in for you."

Better to talk about hockey than the nightmare, she reasoned to herself, certain he'd want to dissect it down to the last scream, whimper and moan. Resolve to avoid all discussions crumbled beneath the caring and compassion on his face. "Why did you call him, Ronen?"

A shrug of those impossibly wide shoulders captured her attention. She couldn't take her eyes off the washboard muscles and light dusting of chest hair. And, of course, he smelled good enough to attack.

"You needed sleep more than practice. Joe agreed." He tapped her nose with the bowl of the wooden spoon in his hand. "As you're so fond of saying, it's no big whoop."

"I made a promise," she muttered, putting only half her heart into it. Those long, lean legs were infinitely more fascinating than shots on goal and defensive drills.

"Hungry?" he asked.

"Starved."

"Tough."

Dragging her gaze back to his face, she said, "Beg pardon?"

"Dinner won't be ready for another hour." He reached out a hand to stroke the side of her face. "Guess we'll have to find something to keep us occupied till it's done."

"Guess we will."

~ * ~

Deep into the night, long after they were both sated on food and other things, Annie was finally able to relax in Ronen's arms. Comfortably somnolent and just ready to drop off, she traced a thumb over the unicorn in her usual pre-slumber ritual.

"Tell me about it," he said.

Playing dumb, she said, "The unicorn? Barbara gave it to me the day I graduated from PA school. Told me it would bring me everything I wanted in life if I trusted in myself—and its magical powers."

"I understand the unicorn is a symbol of chastity and fierceness. Both fit you to a T."

"I don't know about the chastity part."

"I do." Ronen covered her hand with his, keeping her fingers tightly wrapped around the figurine. "Who or what is a tee bore?"

The dregs of her past were the last thing Annie wanted to share with Ronen. With only a week to go before she moved to Syracuse, every second they had left was precious. Each moment with him would have to last for the rest of her life. She chose *not* to spend the rest of that life with the picture of Ronen's face after he learned where and what she came from.

"It's nothing. Just a bad dream."

"That was more than a bad dream, Ann. You were fighting for your life."

He tilted up her chin with a free hand, forcing her to look at him. "Tell me."

Despite her heart slamming against her ribs, Annie stretched like a well-fed cat. "Like many people," she said in an attempt at blithe uncaring, "I have the occasional ugly dream. Luckily, I don't remember them."

Ronen's fingers tightened imperceptibly on her jaw. "You can't lie for shit."

Some of what she'd said was true. She couldn't remember the majority of the nightmare. For that she was grateful. "Tibor was my brother."

"*Was?*"

"He and my other brother Greg died a number of years ago."

"I'm sorry."

This next part was true. "I'm not."

Ronen dropped his hand to her arm. "Sounds like you'd rather not talk about it."

"There's really nothing to say," Annie promised with all her heart. "Ronen, my childhood was not something out of a TV sitcom. Leave it alone. We'll both be better off for it."

"For now," he said. "But someday—"

Hopefully someday will never come. "Perhaps," she agreed, if only to seal the bargain. "Maybe someday."

Ronen opened her hand, took the unicorn between his fingers, examining it with his usual focused concentration. He ran a thumb over the tattered ribbon that once suspended the crystal in the turret window. "This needs to be replaced."

"I keep meaning to do it, but never seem to find the time. When I do have time, I never remember."

"Let me take it," he said, cradling her against his chest. "I have tomorrow off, but the next time I'm on rounds, I'll stop by the What Knotte Shoppe and pick up a piece of ribbon for it."

"I have tomorrow off, too. Let's go together."

"Deal." He rolled her to her back. "But for now—"

"Are you insane?" she shrieked. "I can't possibly summon the strength to make love again."

His kiss silenced her. "Have you ever played cut-throat Monopoly?"

"Not that I recall."

"Chris and I will teach you. Tomorrow is Saturday; there won't be any hockey practice. We'll both be able to rest and regroup. It'll be fun."

The come-hither look on his face told her just how much fun they might have. "With Christopher? I don't think so."

"I mean afterwards."

"What happens afterward?"

He leaned into her ear to whisper exactly what she'd have to do to him. If she lost.

"What if I win?"

"I'm yours to do with what you want."

"Better take your vitamins, pal."

"Promises, promises."

~ * ~

The call from Junior Harbaugh's attorney came just as the three of them were cleaning up after a late breakfast. Chris and Annie had teased and kidded throughout the entire meal, hurling bets and dares at each other over the upcoming Monopoly game. Ronen couldn't recall a time when he'd been so happy. The phone call spoiled it all.

"I have to go," he said, glancing quickly at Annie. "I'm sorry."

"Aw, Dad. Can't it wait?"

Junior Harbaugh's lawyer sounded frantic, claiming someone had gotten to his client. Junior was scared spitless and ready to talk. "There's a problem at the county jail with one of the prisoners. On the way, I have to stop at the barracks for his paperwork."

He looked to Annie for support. "I won't be long. I promise."

"The sooner he leaves, the sooner he gets back, Chris," she said. "You can help me put munchies together for this big whooping game." Behind Chris' back she aimed a sultry look in Ronen's direction. "Since I plan to win big. I'll need... fortification."

The promise in her eyes went straight to his gut, then took a sharp turn south. "I'll keep that in mind." The interview with Junior would break the land speed record.

Annie grabbed his T-shirt, bringing him close for a hard, wet kiss. "Make it snappy, Captain. I tend to get very demanding."

~ * ~

For a Saturday afternoon nearing change of shift, the sub-station was oddly quiet. Usually there were a couple of troopers hanging around, shooting the breeze while waiting for their shift to end or begin. Ronen told himself it was foolish to be so jumpy. His footsteps echoed off the walls of the empty hallway as he made his way toward his office in the back of the building.

The door opened at the touch of his hand. "What the hell?" He moved immediately to the locked file in the corner.

By outward appearances the four-drawer cabinet appeared untouched. Except that the tell-tale, a strand of hair he'd secured to the edge of the drawer before he left yesterday, was gone. "Shit."

Keeping his emotions under tight control, Ronen clumsily inserted the first key into the lock on the front of the cabinet. Then he stretched around to the back to take care of a second security lock. As extra precaution, he'd installed the back lock himself several weeks ago.

There was only one back key; he kept it in his wallet. Someone had tried to get into the file. They failed.

Still, he couldn't control the deep sigh of relief when he found the Harbaugh file where he'd left it—buried beneath last month's activity reports and assignment rosters.

Ronen yanked out every folder relating to the murders. The aborted break-in reinforced the necessity for added security. If he had to take his notes home to keep them safe, so be it. He tucked the files beneath one arm and proceeded back down the dimly lighted corridor. He'd hit the jail, cool the attorney's jets, take Junior's statement, then get his ass home.

Home. To Annie.

As he approached the front of the building, he had the strangest sensation that he could hear Annie's voice. Can't be, he reasoned. She's home with Chris, waiting for me.

"Ooh, Captain."

It *was* Annie; he'd know that moan anywhere. Ronen stopped. Listened intently.

There it was again. He heard her laugh as she teased him about his underwear. An image of her kitchen flashed into his mind. He moved closer toward the sound of her voice.

"I bet there's a whole herd of horny women out there willing to lay out some major bucks for a cop calendar. Would you pose for Mr. April, Captain Marvel—that being my birthday month and all?"

His garbled response came through the door of the break room just ahead. "*I don't pose for pictures, in any style of dress.*"

It all made sense. Bizarre, sickening sense. Every step he'd taken, every move he'd made, had been monitored. That explained the missing Nohmensville PD reports and 'unavailable' personnel files on Randy Terrance and Bobbie Claun.

For how long had it gone on? How many bugs were there? And where had they been placed?

"*It's your turn for a complete physical exam.*"

Rage coiled like a snake ready to strike.

Standing outside the break room door, he heard the gruff demand, "Where in hell did you get a copy of that?"

Distinctive, unmistakable, the voice of betrayal ignited Ronen's rage into a full, rolling boil.

"The boss made me copies."

He didn't know the second voice, but recognized it as that of a younger man.

"Said I should listen, maybe pick up a few pointers to keep the wife happy in bed."

"For Christ's sake, what possessed you to bring it here?"

"What's the big tickle? Nobody's here but you and me. Marvelic is on a day off; he'll never know." The younger one went on, "Wait'll you hear the next bit. Wolfgirl calls him Captain Marvelous and, baby, he's been keeping her on her knees—literally."

"Hell, I didn't think she was into men."

A lewd chuckle erupted. "From the sounds of it, Marvelic is into her. Big time."

It went against all his training and experience, was contrary to everything he'd preached to younger officers about personal safety. Ronen no longer cared about rules, regulations, or procedures.

He drew his weapon from the holster at the small of his back and kicked open the door. Trooper Kevin Dolan jumped in surprise.

Major Jim Valetta jumped higher.

~ * ~

"That's a begonia leaf," Chris offered. "Not a weed."

"Begonia, shmagonia," Annie muttered and kept on yanking what she figured were the ugliest things God ever created.

"Stella will kill both of us if she loses even one bud."

Annie gave him her best I-doubt-it look. "Me, maybe. The woman thinks the sun rises and sets with you, pally. I doubt she'd lift a finger to you."

To pass the time waiting for Ronen to return, she'd taken to puttering in the landlady's flowers, pulling deadheads and yanking weeds. Chris and she had been at it for well over two hours. *Where is Ronen? What's taking so long?*

If anything, Chris was rapidly becoming more annoyed with his father's absence. "Wish he could have spent one whole day doing nothing," he grumbled. "Dad doesn't relax enough."

She grinned and pulled another intruder from the neighboring patch of petunias. Ronen had relaxed just fine last night. She'd made sure of it. "That's why he's so successful at what he does, honey. Captain Marvel never gives up."

"Never giving up put Dr. Latimer straight into an ICU bed," he retorted. "As much as those machines and gizmos fascinate me, I don't want that to happen to my father."

"I'll keep my eye on him after you leave for school." She would, she amended silently, for as long as she remained in town.

Leaning back on folded legs, Chris squinted into the darkening sky. TV weathermen had been forecasting thunder showers for the past several days. So far, none had materialized. Annie wasn't holding her breath for a promised break in the heat.

"You like him," Chris said. "Don't you?"

"A lot." *More than a lot.*

"Are you going to do something about it?"

"I have a career to think about, Chris. A whole new life that doesn't include—"

"A home," he stated. "Family. Kids."

"Don't go there, Christopher."

"Seems to me a girl—I mean, woman—could find a way to do both. If she wanted it bad enough." His vibrant blue gaze bored a hole into her heart. "If she cared enough."

So like his father, she thought. "Chris—"

"You're a stubborn woman, Annie Wolfe."

She came to her feet, wiping her hands on the seat of her jeans. "I'd never deny that description," she said. "I'm going inside to put some sandwiches together. You can grab chips for yourself, fresh veggies for His Highness, or you can sit here feeling sorry for yourself."

"Aw, geez," he muttered. "You win. This time."

Where is Ronen, she wondered again. *What's keeping him?*

After she and Chris washed their hands at the spigot at the side of the house, Annie remembered she'd left her work bag in the gazebo before she went to see John at the hospital. Since the bag deserved cleaning out and replenishing, she said, "Go on ahead. I'll meet you upstairs."

Chris opened the back door, then stopped. After a moment, he turned to her with a grin. "Dad's back. He must have parked on the street, but I can hear him talking to Miz Grover in her kitchen."

"We'd better get moving then."

Mounting the steps into the gazebo, Annie found the contents of the ditty bag strewn across the wood planks. "One of these days, I'm going to throw half this crap out," she vowed as she stuffed a flashlight, pepper spray, and stethoscope—along with any number of drug inserts, disposable gloves, and rolls of non-allergenic tape back into the canvas satchel.

A puck from the last hockey practice had somehow ended up in the bag. She didn't have time to question how it got there, only knew it needed to go back into the trunk of her car. She tucked it into the front pocket of her jeans until she had time to put it away where it belonged.

She was coming down the gazebo steps, slinging the work bag over her shoulder, when Chris staggered out the back door of the mansion. Even from a distance, she could see he was pale as death, eyes wide in surprise, or shock. Stella followed him onto the stoop.

Alarmed at the boy's obvious distress, Annie took a quick step forward. "What's wrong?"

"Dad—"

Stella's cheerful answer allayed her anxiety. "Nothing's wrong, dearie. Everything's fine."

"Annie, get—" Chris pleaded.

Without warning, Stella gave him a hard shove down the steps. He landed on his knees on the sidewalk. When he didn't move, she barked, "Get up, you little snot," and shoved a gun into the boy's flank.

"Jesus, Mary and Joseph, Stella! What are you doing?" Annie raced toward her and Chris.

The gun stopped her. "Cleaning things up for that fool Jim Valetta," Stella breezed—as if waving a pistol at people was a regular part of her activities of daily living.

"Clean up what for Major Valetta?" She took another step. "What's going on?"

Stella waved her back with the gun. "Jimmy was all right for some things, screwing with the computers, hiding files and such." She kicked at Chris with the toe of her spike-heeled sandal. "If this one's daddy hadn't nosed into things, we could have cleaned the lot of those filthy animals out of town."

Filthy animals?

"Annie," Chris moaned. "She's got a tape of you and Dad."

His cheek split beneath a rap from the barrel of Stella's weapon. "I told you to get up," she shrieked, jerking him to his feet. "Stupid, stupid boy. Coming into a body's home without knocking. You'll pay for that."

"Put the gun down," Annie ordered.

"Too bad, Christopher," Stella said in a weird sing-song croon. "I'd taken a fancy to you."

She whipped the gun in Annie's direction. "It's all your fault, missy. Preaching high and mighty ideas about civil rights, equal treatment under the law to that scum when not one of them could speak English. Dirty, filthy animals, spreading their legs, enticing my poor Henry to his death."

God in heaven, Annie thought, Stella was in on the murders. She was *part* of the murders.

The woman who'd treated her like a daughter, fussed over her when she worked too hard, who cheered and hollered louder than anyone at Nuggetts' games, was capable of such depravity. Annie wanted to scream. She wanted to throw up.

By Stella's own statements, the evidence was right there in front of her. Annie still couldn't fathom the depth of her hatred, the lengths she would go, to take revenge against innocent women.

Stella turned the gun back onto the trembling Chris. Annie's fear faded. In its place rose a tidal wave of maternal outrage. Poking her hand into the pocket of her jeans, her fingers closed around the hockey puck. "Touch him again, it'll be the last thing you do."

"You're as bad as that nosy social worker," the landlady sneered. "Butting into things that were none of her concern." She pointed to a spot on the sidewalk in front of Chris. "Move."

He looked at Annie with wild, pleading eyes.

"Kid?" Annie murmured, slowly withdrawing her hand from her pocket.

"Y-y-yeah?"

"Remember the day we met?" Her fingers tightened, wrist poised.

"Uh huh."

"I told you a woman gets herself out of her own jams?"

"Yeah."

"*Duck!*"

Chris went down as Annie winged the puck into Stella's chest. Wordlessly, the older woman toppled like a sack of grain. The pistol spun out of her hand and landed in a nearby rose bush.

Annie cut the distance between her and Chris in less than a second, flipped Stella onto her belly, pinning her to the grass with one knee. She grabbed the woman's wrists, motioning for Chris to come closer. "She can't hurt you now."

"Aw, I know that. It's just—"

"I know, baby." She tightened her hold, wishing the old bat would struggle. "Get my work bag, please."

"I can't breathe. Get off me!"

Annie took a few bounces on the scrawny buttocks beneath her knees—just for grins. "If you can talk, you can breathe."

"Will that hold her?" Chris asked as she used a roll of tape from the bag to wrap Stella's wrists in multiple layers.

Annie grinned. "The more she struggles, the tighter this stuff gets. Go into the house. There's some clothesline on the service porch. After we tie her up, call 911. Tell your father to get his ass home. I need him."

I need him. The thought came as natural as breathing.

"Annie," the boy stammered. "Miz Grover—she was listening to you and Dad while you guys were—"

Stella moved suddenly, and almost succeeded in bucking Annie off. Almost doesn't count. "I'll fix you, bitch! See if I don't."

"You're really scaring me," Annie advised. To Chris she said, "We'll discuss everything later. For now, it's important to be sure this witch can't go anywhere."

"Yes, ma'am." He took off into the house.

After Chris was out of earshot, Annie leaned over Stella's shoulder. The faces of her dead friends, the hideous injuries she'd seen on their bodies, flashed before her eyes: Maria Salvado's torn, bloodied mouth. The broken teeth Annie had to pull from the back of her throat in a futile attempt to establish an airway. Luba Sanko's arms, so bruised and limp, even in death it was clear every muscle and tendon had been ripped to shreds. Kathy Baker. Thank God she'd never seen her body. Gossip about the position they'd found her in was bad enough.

And Barb. Ronen said she'd looked like the rest of the victims. Annie couldn't think about it. Not now. She jerked Stella's elbows toward her shoulders, giving her a brief taste of her own medicine. "Give me a reason to hurt you, old woman."

"Bitch."

"Lady, and I use that term very loosely, I am the woman your mama warned you about."

Fourteen

"Hold still, baby," Annie murmured as she finished cleansing the laceration on Chris' face.

"I'd like to say, 'aw, shucks, ma'am; it's just a scratch' but it hurts like hell."

"Almost done." Holding a butterfly dressing over his cheek, she said, "Last chance, my friend. We can still go the ER for a plastic surgeon's opinion."

Chris looked to his father.

Ronen shook his head. "It's your face; it's your choice."

"I'll pass," Chris said. "I don't mind watching others get sewn up, but nobody's coming at my face with a needle and thread."

"What'd I miss?"

A new country heard from, Annie thought with a groan. She glanced up from first aide duties and gaped. Rachel Floyd, the housekeeper from the hospital, stood there with a satisfied grin on her face.

"Aunt Rachel!" Chris yelled. "Wait till I tell you what happened."

"Fine time for you to take a day off, sister dear," Ronen sniped.

Speechless, Annie's head whipped back and forth between the three people in her kitchen.

"Bite me, Marvelic." Rachel pulled off her shoulder harness and slung it over the back of the nearest chair. "Man, it looks like dollar-doubler day at the supermarket outside. Cops all over the place, reporters, a bunch of hockey players wanting to know if the Wolfgirl can come out and play."

She stuck a hand out to Annie. "Nice to finally meet you up front and personal. Heard you nailed one of the bad guys with a hockey puck. Good going."

"You're the US Marshall?" Annie's mind could never move as fast as Rachel's mouth. She simply took it all in, putting the pieces together while Ronen's sister went on talking.

"I'm on extended leave because of this." She raised a hand to her cheek. "Getting more than a little bored, sitting around staring at the four walls, twiddling my thumbs. So when the big guy called and said he needed help, I couldn't get down here fast enough." She reached over to give Ronen's shoulder a squeeze. "Nothing's too good for my big brother. Even if he is a world-class jerk sometimes."

"Rachel," the brother in question sighed.

"Can't say I'm sorry this one's over," Rachel advised in an aside to Annie. "If I had to sling that mop one more day, I swear I would have done some major damage to the next fool who mucked up my nice clean floors."

"Now, Rach," Ronen teased. "Perhaps you needed a little more experience. Who knows, you might be on the brink of a whole new career."

"You'll never live that long, darling," she promised, taking a seat next to Chris. "Let me take a look at your boo-boo, kiddo. Give it my expert opinion." After a moment she quipped, "That sucker is gonna impress the hell out of all those Cornell women."

Chris blushed. "Aw, geez. Don't tell Nana, okay?"

"Probably already knows," Rachel said. "It's called Nana Radar."

Ronen took his sister's hand in his. "I haven't taken the time to thank you properly, Rach. Annie didn't want someone who would stick out in a crowd and I needed somebody I could trust to keep her safe."

Annie smiled to herself. He had listened to her. "She stuck out all right, only not as a cop."

"Nicest compliment I ever got," Rachel said.

"We're done here, Chris," Annie determined once she was certain the butterflies would keep the wound edges approximated. "Be sure to keep ice on it. It'll keep the scarring down."

"Trooper Johnson is downstairs in Miz Grover's apartment, son," Ronen said. "Waiting to take your statement."

"C'mon, kid," Rachel said. "I'll hold your hand while you talk to the big bad copper. If he pulls out a rubber hose, I'll deck him."

Annie waited until she heard the thundering feet take the stairs to the first floor. "Thank you."

Ronen shrugged. "Just doing my job."

"You didn't have to bring your sister down here just to ease my concerns."

His features darkened with purpose. "I'd trust Rach with my life. She needed something to keep herself busy." He took her hand in his. "I hope you and she will become friends."

"We'll see."

Now that that was over with, Annie decided to deal with other, equally important matters. Boy, would she deal with them. "Is it true?"

At least he had the grace to squirm. "Is what true?"

"You took Dolan and Valetta down on your own without calling for backup?"

"They're in custody. Doesn't matter how."

She waved unused bandages in his face. "You're next in line for first aide for doing something as dumb as that."

Rick Thurrell breezed into the kitchen, dropping several dime-size buttons on the table. "Okay, Cap. Your place and office are officially debugged. "Want me to start in here next?"

Annie stared at Thurrell. "Love the outfit. What's the box for?"

Rick glanced down at the vibrant orange and green plaid shorts and white tee shirt that proclaimed *Women Love Me... Fish Fear Me* and shrugged. "Sorry I missed the action. Heard you took old Stella down with a hockey puck, Wolfgirl. The Rangers call you yet?"

"Sorry. The Mets beat them to the punch."

Ronen's heart dropped to his knees when she repeated, "What's the box for?"

He started to explain. "Annie, something came up during—"

"Gonna debug you, Wolfgirl," Thurrell chirped. "Where you want me to start?"

"*Debug?*"

Horror made slow creeping movements over her face. She glared at the table with what could only be described as disgust. "What are those things, Sergeant?"

Figuring truth, fast and brutal, was the way she'd want it, Ronen said, "Listening devices. Stella had Jim Valetta install them in my apartment and—"

Back ramrod straight, fingers fisting into a white-knuckled grip, Annie looked at Rick. "I take it you found them in Ronen's apartment?"

Thurrell stammered, "Uh, jeez, Annie, I figured he wouldda told you by now." He gave Ronen an imploring look. "Why didn't you tell her?"

Her bark cut the air like a surgical blade. "Tell me, Mr. Thurrell. Now."

The metal box in Rick's hand began to tweak. As he moved closer to the table, tweaking escalated to a steady hum. When he slid the box beneath the table, the hum went to an ear-piercing scream. Rick brought his hand back out and dropped a button on the table. The scream reverted back to a hum.

"I'm waiting," Annie said. Ronen sat by, helpless.

Despite his casual mode of dress, he was proud when Rick went into full alert: stiff posture, clipped tone of voice, detached features. "I found devices in the Captain's kitchen, living room and bedroom."

She nodded. Just once. "You have reason to believe there could be devices such as those—" Her chin jutted toward the buttons on the table. Ronen instinctively covered them with one hand.

"Yes, ma'am. I do."

With another quick nod, Annie said, "Then do it. Start with the bathroom."

"Aw, jeez, Annie," Rick groaned. "No one would be sick enough to—"

"Do it," she snapped.

Rick looked to Ronen.

"Do it," he directed.

Ronen followed the two into the living room. Annie leaned against the wall outside the bathroom door, eyes closed, while Rick Thurrell did his thing inside the cramped space. Within seconds, the screams emanating from the box seemed to shake the walls of her apartment. She made no move, no sound. Ronen's heart broke for the tears sliding down her sculpted cheeks.

When Rick came out, Annie said, "Do it again. Please."

"Annie, there's nothing more in there."

Her jaws tensed, as if she might shatter at any moment. Ronen was reminded of rape victims he'd interviewed immediately after their assaults. "Again," he told Rick.

Thurrell retreated once more into the bathroom. This time, he closed the door. And once again, distinct screams breached the heavy barrier of the wood door. Annie looked at him with such disbelief, he felt his spirit rent into tiny pieces. "I'm so sorry."

"I don't blame you. It's them I hate."

Rick opened the door. He walked to Ronen, dropping two more buttons into his outstretched palm. "Sorry, Cap."

"Don't worry about it. Do the bedroom next. And—"

"Three scans. My word on it."

Annie launched herself off the wall. "Finished in there, Sergeant?"

"All done, Wolfgirl."

"You're a prince." She touched his shoulder, then went into the bathroom, closing the door behind her. The lock's click was as loud, as permanent, as the bars on a maximum security cell.

"Got your work cut out for you, sir," Thurrell offered.

"Tell me about it."

~ * ~

Ronen retreated to the kitchen, listening for two different sounds: water pounding from the shower head and the screams from Rick's magic box. After a while, they intermingled.

The longer the screaming continued, the lower his heart sank.

And the shower kept on running.

Rick took his time, coming out every so often to drop more buttons on the kitchen table.

"How many did you find in my bedroom?" Ronen asked, mainly because he couldn't tolerate not knowing.

"Four."

"Doesn't matter," Ronen muttered, raking his fingers through his hair. "We never did anything in there."

"Cap," Thurrell interjected, "I don't need to know this."

Partly because of Ronen's desire to keep Christopher isolated from his personal life, mostly because the mood only seemed to strike him and Annie when they were in her place, they'd never made love in his apartment. He'd always appreciated her non-verbal acceptance of his need to keep his sex life separate from his life as a parent.

Now, he could recognize that it had been more than that. Certainly, there'd been plenty of opportunity for Annie to take the role of initiator wherever they were. She'd only assumed it when they were at her place, on her turf. Almost as if his apartment, and Chris' presence, whether his son was physically absent or not, somehow made his home sacrosanct. To make love in his apartment would have been a violation. If he loved Annie for no other reason, it was because of her regard for his son.

Whenever Ronen put the moves on her, she always laughed. He could see, now, it diverted him from acting on those moves until they were in her place. Once they got there, hell, he wouldn't have cared where they were. As long as he could feel her satin skin sliding against his, experience that indescribable sensation of being inside her, muscles contracting around him, they could've been in the middle of Main Street at high noon—as long as Annie was in his arms.

The loud click of the lock on the bathroom door instantly brought him back to reality. Annie needed to work through this, on her own time, in her own way. There was nothing he could do for her now, other than be there for her when she was ready to talk.

If that time ever came.

Thurrell mumbled, "I can't tell you how sorry I am that things came down to this. Hope the DA goes for the needle on all of them."

"Thanks."

Rick dropped several more buttons onto the table. "That's the last of them. Written in stone," he said, as if to offer Ronen reassurance, then raised one palm. "I ran scans on Miz G's place before I started on yours. All the stuff is confiscated."

Disgust, as well as ire, threatened to suffocate him. "I don't care what it takes. Get search warrants for homes, garages, workshops, dog houses, outhouses. Any place Dolan or Valetta had room to stash recording devices or tapes." Ronen looked at his sergeant. "Anything you find, bring to me. Nobody else."

"Gotcha, Cap." Rick turned to leave, then said, "What'll you do with them?"

His goal was to protect Annie at all costs. The DA had already made a solemn promise the tapes would never leave his possession, and that no one but he would listen to them.

Ronen wasn't comforted by solemn vows. If the DA had done his job and stepped in immediately, fewer women would be dead—and the woman he loved wouldn't now be scrubbing herself raw. With the added possibility that copies of the tapes were currently circulating among the local population of perverts, he had to protect Annie at all costs. And damn the consequences.

"Cap?" Thurrell repeated. "You wouldn't destroy—"

"I don't know what I'm going to do."

"You need to know," Thurrell said after a moment. "I'd do just about anything to make the Wolfgirl feel better."

Sensing the worst was yet to come, Ronen said, "So would I."

~ * ~

Annie couldn't get clean enough. Couldn't erase the invasive feeling of violation.

"Bastards," she muttered, as she scrubbed herself again, even after the shower turned from tepid to frigid. She didn't care anymore. Nothing would ever make her feel clean.

"Bastards."

Glancing down, she discovered her toes were close to cyanotic. She had to get out of the tub and warm up. Would she ever feel warm again? Safe again? Clean again?

She doubted it.

Would Ronen understand?

Yes, she admitted, he probably would. Not that she was in any mood to discuss her feelings. Not that she'd ever let him, or anyone, say or do anything to her inside this... prison again.

Someone might hear it.

Someone might get their rocks off listening.

Acceptance would always be there on Marvel's beautiful face. Understanding and concern would caution his touch.

"Shit on a shingle." Annie didn't need concern, acceptance, or understanding. What she needed was for everyone to leave her the hell alone. She needed to get the hell out of Dodge and never look back. To hell with John Latimer's offer of the practice. To hell with everything.

Illiana Lupo was a person in her own right. Worth infinitely more than an object for someone's pleasure. And screw everyone who believed differently.

~ * ~

The Deputy Superintendent for Personnel phoned while Ronen was pulling dinner together for Chris and Rachel.

"Congratulations, Marvelic," the Sup's voice boomed.

"Thank you, sir."

In typical fashion, the man relayed his thoughts in quick, AK-47 type bursts. "Yes, well. Albany will send someone to cover Valetta's spot. Don't expect you to wear those shoes, too."

Ronen tried to interject thanks; the sup continued. "Take a few days. Consider your options. Offer still holds. Any assignment. Any questions? Good. Let me know."

"Thank you, sir," Ronen mumbled into the droning receiver.

"Anything important, Dad?"

With a thought for the woman in the apartment across the hall, Ronen said, "Only the rest of my life."

Rachel took the phone from his hand, placing it back in its nest. "How long has Annie been locked in her apartment?"

"Feels like hours."

His formerly loving sister exploded, then got in his face. "Christ on a sidecar! Has it entered your mind to knock on her door? Ask how she's doing? Is there's anything she needs? *From you?*"

"Annie will come out when she's ready."

"And baby, the rain might fall."

"What do you want me to do, Rach?"

"If victim stupidity was an affirmative defense, I'd shoot you dead and no jury in the world would convict me."

Ronen raked at his hair with both hands. "Give me a break, Rach. I know what she's going through. I feel the same. When she's ready, she'll talk to me."

"Captain Marvel, you don't know shit."

At wit's end, he muttered, "So tell me what I don't know shit about."

~ * ~

He picked the most exclusive, most secluded, Bed and Breakfast he could find inside the contiguous four counties. Luxury personified, the Brooklea was worth every penny. Their room, with wall-to-wall windows on three sides, opened onto gardens he's only seen on cable TV shows featuring estates of the rich and famous. Cost didn't matter. Ambiance did.

Thin, gauzy curtains covered the floor-to-ceiling French doors that opened onto a slate patio. Just outside the doors, a wrought iron furniture grouping enhanced a hot tub surrounded by pots of exotic flowering plants. Beyond the patio, spreading in all directions, a meticulously manicured garden offered an impression of sensual delights in the midst of a wilderness.

Their own private Garden of Eden.

It was Rachel's suggestion that while she stayed with Chris, he take Annie away for at least one night. Annie gave mute consent by silently packing a small bag. During the two-hour ride to Brooklea, she maintained her own counsel beneath a veil of stoney composure. Once inside the room, she headed straight for the bathroom, and remained there for over an hour.

The proprietress checked to see if all was well, leaving a plate of hors d'oeuvres and a carafe of wine. If she chose to believe they were honeymooners, Ronen elected not to correct her.

Fearful of mussing the lace bed covering, he sat in an antique oak side chair—and waited for Annie to come out of the bathroom. And waited.

When she finally entered the bedroom, with a hasty 'I'm sorry', he shrugged as if nothing of importance had occurred. "The owner left us a carafe of chilled wine. Along with munchies."

"I'm not very hungry."

"Do you mind if I have something?"

"Of course not." Annie moved restlessly around the large bedroom, pausing momentarily to check out the patio. Thunder rolled beneath flashes of lightening in the distant skies. A yet to be delivered promise of relief from the oppressive heat.

"Looks like we might finally get some rain," he murmured after a sip of an uncommonly good Merlot.

"Might," Annie said in a tight, clipped tone. She paused her pacing to ask, "Where'd they take Stella?"

"County lock-up. The DA has asked for an emergency psych evaluation."

"Good. She needs one." She looked him in the eye for the first time in hours. "It's hard enough to believe Stella was the ringleader of all this—but Jim Valetta? That bites."

"Junior Harbaugh is singing his corrupt little heart out to the DA. He claims Randy Terrance did most of the brutality, also swears Bobbie Claun was never involved."

"Is Terrance in custody?"

"Not yet. We've got a statewide alert out on him. Every airport, train and bus station is being surveilled."

A breeze suddenly picked up, billowing the thin draperies covering the patio doors against Annie's haunted features. Over her shoulder she said, "He called me while you were talking to the reporters."

Ronen almost choked on a cracker and *pâte*. "Randy?"

"Bobbie Claun. Isn't that a kicker?" She rubbed her hands up and down her arms. "Said he needed to apologize."

"Was he drunk?"

"Don't think so. Said he didn't have a clue about any of it. Randy always treated him like one of the guys, so he did whatever he was told, never gave it two thoughts."

Ronen leaned back in the chair. "Takes a big man to admit he's wrong."

"That's what I told him." She continued to pace.

"Please sit."

"Okay." She took one of the barrel chairs, drawing the heels of her feet to the curved edge. Her long, slender arms wrapped around her knees in a cocoon. "Tell me the rest, Ronen. All of it." Her voice sounded brittle, ready to crack. "I need to know every gory detail."

He told her what he knew so far. "Apparently Henry Grover patronized prostitutes when he was stationed in Thailand. He came home with one of those social diseases which don't respond to the usual antibiotics."

"Stupid jerk." She looked up at him. "He transmitted it to Stella."

Ronen nodded. "She became sterile as a result. Before he died, Henry apparently shared his gift with a number of local women."

"But I would have known if—"

"Was every woman in that compound one of your patients?"

"Of course not." For a moment she went back to contemplating the surface of her knees, then asked, "Did he really die in a car accident, like Stella said?"

"Yes. But he wasn't alone."

She rubbed one cheek, then the other, over the smooth skin of her knees. "It all makes sense now. Whomever he was with had to be a woman from the compound."

"The one you said liked to party with some not so nice guys."

"Exactly. And it all started with her." Annie's crouch tightened over her drawn-up knees. "Stella couldn't retaliate against Henry, so she went after the symbol of her husband's betrayal." Her head came up suddenly, hands tightened with a white-knuckled grip on the arms of the chair. "Doesn't explain why she went after Maria and Luba. Or Barb."

Ronen pushed the plate of hors d'oeuvres toward Annie, pleased when she took a wedge of cheese and a slice of apple. "We don't know about Maria or Luba, perhaps that was Randy Terrance working on his own. But I figure while working with the folks at Harbaugh's, Barbara must have heard the stories about Henry, so she did some digging. The threat she aimed at Randy that night in the ER was enough to alert Stella that she needed to be silenced."

She reached for a triangle of melon. "I can't see Jim Valetta taking a bat to someone. That's not his style."

The next was ugly, but Ronen harbored no sympathy for his former commander. "He claims he stopped at a tavern in Bainbridge one night after work. A young woman, looking down on her luck, approached him for a ride. He agreed. Once he had her in the car, one thing led to another."

"Meaning?" Annie prompted, reaching for a strawberry.

"During sex, she bit him. He chopped her in the back of the neck hard enough to stop her breathing."

"Do you believe him?"

His hands raised, then dropped. "Doesn't matter what I believe. Instead of helping the girl, he dumped her body in the trees lining the interstate. Somehow, and we may never know how, Stella learned the truth, then held the information over his head. Once I became involved, she expected him to stall my investigation."

"You mean the bugs."

"Yes. With the listening devices in place, he knew each step I planned to take, then made sure to put up roadblocks. I think when you reviewed the medical records from the office, Stella panicked and sent the boys after you."

"Instead," she mumbled, rising from the chair to begin pacing again, "they picked up Kathy Baker, mistaking her for me." She stopped abruptly, whirling around to face him. "What happened to make you figure it out?"

He told her about Junior's 'lucky seven' slip at the Baker crime scene. "I don't think I ever would have tied it together if you hadn't mentioned something about needing seven days before John's prognosis could be determined."

"Thank God for cardiac enzymes."

"Thank God I came to the ER to find you."

Annie gave him a crooked grin. "We're a pretty good team, Captain Marvel."

Ronen had reached his limit for her delaying tactics. "Talk to me, Ann. Please."

"What's to say?" she asked with a shrug. "A bunch of lowlifes eavesdropped to figure out what we were doing. No big whoop."

"It is a *whoop* when it makes you spend hours in the shower—not once but twice."

"I didn't—"

Ronen came out of his chair slowly, crossed the room, than took her in his arms. "Yes. You did."

"I'm sorry."

"I don't want apologies, Ann. I want you to talk to me."

"Maybe you should take me back," she said with all the enthusiasm of a wilted radish. "I'll pay for the time we've spent in the room."

His heart plunged to his knees. "Do you want to leave?"

Within the span of his arms, Annie looked around the room. "Of course not," she sighed. "It was sweet of you to take me away from— all that."

Ronen sank to the side of the king-size bed, bunching up the lace-edged coverlet beneath his fanny. "I don't know what to say. Don't know how to make you feel better."

He watched her walk through the door to the patio, then bend from the waist to sniff at a bloom on one of the lush flowering plants, kick off her shoes and raise her face to the sky filled with black, ominous clouds. "Ever make love in a rainstorm, Captain Marvelous?"

"Can't say that I have."

She reentered the room, slowly stripping the clothes from her body. "It's a trip you don't want to miss."

Fifteen

Laying placid and languid in her arms, Ronen broached a subject he'd been avoiding. "Ann?"

"Not again. Not yet."

He had to laugh at the response that usually fell from his lips. "I have an opportunity I'd like to discuss with you."

She snuggled against his side. "What?"

"When I took on No Man's Land, the brass promised if I succeeded I could pick anywhere I wanted in the state for my next assignment."

He waited for her to respond. When nothing came, not even a twitch, he continued. "I'd like to check out the Syracuse area. We could look for a house. Get married, of course. My mother would shoot me if I didn't do things properly. After a couple kids, you could start med school."

Annie abruptly sat up, keeping her back to him. Ronen scooted up behind her to wrap his arms around her and nuzzle her neck. "What do you think about my idea, honey?"

She glared at him over her shoulder. "I think it sucks."

The resulting silence came close to deafening. Annie closed her eyes, buried her chin in her chest, and bit back the sadness. It was for the best, she chanted silently. Med school was her dream. All she'd ever wanted.

"What's wrong?"

The light kisses on the back of her neck irritated her to no end. "Nothing."

"You're more tense now than when we first arrived." She felt his chest rise against her back. "Having second thoughts?"

"About med school? Never."

"About us?"

Ronen was holding her too close, tying her into a role she could never fulfill. She pushed him away before getting out of bed and slipping on the Rangers' jersey. Standing at the French doors, she saw that the rain had not lessened during their lovemaking, and continued to come down in pitchforks and hammer handles. "There is no *us*. Never was, never will be."

He came off the other side of the bed. "How can you say that after—" He made a sweeping gesture toward the covers on the floor.

"After what," she asked, perilously close to tears and hating the slightest show of weakness. "Great sex?"

Before she could take her next breath, he came toward her and grabbed her arms, as if he could shake sense into her.

As if she was too stupid to know what was best for her.

"I'll be damned before you bring what we've shared down to tearing up a set of sheets."

"What would you prefer?" Annie looked at his face, so elegant, so furious. "Delete that last question," she said with quiet resolution. "I know what you want. Home and babies."

"You don't need to sound so appalled."

"I have the right!" she spat. "You obviously haven't listened to one word I've said since we first met."

"Ann—"

"Do not patronize me, Ronen! I am a person in my own right and I deserve respect. Something I'm clearly not getting from you."

"I respect you, honey."

"Do you? How would you feel if I asked you to quit the Troops? Right here. Right now. Give it up to play... pig farmer?"

"Don't be ridiculous."

"It's no more ridiculous than this bright idea that I'd be willing to make a home with you, have a baby with you, play mother to your children."

He sank to the side of the bed, taking her with him. "Is it so hard to conceive? You'll be a wonderful mother."

She didn't bother to spare his feelings by containing her shriek of disgust. "A regular June Cleaver, that's me. After all, I had the best role model in the business."

"Is that what this is about?" he asked. "Because your father abused and neglected you?"

She almost laughed in his face. "Only you would term an eight-year-old who rolled johns for their credit cards and pocket change *abused and neglected*, Captain."

His hands loosened. Exactly what she'd expected he'd do. "He made you do that?

"Not him. *Her.* My mother. Bella Lupo, queen of hookers. When her customers started paying more attention to me, she got pissed, and said unless I came home with a minimum of a C-note each night, the door would be locked."

"Good Christ."

"That was nothing." *Captain Marvel wanted to know it all?* She'd give him both barrels.

"My birth name was Illiana Lupo. We lived in a cold water flat a couple blocks from Times Square—made things easier for good old Mom. I didn't know there was such a thing as a hot shower until after Barb rescued me. But, I digress—"

"Annie, please."

She ignored him. "In order to eat, my brothers and I scavenged dumpsters behind restaurants. I liked Italian; Tibby favored Chinese. Gregor didn't care."

Annie began to pace again, deliberately, to put distance between them. It was easier to do it in the dark. She wouldn't have to see his face. "The nightmare you wanted to know about?"

"You don't have to—"

"Yes, I do. I want you to know what I would tell our children if they were to ask, 'what did you do for fun when you were a kid, Mommy?'."

"Go ahead."

"Bella and Gabe sent us out to scavenge one night. It was cold, misty. The alley we picked stunk of rotted food... and other things. I was the lightest, so Greg and Tibor lifted me into a dumpster to see what was there. I don't know how long it'd been since our last meal. I only remember we were so hungry we would have eaten just about anything."

"Annie, please—"

She went to him. Knelt on the floor in front of him, put her hands on his knees. "Listen to me, Ronen. Listen to me real good." When he made no response, she told him what no one—except she and her brothers—knew.

"Greg thought it would be fun to leave me in there, so he put Tibby on the top to hold it down."

"To scare you."

"Partly." She looked at him dead-on. "Mostly to see how I'd react to the rats he threw in on top of me."

Ronen covered her hands with his. "Ann—"

"Eventually, I got out. Greg and Tibby had taken off. I ran home to tell Papa about what his sons had done to his only daughter. But before I could tell him, I heard him making the deal to sell me to a pimp. The kind whose customers liked kids before they reached puberty."

Exhausted from the disclosure—and his damnable stone-like acceptance, Annie came to her feet. "So, tell me, Ronen. You really want someone like that for a wife? Someone like that for the mother of your children?"

"Annie, for Christ's sake! None of it was your fault. *None of it*! You did what you had to do to survive."

"That's right, I did. And I still do what I have to do to survive. And that means medical school. Not a white picket fence, two AM feedings, and dirty diapers."

"I want that with you, Annie."

"I don't."

~ * ~

The day finally arrived.

The day Annie had been dreading since she first saw Chris Marvelic standing in the hall outside her apartment door. The young man she had come to view as a surrogate son was leaving for college. Leaving his father. Leaving her.

From the turret window, she'd spent the morning watching Ronen and Christopher pack the Bronco with all the essentials of college living. She'd given Chris an area rug from her living room because she knew rugs were a big deal with college kids. And they'd swapped wall posters for his dorm room. Her Shaquille O'Neal for his Air Jordan. She'd found a couple of CD's, ones she had on good authority were favorites among the college set, and stashed them in one of the duffel bags waiting to be packed in the car.

Now came the hard part.

She had to say good-bye.

Annie leaned her head against the window casing, fingering the crystals, breath heaving in her chest. "Please, God. Don't let me cry."

It helped to think of saying good-bye to Chris as if it was one of those distasteful, but necessary medical procedures that hurt like hell but promised a cure. The sooner you get it over with, the sooner you feel better.

She turned and barreled our of her bedroom, racing down the inside stairs to fly out the front door and cut across the front lawn to the parking lot. Ronen and Christopher looked up at her simultaneously. "If you think you can just sneak out of here without saying good-bye, kid, you are shit out of luck."

Chris' grin was as bright as the morning sunshine. The rain that started the evening before had continued non-stop through the night, then moved on as quickly as it came. Left in its wake were cooler temperatures, lush green lawns and vibrant flower beds.

"Hey, Annie. You all packed?"

His question raised feelings she preferred not to dwell on. Her plan, advanced by several days after last night's discussion with Ronen, was simple: Say goodbye to Chris, get in the Mustang, make a quick stop at John's hospital room, and hightail it to Syracuse. No fuss, no muss. No harm, no foul.

Mixed emotions barraged her from all directions. Damn, she never imagined anything could hurt this much. She'd never wanted to feel these things. Never wanted to deal with them.

"You bet I'm ready, kid. I got places—"

"—to go and things to do," Ronen finished her standard line. Solemn gaze fixed on her, he looked sad and lost, putting one last chink in the armor encasing her heart.

"Nothing wrong with a woman trying to better herself," she said, knowing how defensive it sounded, and didn't care.

"Never said there was," he came back. "I only question the methods."

"Hey, guys," Christopher called out. "Could my last day with you two end on a pleasant note, please?"

Slipping an arm into his, Annie directed Chris from the parking lot to the sidewalk in front of the mansion. "I didn't realize it felt like that, kid. Sorry."

"You're both acting like jerks," he muttered as they walked. "Are all girls as stubborn as you?"

"If they were," she choked, "the male species would not survive."

"He's nuts about you, Ann."

And I'm nuts about him. "There are issues you don't know about."

Looking down, he quirked an eyebrow in a gesture just like his father's. "You mean the fear of commitment? Yours, not his?"

Wasn't this a new and interesting phenomena? she decided. Being psyched-out by an eighteen-year-old with more insight than men twice his age. "I don't have a fear of commitment."

"Not in the least."

He sounded so like Ronen. "Chris," she started, then stopped. "Whatever is—or is not—going on between your father and me is between us. Stay out of it."

"We're talking about my best friend, Ann."

Ann. Damn. He was Ronen at his most enticing.

"Let's not drag this out into something maudlin," she said, pulling herself back to the business of sending Christopher out into the big, bright world filled with excitement, opportunity, and adventure. "I stashed a few survival supplies into one of your duffels. Condoms and—"

"Annie!"

"Don't sound so appalled. You never know when a... situation might arise when you, or one of your friends, needs protection. The point is to use them."

Finding it increasingly more impossible to keep her hands still, she took to smoothing the collar of his polo shirt. "If you don't need them, give them away." Tears boiled behind her eyelids. "Damn, I never cried till I met the two of you. What is it about you Marvelic men that makes me want to bawl every time I'm near you?"

"Aw, Ann."

She would not cry, she told herself as Chris pulled her into a hug. Could not cry.

Bowing her head against his chest, she sniffed—but only once. Tears would embarrass him. That was the last thing she wanted. Straightening her shoulders, she leaned back to look at him, keeping her palms flat against his chest. One day he would be as strong and independent as Ronen.

"One more thing. Actually—" She paused to clear her throat. "—a couple more things."

"Okay," he sighed. "Lay it on me."

She said in one long breath. "No booze, no drugs, no tattoos."

"Give me a break." *He was laughing. That was good.*

"No body piercings and—"

"Annie!"

"Let me finish," she directed, "before I start to cry then have to blow my nose on your shirt."

"Aw, geez."

"No animal sacrifices."

"Gross."

"I know, I know. But you never know who you might get for a roommate. There are people out there who come from a whole different lifestyle, Chris. People you wouldn't believe could exist on this planet. Stick to your values and don't waver. Don't let some street-smart con artist steer you wrong."

"I won't," he said with steadiness that only came from youth who'd never experienced the seamier side of life. "Promise."

"I want you to know something, Christopher." She looked him directly in the eye. "If I were ever to have a child, I would want him or her to turn out just like you, because... I—"

"Yes?"

"I love you," she said quickly, then took off running for the mansion.

"Annie, wait!"

She could only wave her hand in a sign meant to hold him off from following her. "Gotta go. You be good," she yelled over her shoulder. *I love you, Chris. I love you so much.*

Head down, she didn't see the brick wall of muscle and bone in front of her. Hands took her upper arms in a firm grip. She knew without looking up who was holding her. "Will you be here when I get back?"

"No," she said, and stared at his shirt.

"There's nothing I can say to make you stay?"

"No."

He reached out a hand, gently grazed her cheek with the tips of his fingers. "Promise me one thing."

She closed her eyes against the pain. *Don't drag this out, Wolfgirl. Make the cut clean, sharp.* She nodded silently.

"Promise me you'll get some therapy."

"Yeah, I know. It'll help. Anything else before I dissolve in a puddle on the sidewalk?"

"I love you, Illiana Lupo."

Ah, shit.

~ * ~

"You should have enough money in your bank account to get you through the first semester if you don't go overboard," Ronen said, more to reassure himself.

"Dad." Chris took the Bronco down Interstate 88 toward Binghamton. There, he would catch one of the county roads that would get them to Cornell. "We've been over this a hundred times. I saved everything from Urgent Care. Plus, Nana, Aunt Rachel and Dr. Latimer each slipped me a few bucks. "So, if you even think of putting more money into my account, I'll—"

Ronen wanted to scream. His only child was leaving him. It didn't matter that it was for all the right reasons. Hells bells, sending your kid off to college shouldn't hurt this much. Nothing should hurt this much.

Except losing Annie.

"Hand me a drink from the cooler," Chris directed.

As Ronen slid the plastic Igloo from beneath his seat, his fingers grazed something small and hard. "Soda or iced tea?"

"Don't care as long as it's wet."

He was starting to sound like Annie, Ronen realized. He glanced at the object in his hand. Sunlight sparkled off the crystal unicorn. Choking on the rising emotion, he mourned his failure to replace the ribbon as he'd promised.

"What did you and Annie talk about?"

"Stuff. You know."

The crystal horn dug into his palm. Chris began to ramble, something about getting advice from Rachel and his grandmother. All Ronen could feel was the cool smoothness of the glass. Absently, he traced the pad of his thumb over the carving on the unicorn's flank.

Wishing. Hoping Annie would change her mind and still be there when he got home.

Home. Christ, he must really be losing it if he considered No Man's Land home.

"I imagine Nana gave you the usual grandmother advice—write often, study hard, have a good time."

Chris took his eyes off the road long enough to grin at him. "All that, in addition to the safe sex talk."

"*My mother?*" His mother. Talking about sex. To his son.

"You don't need to tell me. Responsibility is part of the package when you screw around. So—" he asked, "you and Annie been using rubbers?"

"That is none of your business."

"Nana's no dummy, Dad. Neither is Annie. They both told me about the lines that some girls use. I'll protect myself."

"*My mother?*"

Chris just laughed, and kept on driving. The miles seemed to fly. Ronen needed this time with his son to last as long as possible. "Thank God Rachel and Mom didn't decide to make a quick visit to No Man's Land," he muttered. "Wouldn't have surprised me if they pulled up in front of Grover mansion with McNamera's Band in the lead."

"They wanted to."

Ronen's heart sank. "But?"

"I talked them out of it."

Thank you, God.

"Ithaca's closer to Syracuse than No Man's Land. I think they'll join us there. Nana said she couldn't let her only grandson move into a dorm without her first approving the facilities."

Ronen tucked the unicorn into his pocket. "She say anything about me?"

"Why would Nana ask about you?"

"Not your grandmother. Annie."

"What is this—eighth grade study hall? And, no she didn't pass me any notes for you."

"Very funny," Ronen offered in an ugly tone, offended at the thought that he, a command person for the New York State Police Department, one of the premiere forces in the country—if not the world—would act like a high school moron.

"If the question fits," his son reminded him with more aplomb that he would have preferred. Ronen waited. Chris didn't disappoint him.

"She told me what was between you two was none of my business and to stay out of it."

"To which you said?"

"That you are my father as well as my best friend."

Ronen waited a moment before he spoke. Every feeling in the book warred for top prize. "And she said?"

"Nothing." The sign for the exit to Ithaca came up. Chris took it with ease and grace. "But I am going to tell you one thing."

"And that is?"

"If you let her get away, you're a damned fool. Sir."

~ * ~

After parking the Bronco on the street in front of the mansion—only so he could avoid the empty parking lot—and the obvious evidence of Annie's having left him for good, Ronen entered Grover Mansion. Never in his wildest dreams did he think his heart could hurt so much.

He'd lost his son.

He'd lost the woman who'd made him feel whole again.

He might as well curl up in a ball and wait for the end to come.

Thank God his mother and sister never showed up in Ithaca. He couldn't have stood it. As it went, things were bad enough. Christopher put on a brave face but Ronen felt it was all for show, as he watched his son laugh and joke with his new roommate and his parents. All the while, Ronen wanted to scream.

Annie was leaving him.

As he climbed the never-ending stairs to the second floor landing, it suddenly hit him it was dark outside. He'd not realized how long it had taken for the return trip from Ithaca. No matter. His life would never be light again.

Sounds of Chuck Mangione filled his ears as he reached the landing. It had to be his imagination, he decided as he approached the open door of Annie's place. He looked around the empty living room where they'd shared beers and she'd tried to make him understand how important medicine was to her. That family and children were not an option for her.

He could hear her voice. Laughing, then crying. Finally, shouting in release after they'd made love—right over there beneath the poster of one of "her boys".

Without Annie's electric presence, the room felt cold and sterile. Lifeless.

Unable to bear the pain, he walked out the door. During the entire drive back, he'd harbored a fantasy of coming home to find her there—in the dark, listening to one of his CD's.

All he heard was the sound of his own breathing.

Then the sound of his tears.

Sixteen

"Help me, Miz Annie," the child moaned. "I feel sick."

Annie swept Marya Jackson up into her arms, then brushed back the child's damp golden curls off her hot forehead. "I can hear it in your voice, baby. Would you let me take a peek at your throat?"

"Do you havta?"

Having examined the little girl after she first arrived at the domestic violence shelter with her mother and brother, Annie understood why Marya feared anything that even smacked of a medical exam. "Can't make it better unless I know what's making you feel bad."

Marya lifted her head, gazing at Annie through dull, fevered eyes. "You don't need to check me out." Her head dropped like a stone on Annie's shoulder. "I feel lots better now."

She figured the child's head probably felt like it was filled with boulders the size of Rhode Island. Dark circles beneath the sunken eyes were clear indicators of a sinus infection. Plus, the kid talked like she had a throatful of marbles—one of Annie Wolfe's cardinal signs for tonsillitis.

"How's your tummy feel?"

"Hurts. A little."

Un-huh. Add a possible strep throat to the differential diagnosis. "If you mom comes with us into the exam room, would you let me take a peek at your throat?"

"Mommy can be with me?"

"Of course. You can have anyone you like in there. It's your choice."

"But, Daddy never let—"

Annie ran a soothing palm down the child's back, felt the responsive shiver in her too-thin body. Each night after he came home from the office, Marya's daddy, a multi-millionaire surgeon, closely examined his children—and not for medical purposes. At five Marya Jackson had good reason to avoid health care providers.

She swallowed back the desire for ten minutes alone with the man. Do a little *examining* of her own.

"Daddy isn't here now. Here—you're the boss," she promised. "You decide what happens to your body. Got that?"

Marya's smile was weak, but her arms tightened in a vise around Annie's neck. "I'm the boss. Nice."

With Marya still in her arms, Annie found Mrs. Jackson, explained what she felt was wrong with her daughter, then asked if she would join her and the child in the shelter's well-stocked dispensary.

Polly Jackson demurred. "I should call my husband."

Annie took a deep breath, hoping it would quell her rising frustration. "Is your husband Marya's pediatrician of record?"

"Not... exactly, but—"

"Mrs. Jackson, after you and the children came to the shelter, I treated them both for chlamydia and gonorrhea. You may chose to believe your husband wasn't the source of the infections. I, however—"

"Don't yell at my mommy," Marya croaked.

She touched her lips to the child's temple before settling her voice. "Sorry, baby."

As much as she wanted to ask Marya how she felt about her mother consulting her father, Annie refused to put the child in the middle of something that had all the appearances of one of the major scandals in the annals of Syracuse's domestic arena.

"The shelter's counselors helped you obtain a restraining order, Mrs. Jackson. If you call your husband now, he'll claim you weren't serious about filing charges against him and want to come home. Do you?"

Marya immediately stiffened in Annie's arms. "Noooo! Don' wanna go back. What Daddy did made me feel... sceevey."

Annie patted her back. "No one will make you go anywhere you don't want to go, kiddo. You're the boss, remember?"

"Boss," the child said on a moan. "Nice."

"Mrs. Jackson." Annie kept her tone one notch above frigid. "Will you be present while I examine Marya? Or are you going to continue to crap around?"

Polly fiddled with the strand of pearls at her neck. Annie wanted to shove them down her throat, one at a time. "I... I don't... know what to do," she wailed. "Edward always saw to the children's medical needs."

"May I say he did a sterling job of it," Annie muttered under her breath. "Shall we hit the dispensary? I'm on duty at the ER in a couple hours. I'd like to be sure Marya is taken care of before I leave."

"I suppose," Mrs. Jackson sighed.

Turning on one heel, Annie gritted out, "Thank you," And didn't mean a word of it.

~ * ~

After examining Marya and prescribing the appropriate meds, Annie reported to the on-duty staff person, Benedicta Foran. "Why's the director of this joint working on Thanksgiving Day?" She eyed the wide gold band on the woman's left ring finger. "Why aren't you home with your family?"

"I overheard you talking to Polly Jackson."

Annie squirmed beneath Bennie's relentless green gaze. "I was rough on her, I know, but her attitude drives me up a wall."

The director of The Haven, a safe house for abused women and children in the Central New York region, yanked on an errant strand of flame-red hair before tucking it behind one ear. Though she'd not known Bennie Foran for long, one of the things that never ceased to amaze Annie was her endless supply of compassion and acceptance for battered women.

"Polly's not the first client, nor will she be the last, who has difficulty letting go of past coping skills."

"She better learn new ones fast, before Child Protective Services nails her with a neglect citation."

"Annie—"

"Bennie, you hired me to provide medical care to the clients and their kids in exchange for free room and board. It's not that I don't appreciate the shelter's help in paying for medical school, but..."

Annie was on a roll and there was no stopping her. She'd get this off her chest and damn the consequences. Raising a hand for patience, she said, "If Polly Jackson takes those kids back home to that monster, as a mandated reporter I'll blow her into CPS faster than a duck shits on a pond."

"May I say something?"

Today was not Annie's personal best. She didn't need any reminders that she should be a little more supportive, a tad more understanding of the multiple and often tangled issues that surrounded domestic violence.

"It's Thanksgiving, Godammit. These women ought to be thankful they have a warm bed, hot meals, and a safe environment for themselves and their children, not worrying about some scum-sucking, lowlife pervert."

"Annie," she began again. "No one appreciates what you do for our clients more than me. Free medical care, well-child check-ups, immunizations, not to mention all the supplies you've begged, borrowed, or stolen for us, but—"

"No big whoop," Annie muttered. "The drug companies were more than happy to donate meds and supplies in exchange for a little free publicity. And my doctor friend from back home wrote off the exam table on his taxes. I'm happy to do it for you guys. Just don't expect me to be sympathetic to anyone who cannot or will not keep her kids safe and free from abuse."

"Like your mother didn't do for you?"

Annie's head ricocheted off her shoulders. Another thing she didn't need today—someone trying to psych her out. Shit. All she wanted was to do the best at whatever assignment she was given, survive med school and get on with her life. But even she could hear the defensiveness in her voice. "I don't know what you're talking about."

"Of course you do. It's written all over your face."

"Nothing's written on my face!"

Bennie just chuckled, and sat back in her chair. "Annie, Annie, Annie. Each time you have a run in with someone like Polly Jackson your whole demeanor changes. You take the kids in your arms, protecting them like they were your own."

Because I wish they were.

"Yeah, okay. Maybe I do. A little. How did you figure out the thing with my mother?"

One of the few living women whom Annie admired and respected leaned across the disaster area of her desk, and drilled her with a knowing look. "Takes one to know one."

The alarm on Annie's watch beeped, signaling she had one hour before she went on duty at the ER. *Saved by the bell.*

"Gotta go," she said, more than eager to escape her boss' uncanny instincts.

"Let me walk you out," Bennie offered.

In the parking lot, she went to unlock the Mustang's door. The car was surviving Syracuse's never-ending rain and frigid temperatures better than she was. "I'll try to do better with the clients, Bennie. Promise."

"They're a tough population to work with, Ann."

Ann. Man, she didn't need to hear that. Not today. Not any day.

"Dammit," she swore when she discovered the lock on the car door was still frozen from last night's mini ice storm. Giving the lock a hard shot with her palm, she admitted, "You're right. About the protecting thing with the kids. I look at Marya and thank God I escaped before sexual abuse—" She hit the lock again; pain sang up her arm. "Then—I think about my parents and—"

"Damn them to everlasting hell?"

"Only if hell promises no possibility of parole."

"Some people," Bennie mused, "should have been sterilized at the onset of puberty."

Annie gave the door a kick. "Dammit! I'm going to be late. I hate, loathe, and despise being late!"

Her tirade was interrupted when the sound of a tooting horn rang out, accompanied by children's voices that pealed across the near empty parking lot. "Mommy! Mommy! Mommy!"

Bennie Foran's face lighted up like sparklers on the Fourth of July. "Come," she said. "Meet my kids and husband. He's a champ with frozen locks."

The 'champ' pulled a blue and white patrol unit for the Syracuse Police Department to a stop beside them. Five kids of varying sizes bolted from the car and ran to Bennie's side.

"Daddy let us ride with him in his special car for the parade today," one crowed.

"With the mayor herself!" another added.

"Thanksgiving Day parade," Bennie interpreted. "My husband always drives Mayor O'Connell in his chief's unit."

A tall, sinfully good looking cop with a load of fruit salad over the breast pocket of his uniform jacket ambled up.

"Chief's unit?" Annie checked out the cop a little closer. After a moment, she recognized his face from the newspapers and TV broadcasts.

"Annie, this is my husband," Bennie said, giving his broad chest a proprietary pat. "Chief of Police Jorge Morales."

The gorgeous man stuck out a hand. "Heard a lot about you, Dr. Wolfe. Pleased to put a name to a face."

Annie found herself gawking—not only for the man—but for what happened next.

"Group hug, guys," Bennie yelled, opening her arms. Before Annie's shocked eyes, the strong-willed, no-nonsense Director of Domestic Violence Services for Syracuse and Central New York transformed into a lush, willing woman in her husband's arms as well as a loving, expressive mother with her children. The kids wrapped their arms around their parents, sharing hugs and kisses.

An advocate and a cop. Not that Annie was surprised. Cops hooked up with advocates as often as they did ER or ICU nurses.

Each relationship, in Annie's opinion, carried the survival chances of a Popsicle in hell.

The head of a DV shelter and the Chief of Police.

Unbelievable. How did they do it? How did the relationship survive? And *Five* kids. Somebody had to lose out on the deal. It didn't appear to be Bennie, or her spouse. Not the way the two of them were looking at each other.

"Kids," Bennie directed, "go sit in Popi's car while I talk to Dr. Wolfe." She then directed her attention to Jorge the Beautiful. "Could you pull out that thing you use to jimmy doors open? Annie's lock is frozen."

"Sure."

"Thanks," Annie mumbled, more than a little envious of the smile on Jorge's face. On a good day she missed Ronen something fierce. On days like today, needing little provocation to bring on the waterworks, the loneliness rivaled agony.

Bennie touched her arm. "You look a little shell-shocked, Dr. Wolfe."

"Five kids," she mumbled. "A high profile husband. Your job, which probably takes the cake for inducing stress ulcers. Are you a masochist?"

"Is it so hard to believe?"

Frankly, yes. Annie couldn't imagine balancing a home, kids and husband with the responsibility of keeping other women safe. Didn't want to imagine it.

No matter how intriguing the idea may have seemed of late.

"Jorge wasn't chief when we met," Bennie explained, leaning her backside against the chief's unit. "I was Mary Benedicta Foran, a green as grass social worker making my bones in a homeless shelter, frantic to save every dime so I could go to grad school, because one day I was going to save the world. Jorge was pounding a beat in the Combat Zone while finishing his Masters in Police Science. He, of course, had the road to chiefdom all planned out."

Annie waited for the rest of the story. Bennie didn't disappoint her.

"The last thing I wanted," she said, "was a relationship with a culturally immersed, conservative macho man whose ideal woman stayed at home, barefoot and pregnant.

Didn't that sound familiar?

"Then," Bennie said softly, with the most adoring look on her face for the man who was now opening Annie's car door with a quick jab from a lethal-appearing instrument. "The rabbit died."

"Oh, my." On one hand Annie was thankful that the past summer's activities hadn't produced any unexpected gifts. On the other side of the coin, since she'd left No Man's Land a strange longing had found a parking spot just beneath her heart, and demanded—on a daily basis—to be fulfilled.

Her baby. Ronen's baby. *Their baby.*

She paid close attention to the toes of her work boots, then blurted, "Weren't you ever scared one or all of you would lose out? Weren't you concerned Jorge might throw in the towel because you were unavailable so much of the time? Didn't you fear you wouldn't be able to give the kids the love and attention they deserved?"

"Hang on a minute," Bennie interrupted, giving her husband one last kiss before sending him on his way with the kids and promises to be home in time for the feast later that evening. She then took Annie's arm, guiding her in a slow walk around the parking lot.

"Where's all this coming from, Ann? You're an intelligent, resourceful woman with a brilliant future. If—" she added, "—you've got the guts for it."

As far as guts were concerned, Annie was beginning to doubt she had any.

"Is that the problem?" Bennie asked. "Lack of guts, or lack of the right man?"

According to Chris' weekly letters from Cornell, *the right man* continued to police the Catskills, bitching and moaning over the lack of cultural opportunities, and no doubt brewing an ulcer. Damn, she missed Captain Marvelous.

"I always figured I couldn't do both, career and family," Annie admitted. "Never wanted kids. Or so I thought."

"And now?"

"What if it doesn't work?" Annie stumbled over her biggest fear. "What if I fail?"

Bennie smiled. "Believe it or not, Annie, the right man will challenge you to develop strengths you never thought you had. He'll encourage you to try things you never dared before. This person won't deter you from your goals; he'll help you achieve them."

They were back at Annie's car. With a touch on her shoulder, Bennie pushed her into the Mustang. "Think about it."

~ * ~

Irresistible scents of roasting turkey and sausage dressing, as well as the need to spend quiet time with his mother, drew Ronen into the kitchen. "Need any help, Mom?" Easing his arms around his mother's waist, he relaxed in the solace of her familiar scent, her sturdy spirit that always comforted him, no matter the problem. "Can I peel those potatoes for you?"

"I would like that, yes."

Elena Marvelic dried her hands on the towel tucked into the waistband of her apron. Handing him the vegetable peeler, she directed Ronen to the bowl of potatoes waiting to be prepared for boiling and mashing.

Ronen gladly took over the no-brainer chore he'd enjoyed since he was a boy. The rote duty of peeling, soaking and cutting was somehow soothing. Being here, with his mother, eased his troubled heart.

"There is one thing else I would like for you to do," Elena murmured after turning to a mound of fresh green beans on the table behind him.

The serious look on her face sent a sudden terror through him. "What's wrong? Did something turn up at your last doctor's visit?" *Please, God, don't make my mother ill. Annie's not here to take care of—*

Appalled at the unconscious entry of Annie Wolfe into his mind, Ronen's hand paused over the rapidly building mound of potato skins. For months he'd refused to even think about her. With this unexpected intrusion, in his mother's kitchen of all places, came a fierce sting that seared across his chest and rocked him back on his heels. His gut churned in fear for his mother.

"I'm fine," Elena said. "It is for you I am worried."

If the peeler began to work with more force than was necessary, Ronen ignored it. "No need to worry about me, Mom. I'm fine."

Elena peered at him over the top of her glasses. "That is not what Christopher tells me."

It took some moments before Ronen trusted his voice to respond in a calm, emotion-free tone. "College has put his head in the clouds. Pay no attention to what Chris says."

His mother, it appeared, was not about to let things rest. "Who is the woman whom my grandson calls Annie?"

A stronger onslaught of agony forced Ronen to stop what he was doing. As he breathed through it, the grinding slowly eased. "No one special."

"Bah! Do not tell me fairy stories."

"Chris is just blowing smoke. He doesn't know what he's talking about."

"I think he knows, and sees, far more than you give him credit. It is you who is blind. And stubborn," she added.

"Mom."

How could he talk to his mother about Annie? About his feelings—and his failures. "I'm handling it."

Elena moved to the sink, nudging Ronen to one side so she could run cold water over the beans she'd just snipped and cut. "Do you think I am so old that I do not remember what it is to yearn for something—or someone?" She drilled him with laser-black eyes. "Who is this woman who ties my son into knots?"

Ronen sighed. There was no way out of it. Thanks to Chris. Thanks to a mother's unwavering instincts. "Her name is... Illiana Lupo, though she prefers to be called Annie. And—" He paused, waiting for the ache in his heart to recede. "There is no room in her life for me."

"Bah!" Elena repeated, this time with more force. "How could a woman not make room in her life for you?"

"Dad!" Chris burst into the kitchen. "You won't believe what I found in the attic."

As always, Elena offered her only grandchild a sweet smile. "What treasure you have uncovered, Christos?"

"Phonograph records," he announced. "And they have your name on them. My Nana was a recording star!"

Turning on one heel, Elena briskly returned to the beans soaking in the sink. "It was a long time ago."

His mother made records? When? Why? "Mom? What is he talking about?"

"I'm going to play them," Chris said. "Okay, Nana?"

"No!" she said.

"Yes," Ronen directed. "You know how to work your grandmother's hi-fi?"

"Dad. Please. How hard can it be?"

Chris disappeared through the swinging door that separated the kitchen from the dining room. Within seconds, the sounds of "Musetta's Waltz" from *La Boheme* soared from the other room.

Elena stiffened. Ronen saw something flash across her face. A long-buried memory surfaced crisp and clear in his head. "That's you," he croaked. "That's you singing."

"Is someone from another lifetime," Elena maintained, continuing to soak and rinse the string beans. "Of no matter."

"Mom, I know it's you," Ronen insisted. "That's the voice I remember singing Rach and me to sleep."

Another memory came. Elena's sighs when the Syracuse Symphony sponsored an appearance of a famous opera star from the Met in New York. The longing in her face.

How his father's comment to those sighs was a brisk snap of the newspaper in his big workman's hands.

Elena tipped the beans into a colander to drain. "You are mistaken, my son."

"I'm not. Your love of opera is what sparked my interest in classical music. Mom, why didn't you pursue singing?"

"It would have been too hard on everyone. Too difficult."

The sweet, lyrical tones on the recording tugged at Ronen's heart. That pure, young voice he recalled from his childhood. "What happened to make you give it up—?"

Suddenly it was all so clear to him. "You gave it up for Dad."

"I did. Yes."

"Why?"

"Because I loved him. Because he, and the children he wanted, meant more to me than singing."

"You couldn't have had both?"

"Your father wished for me to stay home," she stated simply. "Because I loved him, I followed his wishes."

The aria ended with a flourish. The applause that followed was almost deafening. He pictured his mother, young and eager, taking her bows. Her shining smile must have lit up the concert hall. The same way it had lighted their home for all those years. .

She gave up her dream to keep a man happy.

A sad, sweet smile crossed Elena's face. "Your papa, you and Rachel more than made up for my music."

"Aw, Mom."

Chris burst back into the kitchen. "That was way cool. Who'da thought my nana was an opera star?"

"Not a star," Elena demurred. "I was still in music school when I made that recording. Your grandfather was there, in the audience. He came backstage to introduce himself. Within weeks he offered me more than music. Who could say no to Nicolai Marvelic?"

Stunned by the knowledge of what his mother had sacrificed for a family, a home, Ronen sank into one of the chairs at the kitchen table. *Forgive me, Annie.*

"Okay if I listen to the rest of the records, Nana?"

"If you like," she said.

After Christopher retreated back into the dining room, Elena crossed her arms over her ample chest, then confronted her son head on. "Tell me about this Illiana."

After his mother's disclosure, how could he not tell her? "She brought light into my soul. She made me laugh." He paused. "With her, I was a better person."

"Without her?" Elena prompted.

"I feel... empty, restless. Like a vital part of me has been ripped away."

Elena nodded. "This woman. She lives in No Man's Land?"

Ronen eased back in the chair. "Actually, she's right here in Syracuse. She's going to become a doctor, Mom. And she'll be terrific at it."

"How wonderful."

"Yeah," he muttered. "Wonderful."

Elena's dark eyes narrowed. "You wanted to take her dream away?"

"I tried. Because of that, she left me."

"Did you never offer to help her achieve what she wanted?"

"Not in so many words."

"You, my son, are a fool."

"Yes, I was."

"*Was?*"

"I need to find her, Mom. Tell her how I feel."

"Something is holding you back?"

"I don't know where she is."

"My son," Elena scoffed. "The big shot investigator with the New York State Police cannot find one lone woman in a medium size city?" Elena raised her eyes to the ceiling. "What manner of man have I raised that he cannot figure out who to call to locate his woman?"

For the first time in months Ronen felt a ray of hope. He sprang out of the chair to take his mother in his arms. "Mom, you're the best."

~ * ~

Alone in the ER's charting room, Annie thought about what Bennie Foran said about the right man. Then she thought of Ronen. Not with the pain that always accompanied memories of his beautiful spirit and face, but with a new, different light. The light of success, not failure.

She wondered where he was on this cold, rainy Thanksgiving night. Hopefully, he was with family, sitting around a huge dining room table, mourning a stripped turkey carcass and empty bowls of potatoes, vegetables and stuffing, swearing he couldn't eat another bite. Opera would be playing in the background, of course.

Suddenly, she ached to hear him humming pieces from *Aida*—or the other one she really liked, where the woman coughed her lungs out from end-stage TB. *La Boheme*. That was it. She could almost hear Mimi calling out to Rudolpho.

A nurse stuck her head in the door. "Hey, Annie?"

"Yeah?"

"There's a state trooper out here. Wants to talk to you."

Her heart stopped for a second, then resumed a thundering beat. "Be right out."

Annie came out of her chair, went to meet her visitor. And came to an abrupt stop in the doorway. Standing with his back to her, the trooper maintained an aura of power and control if only by his posture. Unable to see his face, she took in the broad shoulders, arrow-straight back and narrow waist, tight buns and long legs. The tan Stetson tilted forward, exposing thick gold-brown hair, cut to regulation length.

Ronen!

Hope, joy, excitement overwhelmed her. *He's come to me.*

"Ronen?"

The trooper turned. Hope vanished.

Staring into a face that didn't look old enough to vote, she said, "I'm Annie Wolfe. You wanted to see me?"

He removed the Stetson. "Yes, ma'am. My commander got a message from the barracks down in Sydney today. They asked us to locate you, tell you face to face that—"

Thunder in Annie's heart blossomed into a full-blown boomer and threatened to split her chest wall. "What? Is something wrong down there? Has he—someone—been injured?"

The trooper took a step back, cleared his throat. "Guy named Randy Terrance. Know him?"

"Unfortunately."

"He was apprehended last night, ma'am, hiding out in the Delhi mountains. That's near—"

"I know the area, trooper."

"Anyway, the commander down there wanted—"

Hope flared once again. Ronen would do something like this. Keep her updated on the status on the case. She already knew the Grand Jury had handed down indictments for felony murder, kidnapping and rape on Jim Valetta, Stella, Kevin Dolan, and the fugitive Randy Terrance based on Junior Harbaugh's testimony and the wealth of evidence amassed by Ronen.

"Who is the commander, trooper?"

"Gee, ma'am, nobody gave me his name." He ran the edges of the Stetson between his thumb and forefinger. "If it's important, I can—"

"No. It's not important." She didn't need to know who sent the message. Really, she didn't.

"Uh... okay... well, there's more I'm supposed to tell you."

Annie needed to end this. Now. So she could go soak her head. "Okay, spit it out," she snapped. "I got places to go and things to do."

The troop glanced around the bustling ED and shook his head. "I won't keep you, ma'am. Can see you're busy tonight."

"The rest of the message, trooper?"

"Right. When this bird Terrance was apprehended, he was in his van. They said it was filled with all sorts of sh—, uh, equipment that he, Terrance, I mean, uh—we call it a rape van, ma'am. That's where—"

Annie closed her eyes, took a deep soughing breath. "All the tools necessary to grab and subdue a victim, then torture them before dumping the body."

"Photographs, too," the troop added. "Some were of vics—"

Annie winced. "From months, maybe years ago?"

The trooper gaped at Annie like she'd sprouted a third ear. "Commander figures they'll put him away for a long time."

"Better be enough to slip a needle in his arm," Annie growled. "That's one cop who deserves it."

The Stetson went back on, again tilted at a professional angle. "Shit. He's a cop?"

"You betcha, baby." She stuck out a hand. "Thanks for stopping by to tell me the news. I appreciate it."

After shaking her hand, the trooper touched two fingertips to the Stetson's brim in a gesture that was achingly reminiscent of Ronen. "You have yourself a nice holiday, ma'am."

Annie watched him leave. As the straight back and tight buns walked away, images of Ronen's laughing face raced across her mind. An immediate picture of them making love in the middle of a rainstorm followed. Those green eyes, that could flash in contempt as easily as they could in passion, seared her heart. A major league lump rose in her throat.

Not now, she warned herself. *Do not* think of him now.

The two-way radio in the nurses' station squawked. A local ambulance company was bringing in the victim of a drive-by shooting in the Combat Zone on the south side of the city. Estimated time of arrival, three minutes.

While Annie and the staff readied the trauma room, Drew O'Malley, the trauma surgeon on duty, took the information on the victim's injuries and vital signs, sending back orders for the techs to start a second IV line and administer emergency medications.

"Ladies and gentlemen," he barked. "Victim's a cop. We all know what that means."

The scream of police and ambulance sirens sliced the air. The back doors crashed open. Uniformed police officers lined both sides of the on-coming stretcher. Annie saw only the back of a paramedic who straddled the victim's body to deliver chest compressions while another EMT ventilated him through an endotracheal tube connected to an Ambu bag. Everyone, cops, EMT's and the victim were drenched in blood.

As Annie reached for the end of the stretcher, someone called out her name.

She didn't recognize the weeping gray-haired matron in the black dress. The hollow-eyed young man, who had a supportive arm around her waist, was too familiar.

Christopher Marvelic said, "It's Dad, Annie. Help him."

Seventeen

Annie glanced quickly at Ronen's body, lifeless except for the reflexive jerking of his legs each time the EMT pounded on his chest.

"Please, Annie," Chris begged, tears choking his voice.

"Wait here," she said. "I'll be out as soon as I can."

This wasn't time to give in to panic, scream or tear her hair. It was time to act. O'Malley touched her shoulder. "You know the vic?"

Annie nodded. Drew was the only thing she could be thankful for. Known for the fastest hands in town, this surgeon would save Ronen. She was sure of it.

With a gentle tug on her arm, O'Malley said, "Come with me."

"Annie, wait!" A nurse came up behind them. "I've got a thrombosed hemorrhoid in sub-acute B. You have to check her."

"Find someone else." She couldn't take her eyes off Ronen. *Please, God, don't let him die.*

The sputtering nurse followed the gurney into the Trauma Room. "But she's your patient! You can't just—"

O'Malley turned on the nurse. "Find. Someone. Else."

"There is no one else."

"Then slap a little xylocaine ointment on the pain in her ass," O'Malley bellowed. "I'll lance it when I'm finished here."

"Yes, sir," the nurse sighed, and disappeared.

Hands came from everywhere to lift Ronen from the gurney to the trauma table. "Tell me about him," Drew demanded.

"Thirty-nine years old." Annie cut off Ronen's jeans and boxers as she spoke. "Legs look trauma free. The belly's soft, non-tender. That leaves—"

Concentrating on areas above the belly button, O'Malley barked, "Drug allergies?"

"No. His health is excellent except for a few minor GI complaints. GERD, lactose intolerance, maybe a chronic gall bladder."

Without warning, bright red blood geysered from Ronen's upper chest area, coating the overhead spot lights. O'Malley cursed. "It's high in the chest... looks like—ah crud! The entire shoulder's gone." He looked at Annie in silent demand for the rest of Ronen's vital medical stats.

She returned his look. "O pos. HIV neg."

"Okay, boys and girls, I want the on-call vascular and ortho teams in here, like five minutes ago. Ten units of packed cells. Somebody put in a central line on the left side. Let's move, people."

The team responded quickly and efficiently.

"Annie?" O'Malley slipped into gown and gloves. "Up here, next to me."

She stepped forward, panic seeping from every pore. "Drew, I shouldn't even be in the room."

"You see who else is working tonight?"

Annie kept her groan to herself. "Dr. Anders."

"Aberrant Anatomy Anders. The Triple A in all his glory." O'Malley grunted as he packed Ronen's decimated shoulder with thick surgical pads. "You're worth ten of him. Stay right here."

Routine, governed by instinct, stepped in to take the place of terror. "Another suture tray, please," she said calmly. "More lap pads and plenty of saline for irrigation. I want a couple vascular clamps and a ton of sutures, atraumatic."

"I like the free stuff," O'Malley mentioned as he gently explored the wound, dodging bleeders every step of the way.

"Tough. Atraumatics are faster and easier to use."

An anesthesia resident replaced the EMT who'd been bagging Ronen. "Lungs are clear. BP's okay, but it ain't wonderful."

"Open up the IV's," Annie and Drew ordered simultaneously.

"Sorry," she apologized automatically. "I had no right to—"

"Screw the sorries, Wolfe. Just do your job and help me."

"Nice sinus rhythm on the monitor," anesthesia offered. "I'd better slip a nasogastric tube down him."

"Somebody put in a Foley," O'Malley said. "And call for portable films, chest, cervical spines, abdomen and pelvis." He winked at Annie. "Anything else, Doctor?"

"Thoracic spines. Just to be safe."

"Agreed," Drew said. "Nice call, Wolfe."

A cop, leaning against the far wall, waiting for any bullets that might be found, entered the fray of hollered orders and yelled responses. Annie listened with half an ear as she suctioned blood with one hand, cut sutures with the other.

"Sorry son of a bitch," the officer remarked blandly. "Comes to Syracuse to share turkey day with his mom, only he didn't know a couple of gang bangers are cruising the Zone, checking on sightings for the rival bangers who keep a crib next door to Miz Marvelic's house."

"Working up an appetite," Drew mumbled under his breath.

"Exactly," the cop responded, stepping forward with a metal emesis basin after O'Malley signaled with a raised forcep that he'd found a bullet. Annie refused to be rattled by the clang of metal striking metal, and kept on suctioning and snipping sutures.

The cop continued. "She's a real nice lady, Miz Marvelic is. Brews a mean pot of coffee and bakes awesome brownies—from scratch. We try to stop by, check on her every night. Her son being a statie and all."

Clang. Clang.

Bullets two and three went into the kidney-shaped basin. Annie focused on the business at hand, with a tad more attention paid to what the cop was relating.

"Anyway, the family cat goes missing right after dinner. The vic volunteers to look for the kitty, and walk off the meal at the same time. He's coming off the front porch when the bangers come cruising down the street, spraying a little holiday cheer so to speak. The rivals next door return the joy and—"

"We got a mess to clean up," O'Malley said. "Where's the blood?"

"First unit's going up now," anesthesia responded. "Vital signs are better, Drew, but this man's internal organs aren't going to be happy till we get a third line going."

"Anders?" O'Malley barked.

"Yes, sir?" an arrogant voice responded.

"Thought I told you to slip in a central line."

"I'm having trouble with aberrant anatomy, sir. His supraclavicular notch isn't where I usually find it."

"Triple A strikes again," Drew muttered. "Couldn't find his butt with both hands and a working flashlight. Help him, Annie."

"Me?"

Now was not the time to wimp out, she told herself. Ronen's life hung in the balance. Second year surgical resident Stanley Anders ragged on her every chance he got, making snide comments about uppity women in general, and physician's assistants in particular, who *possessed the gall* to rise above servant caste by attempting to become doctors. Anders fell short of the miracle they needed, but he was better than nothing.

"Yes, sir."

Annie scooted around the head of the table, moving to Anders' side. After changing her gloves, she took Triple A's hand, guiding his fingertips over the length of Ronen's collar bone. "Feel for the landmark," she said softly. "Sometimes you need to rotate around the bone." If she embarrassed Anders in front of the team, there'd be hell to pay later.

"Got it," he said after a second, sounding amazed.

"Good. Keep you fingertip on the notch and slip the intercath into the skin just beneath it... Good. Now, ease the needle out... Perfect."

A nurse stood by, IV tubing in hand. While Annie connected the lines, Anders sutured the triple lumen catheter in place. "Nice job, Stan," she murmured, then raised her voice. "Let's hang the second bag of blood."

Residents from the orthopedics and vascular services blew through the doors and moved directly to the table. "Oh, shit," one said after a quick assessment.

"Double shit," the second one said. "Call the OR, tell them to get Room six ready for us."

With three surgeons at the table, Annie stepped back to strip off her gloves and gown, ready to help the nurses.

"Annie?" Drew O'Malley said.

"Yes, sir?"

"Go see to this man's family."

Relief lasted only seconds. What she'd just done paled in comparison to facing Chris and the gray-haired woman whom she assumed was Ronen's mother.

"And Annie?" O'Malley said as she pushed the Trauma Room door open.

Over her shoulder she asked, "Yes, sir?"

"Nice job."

~ * ~

Before facing Christopher, Annie took a moment to bathe her face at the scrub sinks outside the Trauma Room, and prayed for strength. She'd consoled a million frantic relatives in the past, but nothing in the past prepared her for what she had to do now.

"Please, God. Help me to be strong."

With a quick, downward glance, Annie checked her scrub top for excessive blood and gore and decided she looked good enough to face Ronen's family. She straightened her shoulders, swallowed all emotion, and headed out of the scrub room to face the worst.

The hemorrhoid nurse, who obviously had been laying in wait, followed hot on her trail. "A minute, Annie."

Christopher's face, so full of hope and need, appeared in the doorway of the waiting room. "Not now," she said.

"But—"

She whirled on the nurse. "I said *not now!*"

"Well—" The twit drew her shoulders back, chin set at an obstinate angle. "The Chief of ER will hear about this!"

"Leave us alone," Annie ordered. "I'm staying with my family."

The nurse pasted a superfluous smile on her face for Chris and the older woman. "Is there anything I can get anyone?"

The change in attitude from this particular nurse, who in Annie's opinion ranked one rung below Triple A Anders on the food chain, failed to appease. "Peace and quiet."

She closed the door in the nurse's face before turning to the child of her heart. "How you doing, kid?"

"Aw, Annie." He moved into her arms, weeping his heart out on her shoulder. Once the initial flood subsided, he mumbled, "I'm so scared."

So am I.

The woman in black cleared her throat. Chris wiped his eyes. "Sorry for that." Hanging onto Annie, he swung his other arm around the older woman's shoulders. "This is my Nana, Elena Marvelic."

Four months had incurred a significant change in the boy she'd sent off to school with instructions to avoid body piercings, animal sacrifices, and tattoos. Christopher was now a man. The ease with which he assumed responsibility for the care and comfort of his grandmother made her proud.

With the years showing in the lines at her eyes and mouth, Mrs. Marvelic enveloped Annie in a cloud of incredible strength and the scent of White Shoulders. "I'm grateful you were here, Illiana."

Stunned at the use of her given name, Annie drew back to stare at Ronen's mother.

"My son has told me of you. We have much to speak of."

A nurse, not Hemorrhoid Hannah, opened the door. "I'm sorry to disturb you all."

After directing Christopher and his grandmother to the couch, Annie went to the door. "What's wrong?"

"Officer Marvelic's personal effects." The nurse held out one hand. Resting in her palm was a set of keys, a wallet and... a crystal unicorn.

Chris appeared at Annie's side, taking the items from the nurse. "Can you tell us anything?"

"He's..."

Choking back a new rush of emotion, Annie couldn't take her eyes off the unicorn. Anything could have happened in the seconds since she'd left the Trauma Room. "What's wrong?"

"They just took him to the OR. He's holding his own." The nurse gave Annie's arm a squeeze. "Sorry for your trouble," she mumbled, then ducked out as quickly as she'd appeared. Annie stared at the closed door, too numb to feel anything but rampaging fear.

After a moment, she realized both Chris and Elena were speaking to her. She'd not heard them. "Come, Illiana." Elena slid an arm around her waist. "You need to rest."

Annie glanced around the room that was usually packed to the rafters with family and friends waiting for word on a patient. The air was thick with acrid odors of burnt coffee, unwashed bodies, and unrelenting despair.

A battle-worn coffee table listed to one side, sending a motley assortment of magazines and newspapers to the floor. The couch cushions spit shreds of dirty foam through rips and tears in the faded vinyl. The muted voice of a sports reporter rattled off bowl scores from the TV that was bolted and chained to a platform high on the opposite wall.

"Sorry we can't offer more comfortable surroundings," she mumbled.

"The room, it does not matter," Elena said, encouraging Annie to sit. "It is the people who count."

Christopher slipped the wallet and keys into his jacket pocket, then handed Annie the unicorn. "Dad's carried this since late summer. I think it belongs to you."

She cradled it in her palm, studying it for several seconds before curling her fingers into a fist. She sank onto the battered couch, body aching, her mind filled with all the possible complications of a shoulder wound. "Do either of you have any questions?"

Elena folded her hands at her waist, took a deep breath. Annie prepared herself for the expected maternal interrogation: Who are your people? Where do you come from? *How could you refuse my son's attention?*

"Do you love him?" she asked.

Drew O'Malley stuck his head in the door. "Is this a private party or can anyone join in?"

Annie introduced him to Chris and Elena, all the while rubbing the pad of her thumb over the unicorn's edges. Drew sat next to Elena, covering her hand with his. In quiet, clear words he told her exactly what her son faced—if he survived—including the multiple-stage surgical reconstruction of his shoulder.

Chris had a million questions. While Drew answered them, Annie hung on tight to the unicorn and let her mind drift. She remembered the night she and Ronen made plans to replace the ribbon on the piece. Opening her palm, she found the length of frayed red satin still attached to the metal loop on the unicorn's head.

He's carried it with him all this time.

Silent tears rolled down her cheeks. Every feeling, every fear she'd been holding back, from when Bennie Foran advised her in the parking lot to this moment, rose up, pummeling her in a torrent of fear, and regret.

I can't lose him.

Chris was there, pulling her off the couch and into his arms. This time, it was his strength that sustained Annie while she blubbered all over his shoulder. Before she realized it, Drew had left the room; it was only the three of them.

Waiting for word from the OR.

Waiting to know if Ronen would emerge from the first round of surgery intact, mentally and physically. Throughout the next endless hours, she learned that after having raised her children in the Combat Zone, Elena refused to leave her home despite Ronen's pleas to sell the house and move to No Man's Land.

"I could not give up my home."

"Of course not," Annie said. "It's a testament to you and your husband and the life you built for Ronen and Rachel."

"I was hoping you'd convince her otherwise," Chris said. "But my Nana's as stubborn as you, Wolfgirl."

"After what has happened," Elena said, "I am... how do you say? Reconsidering my options." She glanced at Annie. "You will stay with us, Illiana?"

"Of course."

And the waiting continued.

It was shortly after midnight when the surgeons sent down word that Ronen was out of the OR, had been taken directly to the ICU, and invited the family to come up. Ordinarily, family members weren't allowed in the Unit so soon after surgery. Annie suspected Drew O'Malley had a role in convincing the doctors to allow Elena and Chris a few minutes with Ronen before the necessary protocols for monitoring his condition crowded them out of the way.

While Elena and Chris spent time with Ronen, the orthopedic surgeon, one of the best in the country, took her aside to explain his plan of care. "Gonna keep him pretty well snowed for a few days. I'll have the chief of neurology check in regularly."

Annie stiffened. The surgeon shrugged. "We have to be certain he didn't lose blood supply to the brain."

"Yeah, I know." She would have done the same if Ronen was her patient, but still—

"Right now," he rushed to assure her, "all his signs are good. Reflexes and pupils are brisk and reactive. Pressure and pulses are strong. As long as he doesn't clot off the arm, develop an infection, or throw an embolism, we'll be fine. We have to let his body repair itself. Be patient."

Annie's stores of patience were currently lower than a rat's ass. She needed Ronen to wake up, right now, and tell her he'd forgiven her for being an idiot.

"Heard you did a bang-up job helping O'Malley when the patient first came in," the doctor said. "Planning on a residency in surgery?"

"Family practice," she mumbled. "Women's health."

"Stick around, Wolfe. We'll change your mind."

Right now, Annie would give it all up if it meant Ronen's survival. "What about his arm?"

The surgeon's breath hissed out slowly. "Let's get him through the first forty-eight hours, watch for perfusion to the hand, any damage to the nerves. After that, ask me."

Annie nodded understanding. What else could she do? Ronen's life was in this man's hands—and those of the nurses who would need to be sharp enough to pick up signs of complications before it was too late. But right now she'd be damned before she let some twit near Ronen who didn't prove in advance they knew what they were doing.

She glanced up as Elena and Chris, who were looking more confident and reassured as they walked out of Ronen's cubicle. "Take me home, Christos," Elena said. "We must rest, eat, and wait for Rachel."

"But, Nana—"

She held her ground. "Illiana will need relief after a time." She looked to Annie. "You won't leave him?"

Annie shook her head.

Chris didn't argue with his grandmother, however his discomfort with the decision showed on his face. "You'll call if anything—"

"My word," she promised. "Leave me phone numbers."

By the look on his face it seemed that Christopher was torn between allegiance to his father and duty to Elena. Knowing what Ronen would expect his son to do, she took his shoulders in her hands. "Look at me."

Tears welled in those baby blue eyes. "I love him so much, Ann. If I lose him now—"

She shook him. Hard. "There's nothing more you can do for your father except get out of the way and let the nurses and doctors do their jobs."

"I have to stay with him, Ann. What if—"

He dies and I'm not here.

"I won't let that that happen, Christopher," she promised. "Go home, rest if you can, eat something, and I'll see you at—" She checked her watch. "—Six a.m. on the dot," and forced a grin onto her face. "Can't have Captain Marvel waking up to find you looking like death warmed over, can we?"

Their foreheads touched. "I love you so much, Annie."

"I love you, too, kid."

Chris pulled a set of car keys out of his pocket and turned to the stoic Elena. "Ready to roll, Nana?"

Elena hugged Annie. "I can see why my son adores you. Thank you, Illiana."

~ * ~

Despite what the surgeon and nurses were telling her, every hour on the hour, Annie continued to check Ronen's neuro and vital signs for herself until the numbers blurred. Sometime in the middle of the night, when she was too wiped out to care, Bennie Foran and Jorge Morales appeared in the Unit. Jorge assured her the SPD was taking an all out stance to apprehend the shooters, then left to confer with his top investigators.

Bennie stayed with her, offering support and rubbing her tension-filled shoulders. "Care to tell me about this man who would make you pitch a tent in an ICU?"

Annie straightened from her previous slumped posture, shaking off her friend's comfort. "How'd you find out?"

"I have my sources. He must mean a lot to you." With that, Bennie pulled her out of the chair beside Ronen's bed and dragged her down the hallway to the family waiting room. "The nurses deserve their space. And the last thing they need is you hovering, watching every move they make, demanding answers they don't have."

"I've not been doing that."

"Bullshit."

"I haven't!"

"Tell me another fairy story, Wolfe," Bennie challenged. "You're a mess. The sooner you accept that, the better off you'll be."

It was almost too hideous to say out loud. "I'm so afraid."

"Of what? Say it, Ann."

"Afraid of losing what's most important to me."

Bennie kept a tight grip on her shoulders. "He's alive, but appears to be in serious condition. Tell me why he's so important."

Annie related what brought Ronen to No Man's Land and how she'd come to give him up. "I made the conscious choice to give him up so I could go to med school. Now, I might lose him and he'll never know how much he means to me." The unicorn somehow found its way from her pocket into her fist. Idly, she stroked the horn with her thumb.

"Was giving him up your only choice?"

Bennie's physical closeness and accepting tone of voice was exactly what Annie needed to help sort through her feelings. "I did what I thought was best for both of us. I couldn't give him what he needed or wanted."

"From what you told me, he didn't exactly try to give you what you needed either."

"He tried, in his way. I know that now. But, choice has been taken away, and I can't tolerate the thought of a world without Ronen in it."

"And?"

"I know what you meant, Bennie."

"I don't understand."

"You said the right man would help me attain my goals. Ronen is the right man."

Bennie nodded. "These goals are—?"

"A family. With him." Annie felt like smiling for the first time in months. "He wants babies. With me. Can you believe it?"

"Of course I can. You're Annie Wolfe. Who wouldn't want you for a mother?"

~ * ~

"Ronen, talk to me."

Nothing. Forty-eight hours had passed and still no response. The narcotics and sedatives were doing their job, Annie understood that. But he remained so still, and as pale as the sheets covering his legs.

The surgeons finally pronounced confidence that there was no brain damage from the massive blood loss. The patient's neuro signs were intact. They expected no impairment in cognitive function. But none would give an opinion on the status of his dominant hand and arm—except to say time, and the next surgery, would tell. The family needed to be patient.

Annie wanted to tell them what they could do with patience. She told herself she didn't give a rat's ass about his arm. But she did. If Ronen couldn't remain a cop, the ramifications didn't bear contemplation.

Faculty members made random appearances, mainly because, she was told ad nauseam, word had spread on how she'd conducted herself under fire in the ER. Dr. David Murray, the man responsible for accepting Annie into med school, who'd appointed himself her faculty advisor, told her to take as much time off as she needed and not to resume classes until she was certain Ronen was recovering.

Troop brass showed up, puffing and prancing around the halls until she was ready to scream. They left after the attending surgeon stepped in and, as only an arrogant man with a God complex will, threatened harassment charges.

On the Sunday after Thanksgiving, Elena insisted Chris return to classes at Cornell. Obviously reluctant to leave his father, Christopher spent his last hours before he left at Ronen's bedside, talking to him, holding his hand, and finally—for lack of anything else—reading sports reports from the newspaper. If anything would piss off Captain Marvel enough to wake up, he told her, it would be NFL scores.

Unfortunately, Ronen didn't respond.

On the fourth day, John Latimer blew into the ICU like an avenging archangel, identifying himself as Ronen's primary care provider and asked, with all due respect, to review the chart and confer with the surgeons.

"Christ on a sidecar, Wolfgirl," he bellowed. "The man is going to open his eyes, take one look at your face, and wish he was listening to opera with St. Peter himself. Go home, take a shower, sleep for eight hours, and don't bother us. I'll sit with him."

On her last legs, Annie begged, "Promise?"

"Get out of here."

Before leaving the medical complex, Annie sat down with David Murray to request an extended leave of absence. It was granted without a whimper.

~ * ~

"Ronen, quit this crapping around. Wake up and talk to me."

It was her voice. The same one he'd heard in his dreams every night for the past three months. This time, it wasn't whispering sweet, erotic promises in his ear. This time, it threatened serious bodily injury if he didn't give her some sign that he was functioning on all cylinders.

"Godammit, Ronen, you're scaring the spit out of me. Wake up, or I'll... break every finger in your good hand."

The threat was so familiar. So dear. He wished he could summon the strength to let her know he heard and understood. Would give anything for the strength to reach out and touch her. Just once.

He was awake enough to be aware of the ghastly hospital odors of disinfectant and spilled urine. Someone had recently vomited—probably right outside his door. If he could hear all those damn buzzers coming from the ICU monitors, why couldn't he wake up and tell them to turn the damned things off?

Then he tried to move. Understanding came with a blast of agony.

The pain was indescribable. Whatever they were giving him wasn't enough. Still... it allowed him to float away...

The next time he woke up, Annie was still there. How long had it been since the bangers took him down? Couldn't have been much more than a couple hours. Had she stayed with him the whole time?

"I did what you said," she murmured, running her fingers up his good arm. "Got myself some therapy—sort of."

That was good. Real good. Now if only she would—

"I know what I want now, Captain, so I'm going to be very pissed if you don't wake up and talk to me."

He felt Annie's hand cover his; she was talking to him the same way she'd spoken to John Latimer in the ICU. Nonsense things. Stuff about her life in Syracuse. All the gross things she was studying. Living in a DV shelter, for Christ's sake. Checking out kids and their mothers for injuries and other stuff.

The pain in his chest and shoulder didn't hurt half as much as her promises. "Medicine is nothing compared to you." He felt her hair brush his arm. "I'm giving it up."

Pain or not, he had to tell her to shut up.

"I want your baby, Ronen. I'll be the best mother I can—if you'll show me how."

Something wet touched his hand. Tears.

"Ronen, please. None of this means anything if you're not here to help me get through it."

He tried. Tried so hard.

"Godammit, Marvelic, I need you in my life. Wake up, tell me you feel the same."

Somehow, from somewhere, he found the strength. "Don't... yell... Ann."

Three short words sapped his strength. He wished for more.

"You're awake," she said, tears choking her dear, wonderful voice. Lowering her head, she rested her brow on his thigh and began to weep.

"Aw... Annie," he sighed.

Huge gulping shudders escaped her chest. She cried so hard, so deep, the bed shook from the force. With the hand that worked, he cupped the back of her head. "No... more... tears."

Raising her head, she stared at him. She looked like hell.

She looked wonderful.

"I love you, Captain Marvelous. Don't ever leave me again."

"Do my best, slugger," he muttered, and fell back to sleep.

~ * ~

"Okay, here's the deal," Annie said. "If you tolerate soft foods today, the surgeon has promised to advance your diet to regular. C'mon, trooper. One more bite."

Two days had passed since the third surgery. Ronen was thoroughly sick of this place and the food. His arm was better, but it would never be the same. In fact, they'd told him he'd be lucky if he regained even partial use of it. He was okay with the prognosis, but Annie refused to give up.

Reality would set in, he hoped. Until it did, he'd let her feel useful by feeding him. And wasn't that the most ignominious turn of events? Being fed like a helpless infant was bad enough, but if she shoved one more bite of University Hospital slop at him, he might hurl all over the bed.

"This stuff is gross. It probably has a zillion grams of fat in it. How can you stand to eat here?"

"They save the good stuff for the patients."

"That's encouraging."

"Wait till you taste the chocolate chip cookies. The best in all of Central New York."

Cookies didn't sound so bad; chocolate chip was his favorite. "With vanilla ice cream?"

"We'll see. I'll make sure someone writes an order to cover your lactose intolerance."

"I love you, Ann."

She leaned over to give him a quick kiss. "I hope your mother has a spare room, because I can't wait to get you home so you can show me."

In that area of his body, he was doing more than well. *Very well*, in fact. Now if he could only convince her to shut the door, come back to the bed, and slide her hand beneath the sheets...

"Sorry to interrupt," a commanding voice said.

The surgeon. While Ronen had tremendous respect for the man's talents, he had the bedside manner of Vlad the Impaler. He waited through the usual check of his wound, the taking of his pulse and request to wiggle his fingers, then demanded, "When can I go home?"

"Let's see what the OT and PT evals show. We'll take it from there."

Discharge from this hell hole couldn't come too soon. "But I *can* go home?" He and Annie had a date with a priest and an ovulation chart.

"Depends on what the therapists say." The surgeon headed for the door, then stopped and turned back. "Your shoulder took a nasty hit, Captain. Several, in fact. I won't make promises."

"Understood."

"Doctor—" Annie began.

"When are you coming back from LOA, Miz Wolfe?"

"I don't know."

"Make it soon. I need you in the ER. Don't trust anyone else to work up my patients."

"Yes, sir. Thank you, sir."

Ronen waited for the surgeon to leave before he launched his next volley in their most recent ongoing battle. "Told you so."

She sat back down beside the bed, smiled, and picked up a spoon loaded with gray hospital gruel. "Told me what?"

"You should get back to work. The hospital needs you; the patients—"

"Will do very well without me."

"I don't want you missing out on any more classes."

The spoon clattered to the tray. "Have three operations and the anesthesia necessary to keep you unconscious fried a few of your neurons, Captain? Did I hear you say you want me to resume my studies?"

"You did, Wolfgirl."

Annie sat back, astonishment painted all over her face. "What about marriage, babies, and the white picket fence?"

"Can't you do it all? Can't we be together, building a family, while you go to school? Haven't I heard you claim, a million and one times, that pregnancy does not make a woman an invalid?"

"Yes, but—"

Ronen raised his bad arm from the mattress—tried to anyway. It didn't hurt; it just wouldn't cooperate. "It's clear I can't go back to active duty. Probably never will."

"I don't want to hear you talking like that, Ronen. Your arm will come back."

He'd had a lot of time to think about this. "Until it does, there are openings for instructors at the police training academy. If that doesn't work out, I can teach criminal justice courses at a local college."

"They'd be lucky to get you, sir. You could offer tight-ass strutting classes for extra credit."

Fun over, he decided to get serious. Nothing meant more to him than making Annie understand. "The night we were at the B & B, I didn't explain myself very well."

Her dark eyes narrowed; the corners of that beautiful mouth turned down. "How so?"

"I missed out on Chris' early years because I was so busy working and going to school. I rarely saw him, hardly ever spoke to Lisa. This time around, I want to carry the load. Be there when we bring our babies home. This will be a fifty-fifty deal."

"If I go back to school, your fifty might well turn into ninety or one hundred."

"Doesn't matter, because the end will always be in sight for us. I never expected you to do it all; I was a fool for not telling you that then."

"You were a fool? I need to mark this on my calendar."

The beaming smile on her face told him he'd made his point. "Together, my darling Wolfgirl, we can accomplish anything."

"Anything?"

"Sure. I may not be in any shape to push a broom or vacuum cleaner yet. But come the time, I'll be walking the floors at two in the morning. Maybe I'll have enough motion back to change a diaper, give a bottle or two."

Annie offered him a secret smile. "Breast."

"What about them? Yours feel wonderful right now."

"Dummy," she giggled. "Our babies will be breast fed. It's the only way to go."

Wasn't that an interesting avenue to travel?

"Need any help in nipple preparation, Dr. Wolfe?"

"Lots."

Epilogue

"Doctor Annie Wolfe-Marvelic," a sonorous voice intoned.

Holding two-year Barbara Benedict Marvelic in his good arm, Ronen whispered the code word they'd practiced for days. "Now."

Bibi didn't disappoint her old man. "Yo, Mama!"

Even from their seats way in the back of the audience—to make a quick escape in case his daughter decided to get rowdy—Ronen couldn't miss the blush that crossed his wife's face when she heard their child's voice.

Life was good, he decided. Better than good.

They'd found the perfect house on the west side of town right after his discharge from the hospital. Rachel helped them get it ready for their Valentine's Day wedding. Chris stood as best man, with Bennie Foran as matron of honor. Elena moved into the home's attached apartment after she sold her house in the Combat Zone to a minister who was either incredibly brave or profoundly delusional.

After the fourth surgery, Annie finally accepted his arm was as good as it would get. That was okay. He'd discovered he really liked teaching at the academy. He was home in time to relieve Nana from the tortures of caring for a toddler and was able to spend quality time with Bibi before making dinner for his wife.

Annie. The light of his life. Clichéd it may be; it worked for him.

She is the best damn mother in the world. Barbara Benedict was proof of that. Ronen was so proud of Annie for what she'd accomplished. He'd never be able to tell her, would never find the right words to express how he felt about her bravery in facing her demons, then triumphing over them.

Bibi let out another yell for her mom without prompting. Two seats down, John Latimer wiped his eyes and chuckled with the rest of the audience in Manley Field House. Next to him, Elena Marvelic blubbered into a linen handkerchief while Rachel, with a new face and a new husband, beamed.

The recent Cornell graduate offered to take his sister. "Your arm must be fatigued, Dad. Let me hold her for a while."

"No, Chris!" The youngest member of the Marvelic family would have nothing to do with that nonsense. "Do wave for Mommy!" Bibi raised her arms in an imitation of the popular cheer usually reserved for sporting events.

"Whatever you say, kid." Chris' arms went up in unison with his sister's and cheered, "Way to go, Annie!"

"Way go, Annie," Bibi crowed.

The woman in question slowly made her way across the stage. Ronen winced, sympathy rising with each ponderous step. Ignoring the rules of convention, he left his seat and headed for the foot of the stage. He was waiting for his beautiful wife as she came down the steps.

"Everything okay?"

With a hand on her enormous belly, Annie grimaced. "You know that celebration dinner we planned for later?"

"Chinese? My favorite."

"Chinee," Bibi claimed loudly, reaching for her mother. "Fave'rit."

Annie cuddled her daughter to her chest and groaned. "We're going to have to postpone it."

Alarmed at her color, he demanded, "What's wrong?"

"Nothing," she managed after a few hoots and shouts. "Looks like our son isn't going to wait through moo shu pork and shrimp fried rice to make his grand entrance into this world."

Meet Kate Henry Doran

Kate Henry Doran, a nurse-paralegal, travels the length of Upstate New York, investigating allegations of medical malpractice.

Formerly, she served as director of a crisis intervention program, serving victims of sexual violence in Western New York State.

She and her college professor husband have three grown daughters.

*VISIT OUR WEBSITE
FOR THE FULL INVENTORY
OF QUALITY BOOKS*:

http://www.wings-press.com

*Quality trade paperbacks and downloads
in multiple formats,
in genres ranging from light romantic
comedy to general fiction and horror.
Wings has something
for every reader's taste.
Visit the website, then bookmark it.
We add new titles each month!*